T0196349

All My Tomorrows

All My Tomorrows

Gineen Dutkovic

ALL MY TOMORROWS

iUniverse books may be ordered through booksellers or by contacting:

iUniverse
1663 Liberty Drive
Bloomington, IN 47403
www.iuniverse.com
1-800-Authors (1-800-288-4677)

Because of the dynamic nature of the Internet, any web addresses or links contained in this book may have changed since publication and may no longer be valid. The views expressed in this work are solely those of the author and do not necessarily reflect the views of the publisher, and the publisher hereby disclaims any responsibility for them.

Any people depicted in stock imagery provided by Thinkstock are models, and such images are being used for illustrative purposes only. Certain stock imagery © Thinkstock.

ISBN: 978-1-4917-8826-4 (sc)
ISBN: 978-1-4917-8808-0 (e)

Library of Congress Control Number: 2016903044

Print information available on the last page.

iUniverse rev. date: 03/03/2016

"Am I going to die?" the woman asks in a steady voice. "Because if I do, I don't want my mom to know how I went. It would just kill her." The woman is sitting on the edge of a bed, a light-haired man close beside her, their legs touching. She has her arm across his lap, palm up, a belt cinched between her shoulder and biceps.

"You're not going to die," the man replies, his words garbled around the syringe he holds between his teeth. His attention is focused on the blue vein in her elbow. He taps it twice with his fingers and slides the needle smoothly into her skin as she looks away.

That's the way I pictured most of the dramatic events in my life, as scenes from a movie. It was a habit I'd been indulging since childhood. It allowed me to step out of myself and assess life from a safe, less threatening distance. On my more imaginative days I even chose which actors would play the characters and compiled a list of appropriate songs for the soundtrack. A little pretentious to think anyone would want to see a movie about my life but hey, it's fantasy. There had really been nothing dramatic about that day or the action performed. It was a doorway however, through which I passed from one life into another. So maybe drama was permissible.

Chapter One

At four o'clock the summer sun hit my west window at just the right angle. Every day I raced home from work to be there when the miracle occurred and today I was almost late. I hurried up the steps and into the apartment, slipped off my shoes and waited in anticipation. In a few minutes the earth would turn the last few inches needed. I stood still and held my breath, trying to feel the tiny movement. The jangle of keys sounded and the door opened precisely as solar rays infused my apartment with a rich orange glow. My chest rose in a deep breath. Something was going to be different about today and a nagging sense of anticipation tugged faintly at the edges of my consciousness.

"No-vena," Dev greeted me as he came through the door, turning my name into a song. I wasn't sure which brightened the room more, the sun or the man. They came to me at the same time so many days. His voice reminded me of a slow southern river, flowing warm and deep and rich with life. I smiled and felt my heart jump at the affection in his eyes. He was the only person in my life who had ever made me feel like I belonged. Even in my own family I felt like an outsider. With Dev I felt grounded, secure.

"How'd the old people treat you today?" he asked, throwing his keys on the small coffee table. I stood against him and he dropped a kiss on my head.

"They were exhausting. I could just as well be digging ditches for a living as working in a nursing home," I replied. My arms slipped around his lean middle and I rested my forehead on his heart. "The energy has been drained completely from me. If I stay there much longer all my youth and vitality will just be sucked away," I mumbled into his chest, allowing all my weight to sink into him.

Dev chuckled.

"My poor Novena," he patted my back and drew away from me. "You're a bright girl. Why don't you look for another job?"

"Too much trouble. Besides, I've been there almost four years now and I have benefits." I pushed away from him and began straightening the room. Our apartment was small and the furniture mostly second-hand but I liked to keep it neat. It had high ceilings and big windows even though it was the attic of an old mansion and I loved it for its open brightness.

"So you'll just continue to be one of the oppressed working-class slugs like me?" I could hear the smile in his voice and I threw a sharp look at him.

"I don't plan on being a nurse's aide forever you know. I'm just hanging on until you decide to go back to school and finish that journalism degree you've been chipping away at. Then I'll follow you around the world on your adventures and be your kept woman. Sound like a plan?"

Dev snorted with laughter and swatted me on the behind as I bent to pick up a leaf that had blown in.

"You hitched your cute little wagon to one slow horse baby. Let's see, I'm twenty-eight now and I have one year of community college under my belt," he let his eyes roll up and put his finger to his lip as if doing hard math in his head. "At this rate you should be ready to collect social security before I'm a globe-trotting journalist. Will a walker fit in your backpack?"

"As often as you have your nose in some book you'd think they'd just give you a degree and get it over with," I said.

"It doesn't work that way. I like the kept woman part, though. Can I keep you on my house-painter's salary?"

"You could keep me on your way to the poor-house," I said. I tried to sound light but my voice came out low with emotion. When I turned around Dev's dark eyes rested on me with palpable warmth.

"I was over at Mick's," Dev said as I turned back to my cleaning. "I tried some stuff he had and it didn't do anything for me. I knew he was blowing smoke about this dope thing all these years. Give me a good book instead of that stuff any day." He strode into the bedroom and seemed to take the sunlight with him. I dropped the pillow I was re-positioning on the worn sofa and followed Dev down the hall, trying to make sense of what he'd said.

I stood at the door watching him change out of his paint-stained work clothes. He took off his shirt and stood in front of the window fan letting it blow his dark hair away from his heat-flushed face. He turned slowly to face me, his eyes closed, half-smiling as if the feel of the cool air against his bare back was the most enjoyable sensation he'd ever experienced. His lashes made dark crescent-moons above high cheekbones that angled down to full lips. The sun through the window reflected off the pale peach walls and illuminated him from behind, causing a glow to surround his lean body like an aura. He reminded me of a god from some old myth, luminous and otherworldly, appearing like a savior from a stream of light.

Then Dev opened his eyes, smiled mischievously and threw his dirty work clothes on top of the clean ones waiting to be folded in the laundry basket at my feet. I continued to stare at him waiting for an explanation, but he gave none. A cold fear began to build in my chest as it finally registered in my mind that he was talking about shooting heroin. He had done his share of experimentation, but that had been before we met each other.

"If you're stupid enough to try that stuff I can't stop you. But I don't want it here, or anywhere near me," I blurted out. My jaw tightened as I tried to keep from looking too scared. I tossed my hair away from my shoulder and raised my chin.

"Novena," Dev said. "Mick's been shooting dope since he was fifteen. He always talks about how good the high is. I just wanted to try it for myself. It was nothing believe me, I won't waste any money on it again. I'd much rather have a good meal and a movie." Dev's voice was hard. He sat on the bed and clicked the remote, turning on the TV.

"Besides, you sure don't have trouble washing those pain pills I bring home down with a few glasses of wine. This isn't much different," he said, his gaze not moving from the television.

"It's completely different. Heroin's addictive, not to mention illegal. That stuff scares me and Mick's been *hooked* since he was fifteen, that's ten years. Someone with your raging imagination could really get sucked in. I'm surprised he would even expose you to it, as bad as he always says it is," I said. I began folding laundry furiously.

"All that talk about he evils of the street' is just apart of the mystique Mick builds around himself. He likes to dramatize everything, be a tough guy. It's junkie pride," Dev dismissed. Mick had been his best friend for years. His heroin use was common knowledge in the neighborhood but he had such easy-going charm that his bad habit had become an acceptable trait, like the scruffiness of his clothes.

I finished folding my clothes and went to stand at the large bedroom window. I lit a cigarette and blew the smoke through the screen. Dev watched me from across the room. The previously sunny sky was clouding up, the darkness of a storm looming on the horizon. An unexpected gust of wind through the large open window blew the smoke back into my face.

"I just don't want anything bad to happen," I said, continuing to stare out the window. The strange sense of anticipation heightened, becoming a twisting knot in my stomach. As if in response thunder rolled threateningly in the distance. "My mom would call that an omen," I told him, listening to the sound echo through the street.

"You worry too much Novena. We'll always be OK, as long as we're together." Dev said. He came up behind me and surrounded me with his arms, his lips at my ear. His breath tickled my neck and I felt the familiar weakness in my limbs that his touch always induced. "I was just curious. I know my limits. It'll be all right." Dev kissed my neck. "Now let me give you something better to think about," he growled playfully. I sighed and let him shuffle me towards the bed.

A few weeks later we sat in Mick's bedroom. Mick lived with his girlfriend, Francesca, in the same neighborhood as Dev and me. They rented an apartment from Dev's father, Simon, who owned a huge old house on a busy street a few miles from us. He had divided and subdivided the old place over the years into six apartments. He rented these mostly to artists who liked Pittsburgh's North Side for its diversity. We only visited at Mick's place while Francesca was out and we usually sat in the bedroom to avoid being around the expensive pieces of art she collected. She didn't allow smoking in the living room and Mick and I couldn't possibly hold a meaningful conversation without smoking. Booming car stereos thumped through the open windows, sirens wailed, laughter echoed, the noises of a city neighborhood on a warm Saturday night blew in with the breeze. The bedroom was large and airy with room for two stuffed chairs in addition

4

to a four-post bed. I was stretched out on my stomach across the bed while Dev and Mick each occupied a chair. Francesca's old gray cat was purring in Dev's lap.

I loved to look at them together. Dev was tall and muscular with short black hair, a neatly trimmed goatee and dark brown eyes. He had a slightly wild, dangerous air to him and his smile make you think he knew things about you he shouldn't. Mick was short and slight, his long gold hair was wavy and soft, his eyes a gentle blue. Mick always looked a little unsure of himself but was quick to welcome people in a hug. They make me think of Jesus and Satan hanging out together having coffee, discussing the books on the New York Times Best-Sellers List.

"You're telling me you think the world is better now than it was two, three hundred years ago?" Mick asked, his voice heated. He and Dev were debating the state of human kind, one of their favorite subjects. I sighed and rolled over on my back, pretending to snore.

"Wake me up when you start talking about something really important, like what we're having for dinner," I said. They ignored me.

"Sure," Dev responded to Mick's question. "Think about it. People are healthier, we live longer and better than ever before. And I'd say our collective awareness is growing, too. We still have crime, and humans will always be cruel to each other, but it's gotten a lot better. At least now we recognize it as wrong." Dev's voice was low and remained soft, as if he knew without a doubt that he was right. He kept his head slightly bowed and looked at Mick from under dark lashes, his hand continuing to stroke the cat lying across his knees. Mick leaned forward in his chair and he pointed his finger at Dev.

"Our government can let people starve to death in the streets and you tell me we're collectively better off?" he asked, shaking his curly head in disbelief.

"'Our government', you say that like it's a separate thing from us. We're part of it. And we as individuals are just as responsible for each other as the government everyone wants to blame for the problems they don't have time deal with themselves. When's the last time you went back down to the shelter to visit the guys stuck there? Or gave a few bucks to some homeless guy?" Dev smiled to soften the sting of his words. Mick's gentle heart-shaped face flushed with anger.

"Well I'm just saying the power brokers of the world should give the poor a chance. The imbalance of wealth in this country is sickening," Mick sputtered, obviously having trouble making his point. I huffed loudly at hearing the same tired argument made in the same tired words I'd been hearing for years. "Have you noticed the fear and suffering that goes on in this world?!"

"I've noticed it alright." Dev's voice had taken on a tight bitterness. "That lame old line about the rich is just an excuse, an easy out. What do you know about being scared and alone anyway, Mick? When I met you, you had just left your mom's house and were already in trouble," Dev said. "And you," he looked at me. "You hadn't even started to live yet when we first met. Neither of you ever had to go hungry or worry about where you'd lie down to sleep at night, or wake up shivering and alone." Dark clouds had rolled over Dev's usually bright face. Mick swallowed loudly. His flush faded to a pale look of surprise and maybe a little fright. I stared at him wordlessly. Dev seemed to catch himself and his face eased into a smile but it was a hard smile. "And me, I'm just playing devil's advocate. What the Hell do I know anyway?" He let his smile widen to dispel the unexpected tension and I saw Mick shift in his seat uncomfortably. Dev's eyes brightened and his face softened.

"Devvy my friend, even after all these years, sometimes I'm still not sure when you're joking." Mick held the short remnants of a cigarette to his rosebud lips and sucked hard. He exhaled a long stream of smoke, relaxing back into the chair. Dev grinned, rubbed the stretching cat under its chin.

"So Mick, you have anything here?" Dev asked after a quiet minute.

Mick raised his eyebrows and leaned forward in his chair, his face suddenly more animated.

"No but I can call Wilbur," Mick replied, referring to one of the local dope-dealers.

I felt my face flush with anger. Pressure began growing just below my ribs as I saw Mick throw a quick glance in my direction

"He likes me to call early," Mick continued. "He baby-sits his grandkids on Saturday nights. He should be home and he always has good stuff." Mick pushed his long, wispy gold curls behind an ear and reached for the phone. He put in a pager number, hung up and put another cigarette in the corner of his mouth.

My head swung to Dev who had pushed the cat off his lap and was leafing through a magazine, going to great lengths to ignore me. I leaned toward him, giving him the angry-eyed look I'd perfected for when I needed extra help making a point.

"What are you doing?" I whispered harshly as Mick slid to the floor to adjust the volume on the stereo. I thought I saw Mick flinch at the tone in my voice.

"Relax," Dev commanded. He leaned back in the worn easy chair and put his leg across his knee, concentrating on the magazine.

"Relax?! What'd you mean, relax? I don't want you to do this!" I sputtered.

"Leave it alone, Novena," Dev said in a low voice. I recognized this tone. It was the one he used when his mind was made up about something. His face held the look of a big cat preoccupied with its quarry. Mick remained on the floor fiddling with the stereo, conveniently finding the need to adjust and readjust the knobs while Dev and I argued in whispers. I wriggled to the edge of the bed and tried to catch Dev's eye while Mick switched radio-stations, but Dev paid no more attention to me than to the dust particles floating in the pink streaks of setting sun filtering through the window.

Mick stood up and carefully avoided looked at either of us. He lifted his shirt and began an extensive search of his pockets. His too-big threadbare jeans hung below his belly button. He looked at the ceiling and plunged a hand into one side pocket while holding his pants up with the other hand. Coming up empty, he switched sides. That side failed him too and he put both hands into his back pockets, causing his jeans to slide even lower down his thin hips. Mick took his eyes off the ceiling long enough to see Dev and I both staring at him and blushed, then tugged his jeans up and his shirt down over his white belly. He pulled a lighter from one back pocket, held it up triumphantly for us to see, then sunk into his seat and lit a cigarette. Tension hung like our smoke in the air. No one spoke.

We all jumped when the phone rang five minutes later. Mick grabbed the receiver.

"It's Mick, you got anything? No? OK I'll try tomorrow." He hung up and took a deep drag on his Marlborough, then blew it out in a long breath. "Wilbur's all out, he won't have anything till tomorrow." Mick almost looked relieved. "You going to try it too, Novena?" He asked me, suddenly engrossed in rolling the tip of his cigarette against the edge of the ashtray. He darted a glance up at me, caught me staring at him and quickly refocused his attention on the cigarette.

"This whole thing is so weird!" I exploded after a short silence. "It's like having a severed head on the kitchen table and everyone's going out of their way to avoid mentioning it. What is wrong with you people!" I shouted, throwing my hands up. "We aren't talking about having tea and cookies here, we're talking about shooting heroin, for God's sake! You've been planning this, haven't you?" They avoided looking at me, like kids knowing a lecture is coming. "Dev can do whatever he wants, but I want no parts of it," I spat, looking from one to the other. "I can't believe you went behind my back! Once you've made up your mind nothing will stop you from getting what you want, but that doesn't mean I'm ready to give in and make it easy for you." I crossed my arms over my chest and continued to stare at them, taking advantage of the rare power an angry five-foot tall, one hundred pound woman could wield over grown men when they're caught. Mick shrugged his shoulders, screwing his face up into a goofy 'I'm sorry' kind of smile. He looked at Dev for help.

"Don't worry about it Novena. It wasn't meant to be," Dev said lightly. He looked at me from under his thick lashes, testing the waters to see how angry I would be later, already working on his defense.

"There might be some tomorrow. You gotta call early." Mick said before he could catch himself. He looked from me to Dev, eyebrows raised, grubby hands gripping the knees of his worn out jeans. "I mean, you know, if you change your mind," his voice squeaked. He looked back me. "Not that I'm saying you should, or anything, you know. Just, there might … oh Hell," he finished quietly, shaking his head.

"You hate this kind of confrontation, don't you Mick?" I taunted him. "But you hate disappointing Dev more, and that's going to get us all in trouble." I drew my lips into a firm line and turned away from them.

Dev and Mick made half-hearted attempts at drawing me back into their conversation, but I remained icy through the rest of the visit.

"Don't start." Dev said as soon as we were out of Mick's house. "I don't need you to nag me about this."

"Don't need me to nag?" I hissed, and jumped in front of him, halting his fast-paced walk to the car. "For someone so bright, you sure are stupid sometimes! What is it, you can't stand it that Mick knows something you don't, afraid you're missing out? Or is it your big ego saying you can handle anything? You keep telling me it's Mick's junkie pride, so *ignore it!*"

Dev stepped around me and opened the car door, holding it as I got in. I slammed the door and turned toward the window, knowing that silence bothered him more than argument.

"The first time I did it we may have gotten a bad bag. I want to give it one more shot. No pun intended," he looked at me and grinned. I swung around to glare at him. He started the car, still looking pleased with his little joke. "This is just another adventure." Dev's eyes flashed with excitement when he said the last word. "Seeing what it does to my mind and body, how it makes me feel. You never know what you'll learn from something new. I'm going to try it one more time, so I know what Mick is talking about." He looked over at me hopefully, like this would explain things. It had been the prospect of adventure after all, that had first attracted me to him. I returned his look evenly.

"You've tried about every other drug, so this will complete the list, right? What a well-rounded individual you'll be! You don't need college after all. I bet people will be really impressed with your intelligence when your junkie-ass is sitting in prison," I said. He rolled his eyes in exasperation.

"Come on Novena, I'll never be a junkie. I just need a little break from reality once in a while. Like a vacation. A twenty dollar bag of dope is sure more affordable than a trip to Florida. Besides, you're one to talk. You gobble down the pills I bring home like candy and you've been drunk on wine often enough after a bad day at work."

I planted one hand on the dashboard and held the other out to him like I had seen my favorite day-time TV talk show host do every afternoon when she was compassionately trying to figure out why some weeping woman had put antifreeze in her husband's meatloaf.

"Is this about your mother? I mean, she left you when you were really young and you had to take care of yourself. Are your abandonment issues finally coming out? Cause I'm here to help, you know." I pressed my lips together in what I hoped was a look of concerned sympathy.

"This has nothing to do with my mother," Dev's voice broke into a laugh. "And I don't have any *abandonment issues*. You watch way too much TV Novena. I got to start hiding that remote!" He continued to chuckle as he drove and it added dry branches to the flames of my anger. "Why do you always bring that up, anyway? You're the one with family issues. I did just fine by myself. I found you." He squeezed my knee and flashed his smile. I jerked my leg away and pressed myself up against the door of the car for effect.

"Stop making fun of me. How the Hell do I know what goes on in that brain of yours? You never talk about her, your dad never talks about her, but sometimes I'll look over at you and see this lost sad look on your face." I continued to stare out the window of the car. Tears stung my eyes and blurred the passing lights in the darkness. I willed them away.

Dev brought the car to a stop outside the house. The seat creaked as he turned to face me.

"This has nothing to do with my mother, my father, or anyone else, Novena. I can't explain it to you. You know how it feels when you have a handful of pills and a glass of wine? This is the same thing, just a little bit of relief from the day-to-day grind. It'll be OK."

I shook my head slowly. He often 'borrowed' pain pills from the houses he painted. It had started when I pulled a muscle in my back before I had health insurance. Dev found some old unused pain pills in someone's medicine cabinet and brought them home for me. They did more than take the physical pain away. It was the first time I'd ever felt free. The scattered chit-chat of thought that created a constant buzz in my mind stopped. For once there were no worried thoughts tugging at my consciousness and the subtle fear that nagged me like a low-grade fever my whole life disappeared. He brought pills home every few weeks and I saw no harm in taking something that wasn't being used. I looked forward to the feeling of well being, only indulged in occasionally and approached with great ritual. We would open a cheap bottle of sweet red wine and use the special fancy glasses I had found at Goodwill. He'd count out our pills and we would spend the evening listening to music. It was just fun, not scary like actual drug use.

"You say sometimes you feel like something is missing and you don't know what it is or where to find it," I reminded him. "It scares me to think that you might try to fill that hole by doing something dangerous," my voice squeaked as I tried to keep from crying. Dev's warm fingers laced through mine where they were clenched on the seat. I pressed my other hand to my lips.

"I have everything I need." His fingers tightened around mine. I squeezed back and took a deep breath to calm myself. "I want to see if I can help Mick kick this shit for good. If I show him I don't need it and we quit together, maybe he'll finally be free of it." Dev sat back in the seat and waited for my response. "Does that make sense?"

All right, so he had finally hit on an argument I could understand. He had spent countless hours trying to talk Mick into kicking his habit thinking that all Mick needed to quit was a few days clean to see that he could live without heroin. He was trying to help his best friend. My DeValera, named after his father's favorite Irish hero. I nodded, wanting it to be the truth. Wanting him to be doing it for a romantic, altruistic reason.

The next morning we were sitting on the neatly made bed having coffee and reading the newspaper. The small kitchen was dark and drab so we spent our weekend mornings in the bedroom, enjoying the sun when it made an appearance.

While Dev paged through the paper I read the most recent post card from my mom. On the front was a photo of two smiling bald monks in orange robes arm in arm beside a temple. My mom had left Pittsburgh when I was nineteen to teach English classes in Japan. She stayed, traveling between semesters, coming home infrequently to visit.

I had never felt at home in my family. My father, mother and older brother were outgoing, gregarious and confident. I was timid, unsure of myself. I could barely bring myself to dip my toe into the pool of life while the rest of my family dove in headfirst. I wanted so much to be like them. I envied how easily they talked to people, how comfortable they seemed in every situation. How unafraid they were. I tried to be like them. I pretended to be the cool collected and utterly unflappable female hero from every movie I saw but my life seemed more like a long string of blundering Lucille Ball moments and I felt like I never measured up.

My mom and dad had met in college and married in 1965. In their wedding picture she was a beautiful barefoot flower child, he was tall, tan and athletic. My brother Jamie was born a year later. My parents were both teachers. She taught English Lit at the local community college and he taught math at an exclusive private school. For the first few years of their marriage they traveled to a different place each summer, teaching as volunteers. I used to pour over the old photo albums full of pictures of them in villages in Mexico, rural towns in the Appalachian Mountains, Reservations in the Southwest, even an Inuit village in northwest Canada. They were smiling, usually wind blown, my brother just a baby in someone's arms. After my dad landed the big job at the important school the travel stopped.

We lived in a middle-income suburb; grass, trees, families, very average. Dad coached soccer and rowing. Strong and steady, he seemed to have the answer to every question I could come up with. Mom volunteered at the local food-bank and the women's shelter. She led drives to collect coats for the homeless while the other neighborhood wives were hosting Tupperware parties and having their hair done. She seemed to have an endless supply of love. Flamboyant in her bellbottoms and red cowboy boots, long hair flowing, I guess I should have been proud of her but she just made me feel different than the other kids.

My brother and I went to public school. Jamie was athletic and adventure-seeking, up to any challenge. He was popular and had many friends. I was shy and had just one friend, a self-proclaimed outcast like myself named Rachel. On the first day of kindergarten I had walked into class with a book-bag crocheted by a woman whose hands had been blown off by a landmine. Mom had bought it for me, to support the organization the woman was representing. One of the boys had run up, yelling, "that bag looks like somebody knitted it with their toes!" which of course somebody had. I was mortified that I'd been singled out and tried to make myself disappear into the air around me while the other kids laughed. Rachel came to my defense by pushing the boy into a trashcan, making him the center of attention. We were friends from that moment. I threw the offending bag away on the way home, telling my mom that I'd lost it.

It was easy for a plain quiet girl to become invisible and that became my strategy for surviving the awkwardness I felt every day at school. It was just as easy at home where my father was always working on advancing his career, Mom was saving the world bit by bit and Jamie was winning some new award. I felt protected by the wall of personality my family represented to me and I could remain safely behind that fortress, surrounded by their energy and enthusiasm without actually having to accomplish anything myself.

When I turned twelve I began to notice the tension between my parents. My father was trying to get ahead at the stuffy prep school where he taught and Mom refused to socialize with the other teacher's wives to help him. I'd hear them while I was in bed at night, after she'd come home from passing out expired canned goods at the food bank.

"Can't you just tone it down a little, for me?" He'd ask in a clipped, tight voice. "Would it hurt you to dress a little conservatively and attend some of their parties?"

"So all you're asking is for me to change completely?" She'd say. "You'd rather I worried more about my hair and nails than the fact that there are children starving in our own city. Go to jewelry parties and giggle like a silly girl instead of helping adults learn to read? Is that all? Fit in? You just want me to stop being me." She'd state it all matter-of-factly, sounding emotionless. Lying stiffly in my bed I'd plead with her silently, 'change for him, don't let him leave, what's wrong with you? Why can't you just be normal?' I'd fall asleep praying that God would make my mom change so my dad would keep loving her.

But eventually he left. Dad moved to upstate New York, taking a teaching job in an even stuffier prep school and he remarried. My brother Jamie left right after he graduated high school to go west. By the time I was fourteen it was just me and Mom. I hated that my life had changed so much and longed morosely for the days when my family was whole. I became even more awkward and uncomfortable, dressing in black and moping a lot. Mom, God bless her, tried to get me involved. She took me with her to pass out homemade bagels and dollar store candy to the homeless people downtown, but the desperate dirty people scared me. I was dragged to the children's home to read books to the kids but I didn't know what to say to them. Mom encouraged me to take art classes in the summer, learn to horseback ride, offered all kinds of opportunities, but I was so afraid of failure that I just refused. Reading was my escape and I retreated into books, fantasizing about doing adventurous things in exotic places instead of hiding in my room. It's not that I didn't want to live and enjoy life, secretly I very much did. But I wanted to do it with one hand on the pull-cord so I could ring the bell and get off the bus, so to speak, if I didn't like the direction it was taking.

As I got close to graduation Mom sent away for college information but one look at those perky coeds in the colorful brochures and I knew I'd hate it. I drifted along directionless till the end of high school. The same day I picked up my diploma I got a job at the local nursing home where they'd trained me in basic medical care, first aid, CPR, drawing blood. It was hard physically but it didn't require much thought. The confused old people I worked with didn't care what my plans for the future were as long as their simple needs were met. Mom finally gave up and took a job teaching in Japan, something she'd always wanted to do. I felt like an orphan, abandoned and family-less. I still resented her.

"What does your mom say?" Dev asked.

"Same old stuff," I grumbled. "Life is wonderful, she's wonderful, blah, blah, blah."

Dev chuckled. "Where is she?"

"Indonesia." I yawned for effect then threw the card on the floor. Against my will I felt the familiar ache that always panged in my chest when I missed my mom.

Before we had finished our second cup of coffee someone was banging heavily on the unlocked front door downstairs. We heard it open and close quickly then Mick came loping into the bedroom with the serious pre-occupied look he got when he had dope in his pocket. A puff of dust rose around him as he plopped onto a chair in the corner.

"Mornin' John, Yoko," he said, making reference to our always sitting on the bed. Dev looked up from the paper he was reading. I stretched and yawned, not quite ready to be social this early.

"You need to dust off when you come in," Dev scolded, rubbing his neatly trimmed beard and straightening his sweatshirt, as if to set a good example. Mick lit a smoke and crossed his legs.

"This is the result of honest labor," he protested, holding out his arms to indicate the seemingly ever-present coating of dry-wall dust he wore. "I'm in the same line of work as Jesus you know." Mick winked at me and took a long drag from his cigarette as Dev rolled his eyes.

"I bet Jesus didn't trail wood chips everywhere he went. I'm gonna have to start brushing you off before you come in, like a shaggy little dog," Dev's face broke into a wide smile as he rolled up the newspaper he was reading and reached out to swat Mick who flinched reflexively. Mick caught himself and shifted position, as if to signal a change of subject.

"I already been down the street. Got some of Wilber's finest," Mick said and opened his mouth. Under his tongue were three tiny colored round bundles. He closed his mouth and smiled.

"Wilbur came through." The absence of Dev's hand left a cold place on my thigh as he got off the bed. He crossed the room and stood in front of Mick, smiling down at him warmly. Mick's face softened as his eyes rested on Dev. I hated being the third person and I had spent lots of energy trying to become a part of the relationship the two of them shared.

Dev and Mick had a love for one another that sprung from being the youngest residents at the Salvation Army Shelter years ago. Dev had just come back from the west coast and hadn't found a job or a place to live yet. Mick had been kicked out of his mom's house for getting high. On their first night in the shelter, Dev had saved Mick from being beaten up by another resident. Mick returned Dev's favor by helping Dev get a steady job so he could move out of the Sally and they had remained best friends ever since. They had known each other before I came along and although I'd never admit it, I resented their connection. Sometimes it seemed like they had a secret understanding, an energy that vibrated between them when they were together. It was something I wasn't a part of and it drove me crazy with jealousy.

Mick was already at the dresser, getting a spoon and lighter out of his pocket. I was fascinated by what was going but didn't want them to see my curiosity. I flipped through the paper Dev had left on the bed, determined not to show interest. From the corner of my eye I could see him flicking the lighter and an acrid smell drifted over to me.

He drew up two syringes, gave one to Dev who took it to the corner chair and proceeded to cinch his belt round his arm just above the bicep.

15

No longer able to contain my curiosity, I threw down the paper and huffed loudly. Mick's eyes locked mine. "Do you want to try Novena? It won't hurt you, I promise. I'll just give you a little bit so you can see what it's like." He stood looking at me.

I was standing at a fork in the road. Dev was setting out on the path in one direction. I imagined his lean form disappearing into the distance, fading from my view. As much as I hated the thought of sticking a needle in my arm, the idea of remaining behind alone scared me more than the danger of Mick's offer. I swallowed, brushed the hair off my forehead, hesitated for a second and took a deep breath. Then I plunged ahead and held out my arm to Mick.

"You have to do it for me. I don't know how," I said, the words rushing past my lips. Mick smiled, sat close beside me on the bed and wrapped his belt around my arm.

Dev had missed the whole exchange between Mick and me. He was sitting in the chair looking happy and breathing deeply, as if savoring the taste of the air. I glanced at him and then my attention was all on Mick. My breathing quickened, my heart pounded with nervousness. I had no idea what to expect and the fear was a little exhilarating, like I was jumping out of an airplane with a parachute for the first time. Mick guided the needle smoothly into my vein, I hardly felt it. Then a slow warmth spread through my body and then my limbs, as if warm honey was being poured into me.

I looked at Mick, who had his eyes on my face, judging how much heroin to give me. "I feel all warm," I said. "Not good though, more like I might throw up."

Mick smiled. He took the belt off my arm and went to the mirror. He shot a syringe full of the cloudy stuff into the vein in his neck.

"A lot of people get sick from dope the first time. If you do it enough you get over it," Mick said.

"Great, something to strive for," I said, wrinkling my face against the nausea. Mick didn't hear me. His eyes were softening and his face relaxing as the drug pulsed through his vessels, relieving the ache in his muscles that he said began every morning when he woke up. I pictured his cells screaming out for the drug after a night of not using. He smiled at me and kissed my cheek as I continued to watch Dev from my seat on the bed, trying to will the discomfort in my body away.

"This is some good stuff," Dev said from the corner, his eyes were bright, his face smiling. "Hey Novena, let's go see a movie. Mick, you going to work or you want to come with us?" He stood up and stretched slowly.

"Got to make money," Mick said. "I'm putting a roof on this place across town. The owner is some rich guy and I can usually skim a few hundred in cash off him for dope money." He seemed to have new energy, like a toy just wound. He slipped out the door, waving as he went. The sleeve of his faded too-big work shirt hid his hand, making him look like a child late for school.

"Well, how do you feel, Novena?" Dev asked, dropping to the bed beside me. He smiled and draped his arm around my shoulders. "I knew you wouldn't be able to resist when the time came. We have the same sense of adventure, you and me. That's why we're so good together." He kissed my forehead and his smile grew wider as he looked into my face. Without waiting for my response he got up and ambled to the dresser where the evidence of our adventure was still displayed.

I studied Dev. His face glowed. He looked comfortable and content, humming to himself as he picked up the pieces of balloon and plastic bag the heroin had come in. How can something that makes him so happy be so bad? And why don't I look like that? I wondered.

"I feel weird," I said in a low voice.

"It'll pass. The first time is a let-down. It gets better," he assured me absently, busy cleaning up. "Go get that bottle of bleach in the kitchen. I want to clean these needles."

I got up reluctantly and plodded down the hall, found the bleach and clomped loudly back into the room, hoping my pace conveyed my opinion of the day's events. Dev just took the bottle and poured bleach into a cup, filled each syringe and let them sit. Then he cleaned the spoons and wiped the dresser. "Bleach kills everything," he smiled. He was very careful not to spill any on his jeans.

"Hey, how'd you know how to do this?" I asked, noticing how naturally he seemed to be carrying on about his business. "I thought you just wanted to try it 'one more time'?"

He blushed a little and dropped his eyes, but his face remained relaxed.

"I did it a few times with Mick," he admitted. "We thought we should just ease you into the idea, let you make up your own mind. I'm only going to do it for a while. Mick promised to quit when I do," he explained. "If we do it together, maybe he won't have such a hard time. I can set a good example." He raised his eyes to mine from across the room. "What did you think?" He asked. I just shrugged. He held my gaze. "You know," Dev continued, "you didn't have to do it. I wouldn't have been disappointed if you refused. I just wanted you to have the choice. I know how you hate to be excluded," he said, smiling. "You aren't still mad at me are you?"

I had compromised what I believed, done something I thought was wrong to go where he went. No, I was no longer mad at him. It was a reminder that he didn't need me as much as I needed him and the emotion that evoked was more uncomfortable than anger.

Instead of replying I ran to the bathroom and threw up. The faint nausea had suddenly become severe and I scratched at my skin as if I had a rash. Dev came to the bathroom and leaned against the wall as I continued to vomit.

"Chippy-flu," he told me. "Chippy's what they call beginners. It always makes people sick at first."

"You're not sick," I said from the depths of the toilet bowl.

"You'll feel better if you eat something," he said, patting me on the back and ignoring my remark.

"Sure, we'll eat something. At least that'll give me stuff to puke up. Tell me, why this is supposed to be fun again?" I asked irritably. Dev just laughed.

We went to the movies, had dinner, came home and went to bed. That night I dreamt that our house was haunted. The ghost's presence was oppressive. I could almost see it, like a shadow stalking me, from the corner of my eye. The fear was so overwhelming it almost cut off my breath. In dream-slow-motion I struggled to the door to escape, trying to shake off the force weighing down my legs. When I got to the door and pulled it open the ghost slammed it shut from behind me. I woke up sweating and shaking in the dark. Dev lay sleeping peacefully beside me.

Chapter Two

The next day I replayed our actions over in my mind. I chewed my lip as the familiar fear that simmered below the surface of consciousness boiled at a slightly higher heat. I was used to the feeling. I had been living with it my whole life. This was not the heart pounding fear one might feel while being chased by an angry dog but it was not as mild as say, worrying that I'd wind up with cancer at the age of fifty. It was something deeper and more corrosive. I called it fear of nothing but fear of everything was a more accurate description. To discuss it would blow my cover and reveal me as the coward I really was. Usually I just pushed it down and chugged Maalox straight from the bottle when it manifested as acid rising up to scorch my throat. My decision to follow Dev's lead rolled around with the fear in my mind.

I was uncomfortable about my decision and feeling weak-willed that I had conceded after all the initial raging I had done. But now there was no turning back. I had made my choice. And there was a strange intimacy to the act, as if we were bound, the three of us, by a secret ritual. That's what really appealed to me I decided, that sense of belonging to each other.

Two weeks later Dev asked, "Do you want to call Mick?" We were cleaning up after dinner. Our little kitchen was old and nineteen-forties drab but the fading light from the window over the sink made it dim and cozy. My hands were immersed in warm soapy water, washing dishes. Dev was sitting at the table, swaying gently to an old song on the radio with his eyes closed and a slight smile on his lips. "Listen to that guitar. Beautiful, isn't it? It sounds like the first drops of soft summer rain hitting the leaves." His voice was deep, as if he was talking to himself, lost in the enjoyment of the music. I closed my eyes and strained, trying hard to hear the song the way he did but found myself wanting to watch Dev instead. His eyes opened as the song ended.

"We haven't gotten high since your first time. That shows we can handle it. What d'ya say Novena?" He pushed his chair out and stood to stretch his arms, as if preparing for action.

A muscle in my shoulder tightened. I shrugged a little and continued washing the dishes that were piled in the sink, trying to buy myself some thinking-time. Dev picked up a towel and began drying the silverware. He sang to the radio and did a funny little dance with the towel, raising his eyebrows at me suggestively as his bright eyes held mine and I laughed before I could catch myself. I wanted to touch the life that danced in him, wanted to feel the same freedom that vibrated through him.

"It's the weekend," Dev continued. "We deserve to treat ourselves every now and then and if we share one bag, it won't cost that much."

"OK. I guess we need a little break once in a while and it's cheaper than dinner and a movie," I said, as if that were reason enough in itself, relieved that it provided an excuse to agree with him.

"Novena honey, you can pinch a penny till it screams for mercy!" Dev said approvingly, squeezing me from behind. He planted a loud kiss on my ear and danced to the phone. He called Mick and I made tea, allowing the activity to distract me from observing Dev's joy.

Mick met us at the door with three bags of heroin. They were smaller than I imagined, smaller than my smallest fingernail. Each came wrapped in the tip of a balloon, incase the dealer had to swallow them in a hurry and looked like tiny colorful bundles. Mick carried them in his mouth and spit them into his hand as he came through the door.

"Fifteen bucks a piece, going fast," Mick said as he collected Dev's money. Amazing how much enthusiasm the guy had when he had 'a burden in the hand', as he called it. Dev moved briskly to the bedroom which was in the back of the apartment, and closed the window blinds. Mick filled a small cup with water, fetched two spoons from the kitchen and bent them so the bowls sat evenly on the dresser. I watched thinking how industrious they were, like busy little elves in some warped workshop. Dev cut the balloons and took out tiny triangles, corners of plastic bags filled with a miniscule amount of pale brown powder. He untied the knots in the bags, emptied a whole bag into each spoon and then half of the last bag into each spoon. Taking a syringe, he shot a small amount of water onto the powder, ripped a little piece of cotton from a Q-tip and dropped it in. He used a lighter to bring the contents to barely a bubble and then applied the tip of the needle to the cotton, sucking up the precious fluid. He used a second syringe to draw up a smaller amount and handed it to me.

"Can you do this?" Dev asked.

"Of course I can. I was trained to take blood samples at work." My jaw was stiff when I spoke and my mouth was suddenly dry and cottony. I dropped onto the edge of the bed.

"That's not what I mean." He looked at me doubtfully. Without speaking I reached out to unbuckle his belt and pull it from around the waistband of his jeans. I used it to tie off, holding the end between my knees to pull it tight. I tapped the fat vein that popped up in the bend of my arm. I've drawn blood from hundreds of patients, I thought. I can do this. I used my right hand to hold the syringe, eyed the blue line in my left elbow and took a deep breath. My hand shook and my heart pounded, but the tip of the needle slid easily into my skin and I felt the slight pop as it punctured my vessel. I pulled back on the plunger of the syringe to see the dark blood mix with the light brown heroin in slow billowy clouds, confirming that I was in the vein. My mouth began to water. I pushed the drug in and dropped the end of the belt I held between my knees so it loosened from my arm. In seconds, before I got the needle out, I could feel a warm heaviness begin below my belly button. Another few seconds and it was spreading to my limbs, melting any tension I held in my body and allowing me to sink deeply into relaxation. My chest rose involuntarily in a deep sigh. A glow washed over me and into me in a slow wave. I felt like I was in love. I beamed a smile at Mick who was watching my reaction.

"Instant karma," he said softly, smiling back with a knowing look in his eyes. Dev radiated from his position in the rocking chair. He looked like a smiling Buddha. The three of us sat silently sharing the rush, each knowing that the others were feeling the same thing. The initial intensity passed. I settling into a state of peaceful contentment. We went out for coffee, blessing everyone in the cafe with our soft smiles.

"Maybe that's the thing about heroin that seduces people," I said as I sipped my coffee. "You can still function. I thought I'd be like the junkies on Drag-net, staggering around, blank-faced and looking like death, all pale and skinny and scared."

Mick shook his head and smiled a little.

"Nothing's like it is on TV. You don't get giddy or giggly, you don't feel paranoid or mean, and you don't see visions or find God," he said.

"You just feel really good!" I finished for him. Mick and Dev laughed.

"You have to be careful with this stuff," Mick warned a few weeks later during our regular Friday night get-high get-together. He stood at the mirror and expertly hit the vein in his neck. "It'll steal your soul. Soon you'll be selling everything you own for a hit." His voice was low and he sighed deeply as his heart pumped the drug into his system. Then he slumped into the wooden chair beside the dresser. The yellow-shaded lamp above him made his wispy curls shine like a gold halo circling his head.

"Not me," Dev replied. "You know I'd never sacrifice the things I worked to have." He nodded at his stereo, stacks of CDs, and bookcase full of antique books. They were his only possession of worth, but things he considered treasures. Mick grunted and lit a cigarette. His toolbox and a few thousand dollars-worth of tools was sitting in hock as we spoke. Dev withdrew the needle and sat back, his faced flushed and his eyes shining beneath droopy lids. "Good stuff," he said and closed his eyes to enjoy the rush. Mick watched him and grunted again. I saw the wary look that crossed Mick's soft features as he watched Dev, and the specter of fear that haunted me that first night tapped my shoulder with icy fingers, reminding me of its presence.

Chapter Three

The alarm clock ringing in my dream was way too loud. It couldn't possibly be morning in real life already, I thought as I reached out to turn off the obnoxious buzzing. It was morning, in fact it was past time for me to be out of bed. The alarm was on its third round of snooze. Groaning, I dragged myself from under the warm covers and rushed to get ready for work.

Usually I took the bus to save money on gas and to lengthen the life of my old car but since I was running late I drove. The nursing home was only a few miles from our apartment and at six thirty in the morning, traffic hadn't built yet. I slipped into a parking spot and hurried into the basement where the time clock waited. I saw the large form of my favorite co-worker Lynette, reading the notices beside the racks of timecards.

"You almost late," she said. Her deep voice vibrated while emphasizing the last two words. She was a large black woman in her late fifties and her big brown eyes held affection even though she looked reprovingly down at me from over her reading glasses.

"Yeah, well late is like pregnant. Either you are, or you're not. And I'm not," I said as I plucked my card from its slot and punched it with mere seconds to spare. I darted around Lynette and jumped onto the elevator in front of her.

"Hmp," she exclaimed as she lumbered heavily through the closing doors. "'You either is, or you ain't', she say," I heard her mimicking me in a high squeaky voice, loud enough so I could hear. "We'll see how smart she is when she doin' Miss Weeber all by herself."

"No, Lynette, you can't leave me with her alone, you know she always tries to bite me," I grabbed her fleshy arm and pretended to plead with her.

"You been up all night pleasing that pretty man you got at home. I know that look. When you gonna get off your ass and get a education so you can take care of yourself?"

"I can't leave you here alone Lynette. What would you do without me?"

"Honey, I'm gonna retire soon and then what will you do without me? You got to think about yourself. And when you gonna come to church with me and get to know God? He be waitin' to hear from you."

The elevator door opening saved me from having to answer. We had reached our floor and went into the dingy staff lounge to get ready for the day. I hung my jacket in the beat up locker and reached for the bottle of antacid I kept stored there, swigging from the bottle in preparation for a rough morning.

"You gonna need some kinda religion today, girl, Steph called off again," Lynette said, looking at the schedule.

"Me? What about you and your bunions?" I asked, groaning inwardly at having to work short staffed again.

"I already got Jesus baby, I'll be fine today! Yes, Lord," she crooned, "I'll be just fine!"

We headed out the door together and I grabbed the plastic pushcart to begin collecting water pitchers to fill with ice for each resident. Part of what I liked about my job was how mindless and undemanding it was. It was hard physically, and the residents could be challenging, but over all it asked little more than that I show up. As I pressed each plastic pitcher into the ice machine and filled it, I began thinking about how nice it would be when Dev and I had money and could find a house with a yard, maybe on one of the wide, tree-lined streets in the better part of the city. The fantasy slowly built on itself, opening into a wider and more detailed story. The pleasant daydream continued as I placed each water pitcher back in the appropriate resident's room. I could see Dev and I and maybe a few kids, having dinner with guests on our luxurious backyard deck. I would remain slim even after the kids and of course Dev would get even more handsome with time.

"Where your head at, girl!?" My fantasy was rudely interrupted by Lynette's deep voice. I looked up to see her standing, hand on cocked hip, in front of me. I had pushed the cart right into her wide behind.

"Oh sorry Lynette, I didn't see you!" I blushed at my lack of attention.

"Didn't see me? I'm big as a Volkswagen, for Jesus' sweet sake!" She drew herself up tall, the thick braids piled on her head adding several inches. "What you day dreamin' now?"

"I was just thinking about when Dev and I have enough money to buy a house, maybe with a big yard."

"You'd do best keepin' yo mind on right now, bay-bee," she said. Her slang always intensified when she was making a point. "It don't get any better than today. We each only got today. You better start appreciatin' every minute the Lord gives you, child. Um hum, every minute. No time for livin' in yo mind."

I loved it when she sounded like she was giving a sermon. Lynette got all choked up about Jesus. Sometimes I wished I could get religion. I wanted to feel the kind of passion that was so powerful it left no room for self-consciousness.

"Here and now as good as it supposed to be," she continued. "You got one foot in yesterday and one foot in tomorrow, you pissin' all over today. And today is a gift granted to us by God Hisself. Now help me get Mr. Taylor's teeth in," she said, pulling me abruptly back into that here and now. I looked at the grizzled confused patient waiting for me to bath, dress and wrestle him into a chair and my mind relaxed back into daydream where I could avoid the present waiting for me.

Later that evening I paced nervously in front of the window, looking out every few seconds. I thought about Lynnette's love for Jesus and said a quick prayer for everything to be OK, wondering if Jesus would notice that I only prayed when desperation set in. Hopefully He appreciated any attempt at contact as progress in the right direction.

"What's taking him so long?" I asked Mick, who was sitting on the floor with his legs crossed and his head leaning back against the wall. His eyes were closed and I noticed for the first time the dark circles beneath them. "I know something bad is going to happen. He's either going to get busted by the cops or beat up by the dealers." I shook my head and lit a cigarette.

"Dev'll be fine Novena. He's too big for some scrawny dealer to mess with. He's got to do this so people get used to seeing him on the street. Once everybody gets to know you they look out for you."

"So you're telling me nothing bad ever happens?" I put my hands on my hips and challenged him.

Mick opened his eyes a bit and smiled.

"I been beat up by dealers, beat up by cops, ripped off and scared shitless. Yeah, stuff happens. That's the risk you take." He closed his eyes again. I huffed and turned to the window in time to see Dev running up the steps to the house.

"He's back!" I shouted. Mick rose slowly from the floor just as Dev opened the door.

"Any trouble?" Mick asked him.

Dev clapped Mick on the shoulder, smiled and then ruffled Mick's hair affectionately.

"How quickly the student becomes the master," Dev said, bowing to Mick in mock deference before slinging off his leather jacket and hanging it neatly on the back of a chair. "I got a deal. The guy gave me three for forty bucks."

Mick winked and smiled at me.

"See Novena," he said. "Sometimes it pays to send the big guy. After a few times, Dev copping will seem as normal as taking out the garbage."

It was Halloween. The wind blew through the trees outside, making the dry leaves rustle and scratch against the windows of the warmly lit bedroom, which seemed like a bright sanctuary against the cold gusts blowing in the dark. I loved Halloween since I'd been kid. It seemed so dangerous for to us to dress up and run around parentless at night. In grade school my friend and I would roam the neighborhood in the dark scaring ourselves around every corner. We'd grab at each other breathlessly, giggling in terrified delight and finally we'd run home to count our candy. As a teenager I hated just about everything, especially holidays, but managed to appreciate the darkness of Halloween. It was safe-scary: I wanted to believe a ghostly apparition would float up from behind a tombstone, but I was reasonably sure enough that it wouldn't to still enjoy the experience. This enjoyment followed me into adulthood and my friends and I would plan our Halloween activities weeks in advance so we could be properly frightened on the big night. Séances, midnight walks in the cemetery, ghost stories in the dark, it didn't take much to get our imaginations going and soon we'd be sitting bunched together, clutching each other's arms and jumping at every noise, laughing with fun-scary excitement. My best friend Rachel had to work this year so I had no plans and was feeling restless. Maybe we would get high tonight, I thought, looking forward to doing something illegal and risky to celebrate Halloween.

I jumped onto the bed where Dev was sitting with his back propped against the headboard, a cup of tea on the nightstand, and a heavy book in his hands.

"It's my holiday," I reminded him.

"Don't bounce. I'm reading," he murmured. I poked at his flat belly. "Hmm, what?" he asked in a slightly irritated tone. He sounded far away and didn't look up from the book, 'A Complete History of The British Isles'. *This* couldn't be what was upstaging me, I thought, rolling my eyes. I grabbed the book and dropped it to the floor, then bounced onto Dev, straddling him.

"It's my night. You could have at least dressed up like a Viking and ravished me or something," I complained. With a swift motion he rolled me onto the bed under him and trapped my hands above my head.

"Arr, I'll ravish ye fair maid!" He growled and squinted lopsidedly at me.

"Vikings aren't supposed to sound like Popeye," I squealed when his whiskers tickled my neck. His mouth on mine stopped further complaints.

Dev raised his head and put his fingers lightly on his lips.

"Mmmm. That was a good kiss," he murmured.

"And what was so good about that one in particular?" I asked, clasping my hands around his neck.

He paused, as if contemplating.

"It was as soft but still demanding, like queen whose wish is always granted." He smiled down at me and I laughed softly.

"You are so full of bull-shit," I said. "That must be why I love you." I pulled him back to me and wrapped my legs around him.

We heard Mick's loud banging on the unlocked door just before he walked in. His boots dragged on the floor, making a shuffling sound as he entered the bedroom.

"Jesus, is that all you two do," he asked as he dropped into the wooden chair in the corner and crossed his legs. He slid a smoke between his lips.

"Every time I pop in you're pawing each other," he mumbled around the cigarette as his face was illuminated briefly by the flame of his lighter.

"Then stop popping in," I snapped and sat up to straighten my shirt. Mick ignored me and picked up the half-finished cup of tea I had set on the floor before disturbing Dev's reading.

"So what did you do last night?" Dev asked, his eyes on Mick soft and warm. He was sitting on the bed beside me, our backs against the headboard, his hand resting on my leg as usual.

"We went to an exhibit one of Francesca's friends was showing. At that new gallery downtown," Mick said, making a point of not looking at us. He was paging through Rolling Stone. Dev shot a glance at me and snorted with laughter.

"You mean that one with the ping-pong balls tied to fishing string and hanging from the ceiling?" Dev asked, a taunting lilt in his voice.

Mick brought his head up, eyebrows raised and looked down the length of his nose at Dev.

"I'll have you know there was some very expressive work there," he said haughtily. "And I enjoyed it." He went back to his magazine, which was open to an article who's title, 'OZZY' matched the fading home-grown tattoo that spelled out the name, one letter on each finger of his left hand, of his favorite musical 'artist'.

"Did Francesca make you wash your hair and wear a suit, too?" Dev asked with a wide smile, elbowing me conspiratorially. He kept his laughing eyes on Mick's form, now stiff in the chair. "Son, you better pray she never finds out who you really are or your ass is grass," Dev joked. "I'd pay to see you all cleaned-up and dressed in a suit, strolling around a gallery saying things like, 'this work is very expressive', and trying to look like you know jack-shit about art," Dev hooted. He got up to turn on the stereo, his back to us.

"I may not be *in-love* with Francesca," he paused almost imperceptibly and blushed, "but I can at least keep the woman that loves me happy." A miserable look passed his soft features, and he stayed focused on his magazine. My giggling died away as thoughts of the occasional current that passed between Mick and I rose to the surface of my awareness. Dev turned back to us and the moment was gone before I could grasp it.

"Well, you want to get something? Maybe split two bags between the three of us?" Mick's voice held none of the longing it had seconds ago and his eyes were sharp and bright again.

"Yeah. We got the cash Novena?" Dev asked me. I had no time to think about Mick's words as I fished thirty dollars from my purse. Mick punched a pager number into the phone. He carried on a short conversation after the phone rang back and hung up. Mick stood and pulled a scrap of paper from his worn out wallet then put in another number.

"Wilbur's out with his grandkids," he said, lighting a cigarette. "I called someone else." He exhaled a blue cloud of smoke. When the phone rang this time he spoke in clipped, hushed tones and hung up. "We have to meet this guy at Mallory's Place. I don't know him. We should both go," Mick said, looking hard at Dev.

"Sure. You ready?" Dev pulled on his old leather jacket and grabbed his keys.

"Can I go?" I asked suddenly in an eager voice, jumping up in front of the door. They looked at each other and paused. "I never get to go. I just want to see what it's like." I explained.

"Mallory's Place is that run down bar over on Federal Street. It's in a really bad part of town." Dev said.

"We live in a bad part of town." I reminded him. Mick shrugged his shoulders and Dev nodded.

"I feel just like I did when I went trick-or-treating as a kid," I said, skipping toward the car outside. Dev rolled his eyes.

"Well don't get too excited Novena. You're not getting out of the car," he said.

We drove the short distance to the bar which was in a run down building in a row of other crumbling buildings. Cars were parked all over and we found a dark spot under a broken streetlamp. A small group of young men were slouching on the corner looking menacing, hands thrust into the pockets of their over-sized hanging-off-the-ass jeans. There was broken glass on the sidewalk, graffiti on the walls, weeds growing up from between the uneven and broken pavement.

"I changed my mind. Novena you better come with us. And stay close." Dev said, motioning me out. The odor of rotting garbage, moldering buildings and stale urine hit me as I climbed out of the back seat.

"Ah, urban decay at its finest." I said as I inhaled. That pleasant little tingling of excitement and fear trailed along the back of my neck as we approached the entrance to the bar.

Dev went in first and I watched in awe as his form seemed to grow and become rougher. He lifted and squared his shoulders, lowered his head and narrowed his eyes. His arms hung at his sides as if ready to move into action in a second. His face settled into a look of quiet hardness. I became almost afraid of this Dev I didn't know, but I was a little thrilled by his transformation too. Mick was close behind me and I could hear by his light cough that he was nervous.

The bar was dark, smoke-filled and packed with people. On one side of the narrow building a smoke-clouded mirror hung above a bar. On the other side booths and tables were overflowing with people. The whole place was filthy even in the dim lighting and I hoped nothing would crawl onto me from the floor. The walls were cracked, the ceiling sagging and water-damaged and I almost choked on the heavy smell of stale smoke, urine and alcohol.

The patrons were mostly male, less-than-clean, with dark hard faces. Many had the lost look of hopeless chronic drunkenness. Some had the cold look of men so far gone into badness that the enjoyable fear-vibe I was riding froze into terror as I realized I was way out of my element.

The few women were thin, with empty eyes and faces drawn in pinched desperation. Women who looked like they spent their days passed-out on filthy mattresses in decrepit flop-house rooms and their nights offering what was left of their wasted bodies for drugs. I grabbed a handful of the back of Dev's jacket as he pushed his way through the crowd at the bar and headed towards the back room. Suddenly a huge fat man in a tent-sized leather jacket shoved past us, moving much faster than I would have expected a man of that size to move. He yelled angrily and grabbed a skinny guy in a dirty black t-shirt, lifted him over his head and lumbered toward the front of the bar, the skinny guy screaming the whole way. I tripped over my own foot trying to get out of his path, lost my hold on Dev and by the time I regained my balance, Dev and Mick were nowhere to be seen.

"Damn," I whispered to myself. There was no way someone my size was going to get anywhere in this crowd, I thought. I tried to look inconspicuous and make my way timidly in the direction I had last seen Dev and Mick traveling toward. Someone's hand in the crowd found its way to my butt cheek but I didn't stop moving long enough to identify the body it belonged to. My legs were beginning to shake. I felt small and weak and very vulnerable. The noise in the bar seemed to rise a decibel and the room appeared to narrow, as though it was closing in on me. Bodies pushed at me from all sides and I felt a shaky sense of panic begin to form.

"Hey, little girl, I bet you're here looking for candy tonight, ain't you?" a rough voice asked. I looked up and saw a tall thin man with long stringy blond hair and a droopy mustache blocking my path. His smile was mean, his pale face pulled tight by years of hatred. He crossed his arms in front of him and looked down at me. "How about you do me a trick, then I'll give you a treat." He grinned an evil jack-o'lantern smile full of jagged, broken, tobacco-yellowed teeth. My knees knocked together and my mouth went dry. Then a hand landed heavily on my shoulder from behind and for a second I was sure I was going to throw up.

"Sorry, she's leaving," Dev's firm voice said above my head. He pulled me backward against him and then pushed me in front of him through the crowd, his hands on my shoulders, until I was breathing the cold sweetness of outside, thankful for the air that had almost choked me with it's foulness on the way in.

"Jesus," I whispered, looking at Dev's familiar features with gratitude. "Thank God." I was still shaky.

"Thank me, not Jesus!" Dev said. "Can't you ever stay out of trouble? I should have known better than to take you to a hell-hole like that," he shook his head and spat on the sidewalk. "And that other one is just as bad as you." Dev complained and nodded toward Mick, who was looking equally shaken and was rubbing a swollen red mark on his throat gingerly. "Some junkie on a jones thought he had dope in his mouth 'cause he wouldn't say hello and tried to strangle it out of him. He was almost blue by the time I got there. It's no wonder he always gets into trouble. He doesn't stand up for himself. You got to look like you mean business if you're going to go in a place like that. Next time, I go alone. I don't have time to be baby-sitting you two while I'm trying to cop." He said. "Now let's go home and get high." Mick and I hung our heads and filed to the car. My legs finally stopped shaking, and I remembered that it was Halloween.

My real dose of fear was more than I had needed to feel like I had properly celebrated my favorite holiday.

***

"Hey, Gilbert." Dev said, grasping the thin man's hand in greeting. The needle marks on the man's tan arms were evident as he dropped his hand from Dev's. He was a friend of Mick's who had been joining us when we copped. I watched his slumped frame cross the room. His grey eyes seemed tired all the time and his face was dulled with the look of someone who had seen too much tragedy, but he had a subtle humor and an air of composure that caught me off guard.

"Hello Dev," Gilbert replied. He ran his bony hand through the curly red hair that stuck up from his head in clumps, making it lean to one side a little, like a wave about to crash onto the shore. We were sitting in the bedroom waiting for the phone to ring in response to the page Mick had put in and Gilbert had just joined us. He shook my hand, put his arms around Mick's shoulders in a brief hug and lowered himself into a chair. He then crossed his legs and folded his hands in his lap as if he'd come to high tea.

"Dev if you ever need extra money just call me," he said. "I work for a labor place, carrying bricks, mixing mortar, that sort of thing. I can sign you on any time. I've been there since I dropped out of school. They're good to their employees."

"Thanks Gil, I'll keep that in mind," Dev answered before leaving the room to get spoons and water.

I studied Gilbert closely. He had the diction of a college professor, the appearance of a bum and the quiet steady presence of a yogi master. I had met him a few weeks before and was still wary of him. He was a long-time drug addict and I saw him as being different than us. He seemed scary and distant, further down the path than I thought we would ever get. He'd crossed the line from occasional use to every day need years ago.

"Novena do you by chance have today's paper? I missed the evening news," Gilbert asked. I jumped a little and wondered if he had seen me staring at him. I passed him the paper and he methodically removed a pair of wire-rimmed glasses from a case, balanced them on his nose and opened the paper to the financial section.

"What were you in school for?" I asked.

"I was working on my PhD in physics," Gilbert said. I had to close my mouth, which had fallen open at his words.

"Um, how did you get … here?" I asked, trying not to offend him. He smiled and looked directly at me. His eyes were sparkling. Dev came back in and began the ritual of cooking the dope, his back was turned to us and his attention was focused on the flame and spoon.

"No matter what I say it'll sound like an excuse and I quit making excuses years ago. There was no big event or emotional trauma that drove me to it. I just wandered away and got caught up in it." His face held sadness but his voice was matter-of fact. He struck me as someone for whom drug use held no romance. It had just become a way of life.

"Don't you miss school?" I really meant 'miss living a regular life', but I didn't want to use those words. Gilbert seemed to know what I was saying anyway.

"No sense in missing what I freely gave up," he answered, his attention on the paper. "Things just didn't turn out like I thought they would." I turned my attention to Mick who had crossed his legs and leaned forward to join the conversation. Mick liked to demonstrate his wisdom whenever a chance presented itself.

"I've gotten used to being who I am now, how people look at me, their perception that I'm just a worthless junkie," Mick offered. "Most of us only see what we want to anyway. This world gives us easy ways to hide out. As long as you make enough money, drive the right car or have the right job you're accepted no matter what kind of fucked-up you are. At least in this life I'm faced with all my shortcomings head-on. It's kind of liberating to have your bad habits staring at you every day. No one expects too much from me." He sounded like he was trying too hard for Gilbert, who viewed him with a kind smile in his eyes.

·"*This* is regular life for me now," Mick continued with a sigh. "Anyway, most people living a so-called normal life are probably hiding some horrible vice themselves. At least I don't have to be caught up in how I *appear* to others, or struggle to make myself *look* successful, *act* respectable. It sounds like excuses and rationalizations, but I just don't care about that shit anymore. All I worry about is living my life peacefully and not harming anyone else." He smiled a weary kind of smile. I nodded, seeing his point and enjoying the idea of living out-side convention, of being part of a select group.

"Doesn't it bother you to think people look down on you?" I probed after a minute.

"*I* know who I am, that's what's important. This life woke me up. Most people don't even see the world around them. They have no appreciation for what they have, no idea of how fragile their hold on life is. Me, I know exactly what I've lost so I see clearly what I have," Mick said. He looked from Gilbert to me, eyebrows raised, a look of expectation on his face, as if he were waiting for us to agree.

"Yep, we've left the regular world behind to live like monks, we junkies." Gilbert's voice was gently mocking. "We don't care what you do for a living, what kind of car you drive, or how much money you make. Unless, of course, you're buying the dope!" He flashed a wide grin, then we all got quiet as Dev handed us each a syringe.

***

Dev was reading as I walked in. He sat in the living room in a dim pool of yellow light, his eyes shadowed by the book he held. He looked up and his face brightened, like a dark mountain that's features are illuminated by the sudden glow of dawn breaking over the horizon.

"Hey Novena," he smiled. "Come sit with me." He put down the book and patted his lap. Three years we'd been together and his face still lit up every time I came home. Three years and my heart still jumped each time he touched me. It was a chilly early November evening and I sat across his legs and burrowed against his chest to get warm, listening to the strong slow beat of his heart, drawing warmth from his body. I slid my hand under his shirt and rubbed the coarse hair of his chest, letting my cold hand thaw.

"You hungry?" I asked. "I didn't have dinner and I'm starving," I said, putting emphasis on the last word.

"You're such a creature of extremes," he laughed, pulling my hand out of his shirt and kissing my palm. "Never hungry, always *starving*, not cold, *freezing to death*, and instead of just tired you're always *completely exhausted*." He continued to laugh and squeeze me. I wrapped my arms around him and let my fingers stroke the soft hair at his neck. "I got a call in to Wilbur. I can't leave," he said.

I brought my head up to his eye level.

"You got high yesterday," I said. I tried to sound unconcerned but worry crept over me like a dark shadow.

"It wasn't that good. I didn't get much of a rush and I had a rough day. This cold wet weather makes my joints ache. I must be getting too old to work outside," he smiled.

"We planned to go out tonight. I've been looking forward to it all week," I brushed a lock of thick hair off his forehead. "I'll rub your back later to help you relax," I said in a coaxing voice.

He fidgeted, bouncing his knees and making me flop around on his lap. "I already paged Wilbur. I don't want to not be here if he calls, it isn't polite," he said. "We'll go out tomorrow, I promise Novena. I just need a good high this week." He was quiet for a minute. "Tonight lets stay in, just us."

His dark eyes won me over. I sighed and put my head back on his chest.

The sound of the rain on the window reminded me of the night we'd met. The memory began to play in my mind, and I let myself indulge, as if I were watching an old movie I'd seen a hundred times before but enjoyed every time.

Dev was twenty-five and I was twenty when we met in the laundry-mat on a rainy night. Mom had gone to Japan to teach. She wanted me to move to New York were my father lived but I had refused, reminding her that she had been on her own at 19. She found me an apartment above the garage of an elderly friend of hers and I moved into the tiny space. Alone for the first time, I was terrified but would rather die than admit it. I was perpetually angry and some part of me relished the opportunity for resentment that this new abandonment brought.

I was living in a cold drab apartment, working every day, wondering if I were destined to slack through the years dragging my fear with me. The night I met Dev I was having a particularly miserable evening full of regret and sorrow, spending Friday night doing laundry alone.

I looked up from my National Geographic magazine in irritation as the laundry-mat door jangled opened and Dev strode in with a duffel bag over his broad shoulder. He flashed me a wide smile. His eyes were bright and seemed to dance as they took in the room with a quick sweep, coming to rest on my thin black-clad frame.

"Excuse me miss, did you know that you're breaking rule number two?" He nodded to the sign on the wall above my head and a lock of dark hair fell over his brow. I pulled my eyes from his and twisted to read the sign posting the rules of the place, noting that number two said 'no sitting on machines'. Dev threw his clothes into a washer then pulled himself up onto a dryer next to mine. "If the manager comes in I'll blame you," he said with a wink. I blushed and looked back to my magazine, trying to ignore him. There seemed to be a force surrounding him, drawing me to him. As he shucked off his worn leather jacket the scent of him drifted to me, exotic, like cardamom and sandalwood. "Eureka, I been there," he said, pointing at the magazine that I had let droop from my fingers. "Beautiful place if you like fog and rain." I closed my open mouth and glanced down. 'Eureka, California: Land of Mist', the title said.

"You've been west?" I asked, trying to sound disinterested. I raised the magazine but my eyes remained on his face.

"Yeah, mostly up and down the coast, from Mexico almost to Vancouver. I only got to visit inland once but I want to go back and see the desert." He looked straight ahead as if picturing it in his head. "Someone told me when the sun comes up, it turns the rocks red and the sand glows like crystal. I want to see that." He turned his head and caught me studying him, saw my face flush as I looked quickly away and hid in the article again. He smiled and pulled the magazine out of my hands.

Dev told me about being stationed in Germany and Greece with the Army. About how at seventeen he'd hitched rides from the east coast to the west, then worked on fishing boats and in factories for a few years till he joined the Service. About how his mother walked out on he and his drunken father when he was twelve. He told me that he'd spent hours in the library reading Dickens and Hemmingway and Doyle, the stories inspiring him. As he spoke his rich voice seemed to penetrate the fog that shrouded my life. I hung on every word and began to feel my always-tense muscles relax. I pulled my eyes away from him and shook myself. It's just the rocking and warmth of the dryer I'm sitting on, I thought, as I jumped off and busied myself retrieving my clothes.

Despite my protests he helped me carry my laundry the two blocks to my home and a few days later he was knocking on my door asking me out. I refused, he kept trying. Every few days the familiar knock would sound and I would have my refusal planned. He eventually wore me down by showing up consistently for two weeks, smiling widely and asking if I'd changed my mind.

"Come on, you look like someone who could use a decent meal and a good laugh. I'm great free entertainment," he said, wiggling his eyebrows at me. I agreed reluctantly to one dinner, unable to resist his warmth.

The night of our first date he complimented my beauty and gallantly handed me a single pink rose, to which I rolled my eyes. During dinner he charmed me with tales of his independent childhood and travels. He had a way of making even the worst experiences sound funny. I had to work hard to keep my defenses up. Dev missed nothing.

"How about dinner number two?" He asked with a knowing smile as we stood on the steps to my building at the end of the evening.

"Against my better judgement I might agree to it," my face fell into its familiar mask of gloom.

He took my hand, raised it to his lips like a courtly gentleman and kissed it softly, his dark eyes never leaving mine. A rich orange-pink glow began to gather at the edges of my vision clouding my senses for a minute. I took a deep breath, inhaling the scent of him … and almost swooned. Dev smiled and then he got into his beat-up car and drove away, asking no more from me than the innocent kiss and a promise to let him cook me dinner the next weekend. I carefully preserved the pink rose, admiring it for days in spite of myself.

He was gracious, funny, wise and his insightfulness touched me. When we went out he was as kind to strangers as he was to me, treating even the bums we visited at the Salvation Army like valued friends. The light of his spirit was contagious. I could feel myself being pulled to him like a small dark planet drawn in by the gravity of a bright sun. Soon I was looking forward to our visits. We'd sit on the porch and talk about books and music.

Slowly he charmed me out of my perpetual bad mood, pointing out the innocence of laughing children playing in the street, the tenderness of an elderly couple holding hands in the bookstore, the brilliance of the sun illuminating the glass buildings in the city. Dev reacquainted me with the beauty I'd been overlooking. He was slow and patient as he taught me to enjoy his hands on my body.

With his gentle teasing the hard humorless person I had become began to soften. I felt like I had been given back my life and my cold aloofness melted into a warm feeling of security. The nagging fear that lived in my stomach all my life eased as I began to live with one hand on Dev, as if life were an electric current that was weakened as it passed from him into me at a voltage I could handle. Within a few months he seemed as essential to my existence as oxygen and all that was left of the pathetic creature I had been was lots of dark clothes and a tendency towards drama.

The phone rang, startling me out of reverie. I stirred in Dev's lap and sighed, caught up in the romance of our story as I retold it to myself.

I moved on Dev's legs as he shifted to pick up the receiver. Wilbur had called back and I listened to their short conversation while still wrapped in the warmth of my memories.

"Make sure you get some for me too," I said. He tightened his arms around me and kissed the top of my head. Everything would be OK as long as we were together, I thought.

Chapter Four

"Gotta go." Mick said as he slid out the door one evening after getting high. He was anxious to get home to Francesca. Gilbert raised his hand in farewell then went back to cleaning his needle. I blew out a slow breath and dropped the belt from around my arm when the warm feeling overtook me, wrapping me in an affectionate embrace. I looked at Dev who was sitting on the edge of the bed. He pulled the needle from his arm and immediately began to turn blue. His eyes rolled back into his head and he slumped forward onto the floor. I stared, not quite sure what was happening.

"Fuck," Gilbert swore as he dropped to the floor beside Dev and rolled him to his back. It registered in my brain that Dev had done too much dope. Taking care of an overdose was something every experienced junkie knew how to do, because if you called the medics everyone in the house got arrested. Gilbert swung into action without missing a breath and I frantically followed his instructions, surprised at my presence of mind. "We need to get him into the shower," Gilbert said. My hands shook and I was thankful for Gilbert's quiet steadiness as we dragged Dev to the bathroom across the hall. We propped him against the shower wall fully dressed and held him pinned there. Gilbert turned on the cold water. I didn't feel it as it hit us all. It soaked Dev, turning his red sweatshirt the dark color of blood, and his jeans an inky blue-black. Dev moved a little, raising his hands in slow motion to fight off the water hitting his face, then he went limp again.

'Don't you die, Dev. Please don't leave me,' I pleaded silently with his slack blue face.

Gilbert pulled him out of the tub, holding Dev's weight against himself and pivoting until he could lower his torso to the floor. I hurried to grab his ankles. A rush of anger overcame me as I became tangled in the shower curtain. *'Why do you have to do this to me?'* I thought as I pushed his legs over the edge of the tub.

"Ease him onto the floor Novena, don't drop him," Gilbert said between pursed lips as we struggled to lay him flat. "Bruises won't make him anymore careful in the future," he finished quietly as if he knew what was in my mind. I looked at Gilbert anxiously and felt my own breath coming in short gasps. Gilbert leaned over Dev and breathed into his mouth after pinching off his nose. I felt disconnected, like I was watching a movie, not quite convinced that this was really happening. Under Gilbert's direction we hauled Dev into the shower again, soaked him then put his still body back on the floor. Gilbert began calling his name. I knelt beside him and slapped Dev's face repeatedly. Dev took a ragged breath with each blow, the blueness of his lips changing to pale pink. As I realized that he was going to live, my anger rose and my hand got heavier as I continued to strike him. My jaw was clenched and my breathing heavy when Gilbert finally caught my forearm in mid-slap and held it.

"Honey, stop. You don't have to do that," he said in a low gentle voice. His eyes on mine were soft and sad. I stared at him for a minute then pulled my hand away and hit Dev's reddening face again, hard.

"But I want to Gilbert!" I said before dropping my arm. "I want to."

Dev began breathing on his own, his face slowly returning to pale except where it was red from my hand. We dragged him across the hall and laid him on the bed where he remained unconscious but breathing.

Gilbert sank limply into a chair by the bed. I wanted to crawl into his lap, wanted to cling to him and make him tell me everything was OK, to let his strength flow into me. Instead I pulled a chair close to his.

"I'll stay with you for a while and make sure he's OK," Gilbert told me.

"Thank you Gilbert." My heartbeat finally began to slow to normal pace and I relaxed a little. He nodded and lit a cigarette, passed it to me and lit another one for himself. I pulled in a deep long drag, like someone starving for oxygen, held it for a second and exhaled loudly, not caring how it sounded. Finally I could speak. "How did this happen? Did Dev just do too much?" I asked, biting my lower lip.

Gilbert shook his head slowly. He sucked on his smoke and met my eyes.

"Dev wanted to try a stamp bag. They're hits of almost-pure heroin that come in those wax-paper bags like stamp collectors use. You can't always find them so Dev wanted to get a few while the dealer had them. They're twice the strength of a normal hit." Gilbert looked disgusted. "I should have stopped him."

"It's not your fault. Dev always has to push the limits. I'm just so thankful you were here," I said as I watched him lying pale on the bed, dark circles beneath both eyes. I could hear the crackle of Gilbert's cigarette in the silence.

"How long have you two been together?" He asked me.

"Three years," I said.

"So you knew each other before all this."

"Oh yeah. This is new to us both. Dev thought he'd just try it and I like it once in a while, too. We can quit anytime." My voice was firm but my face felt like it held a question as I looked at Gilbert. He shifted in his seat and looked away.

"How'd you two meet?" he asked conversationally, trying to fill the awkward silence.

"I didn't even want a boyfriend." I began, letting a smile ease the tension in my face. "My whole life I dreamed of traveling," I said, thinking about how to tell the story. "I fantasized about the day I could jet off to some exotic land and take care of famine victims or be part of a disaster relief team tending to earthquake survivors or something really exciting. I spent lots of evenings in the library after work looking at books about Indonesia and South America, planning." I paused, liking how independent and adventurous I sounded when I told the story in those words. Gilbert nodded, encouraging me to go on.

"One night I reached out for a magazine about temples in Nepal and someone else grabbed for it at the same time. The girl told me she wanted to collect a rock from every continent before she got married. Her name was Deb.

We spent the rest of the evening talking and by the time the library closed we were planning to travel the world together." It was true that I wanted to travel but I shuddered at the thought of doing it alone. I needed someone to take me with them on their adventure and Deb seemed like a good candidate to fill the job.

She'd had an old black leather biker's jacket thrown over her pale pink mini-skirt and lacey white blouse. Her thin legs in rose-colored hose ended in combat boots. She looked like an angel who had landed on the wrong side of town when she'd fallen to earth. I could remember the way she flung her long blond curls out of her blue eyes. She was beautiful in a fragile, silent-movie star kind of way but there was a dark sadness to her too.

"I wanted to be just like her. She had been on her own since she was seventeen, wore really cool clothes, lived with an older man and went to night clubs all the time. I started spending most of my time with her. I went to their house after work and stayed the nights in their spare bedroom. It was fun at their house, people coming and going, things happening all the time." It was a new experience for me to have friends like these, friends who made exciting things happen and I was flattered that they wanted me around.

"Deb's boyfriend Roy was about thirty-three, a short thin guy with stringy brown hair that made him look like a mean little dog. He liked the fact that he had two young girls staying with him and we liked the fact that he got us into bars and nightclubs even though we were underage." Gilbert grunted.

"I bet he liked it," he said.

"Roy was a used car salesman and he did a little drug dealing on the side, mostly pot and some coke. We rode with him sometimes when he made drug deliveries. I took the diet pills he brought home to stay up for work after being awake all night but mostly I would just drink while they got high." I looked at Gilbert for approval and he nodded. In reality I was scared to death to try the cocaine they offered me even though Roy told me the "diet pills" were not much different.

"Roy always had friends and 'clients' at the house. He said entertaining was good for business. It was one big party all the time. After a while though, things changed. Deb quit her job as a checkout girl and she had to rely on Roy for money and a place to live. He treated her OK, but every once in a while he would get all coked-up and hit her." I paused, remembering standing in the doorway of the bathroom, watching Deb look at her reflection in the mirror while she covered her bruises with makeup and snorted lines of coke to numb her swollen face.

Gilbert clucked his tongue reprovingly and drew a deep lungful of cigarette smoke.

"One night I thought he was going to kill her and I tried to call the police but she stopped me. A few weeks later, Roy and I ... had a fight and I left and didn't go back," I paused for a second to take a deep breath. I hated this memory, I hated how it still made me feel shaky with emotion. "After that, after seeing how he treated Deb, I decided never to trust men. Then I met Dev and I ... changed my mind."

"Maybe you should have stuck to your original plan," Gilbert said with a gentle smile and reached out to touch my hand. I smiled too, feeling shy all of a sudden that I had told him so much.

Later that night after Gilbert left I crawled into bed, curling myself against Dev's warm back. My weary mind drifted uncontrollably like an unmanned boat towards the rapids, and crashed into the part of my story I hadn't told Gilbert. To say Roy liked having Deb and I around was an understatement. He strutted around talking about his girls like he owned us both. At first I felt like he thought of me as a little sister. As time went on it became clear that his intentions were not brotherly at all. He began to make it known that the time would come when I would have to pay for being at the parties, the places he took us, his acceptance of me into his house. I tried to ignore the not so subtle advances he made, thwarted them by pretending I didn't notice. Deb seemed oblivious. I was always able to dance away from him, remaining just out of reach of his pawing hands and leering mouth. One night he finally lost his patience. Deb had run from the room when it started.

Even now in the darkened room, my face burned with shame when I remembered his rough hands tearing my clothes, roaming my body, how powerless I was to stop him as he held my flailing arms and pinned my kicking legs. My shame deepened as I heard my desperate voice pleading with him, my cries becoming hysterical sobs. Finally he had spit in my face, told me I wasn't worth the fight and rolled off me. I had run from the house, devastated that Deb hadn't tried to stop him. I sobbed and cursed myself hotly for being so stupid, hunching my shoulders and holding myself tight as I staggered to the bus station. I spent the night there in a hard cold plastic seat, drinking stale coffee and shaking, afraid to go home in the dark. I never saw either Roy or Deb again but the distrust and bitterness left was like an ugly taunting creature that lounged around the edges of my consciousness, casting a shadow over my days until Dev's light chased it away.

I let the wave of sickening feelings crest and eventually ebb. With effort I wrenched my mind away from the past and placed it on the events of the evening. I wondered where the physical strength had come from to help move Dev's limp weight around so easily. I puzzled over my reaction, admiring my ability to follow Gilbert's instructions without panicking. I thanked whatever god had been with me and edged into uneasy slumber.

The phone rang early the next morning, waking me. Dev grumbled and turned over as I answered it. The events of the past night came crashing into my mind.

"Novena it's Mick, how you doin'?" he asked.

"Dev overdosed after you left last night," I said in a rush, feeling a need to say the words out loud. There was a silence on the other end.

"Is he OK? What happened," Mick's voice held concern and reluctance, almost like he didn't want to know.

"Yeah he's OK. Gilbert was here, thank God. Dev just started to turn blue and then he fell over. We put him in the shower and after awhile he was breathing on his own. He's still sleeping." I could hear Mick sigh on the other end and the muffled sounds from his fidgeting with the receiver.

"Dev takes things too fast sometimes … he thinks he can handle anything. I'm sorry I wasn't there," his voice trailed off and he was silent for a minute. "Dev scares me sometimes. He's so intense," he said quietly. Then his voice gained volume and conviction. "But he's so sure of himself and more in control than anyone I've ever met. This was just a freak thing. It happens to us all in the beginning. It'll be all right, Novena. Tell him to call me when he gets up," Mick said before we hung up. I sighed, not at all comforted by what Mick had said.

"Think about it Novena. I was on the edge of death," Dev said later, after waking up and hearing the story from me. "I don't remember it, of course, but what a trip!" He flashed a smile at me and there was awe in his voice. "Just to know I was that close …" He caught my hard stare.

"You think it was some kind of adventure? I should slap you harder for that than I did when you were on the bathroom floor," I told him.

"Don't get all pissy, now. I'll be more careful. Besides, you're a trained nurse's aide, you know what to do. I'm safe," he said, shrugging his shoulders.

I ignored him and went back to watching TV, but I reached for my bottle of Maalox when Dev came home later that evening and cooked his dope. My stomach churned as I watched him closely for signs of impending overdose and I exhaled my pent up breath when nothing happened.

I shrugged off the lingering feeling of apprehension as I took the syringe he offered me. Shooting heroin had become just another part of our lives. We went to work every day, visited Dev's father and spent time with other friends. Nothing had really changed, I thought as the rush washed over me in warm comforting waves, dispelling the rest of my fear.

"Relax," the drug whispered in my ear. *"Things are completely under control."* I succumbed to the soothing voice and tried not to think about Dev's blue form lying on the bathroom floor that night.

***

It was two weeks before Thanksgiving and our apartment was freezing cold. We lived in Manchester, an old section of north Pittsburgh that boasted wide straight tree-lined streets and huge houses dating from when steel industry giants built homes beside the river. It also had the highest crime rate in the city. Many of the old places had been destroyed during the riots of the sixties and I liked the contrast between burned-out skeletal remains of destroyed houses along side neatly kept flower gardens and restored mansions. Our little space was stifling hot in the summer and frigid in the winter, but I loved living in the attic anyway. I felt above and out of reach of the interesting characters below, yet I could still be entertained by their antics from the safety of my window. As I sat curled in my rocker I was watching two young men trying to decide how to get into their car. Someone had left a big mean dog chained to the lamp post beside their vehicle. Every time they got close to the doors the dog went into attack mode and they would scream and run away. Finally they climbed through the hatchback, into the front seat and drove away. I picked up the phone to call my mother for our bi-weekly check in.

"Hi Ma," I said as she answered.

"Hi, Baby," she crooned, "it's sooo good to hear your voice!" she finished in an enthusiastic voice. My mom always sounded over-excited when we spoke. "What's new?" she continued. "How's Dev?"

"We're both fine," I said. "Nothing much new, job's the same, we're both OK." Mom had met Dev when she was home to visit the year before and of course they loved each other.

"Have you talked to your father lately?" It was always in the first five minutes of the conversation that she asked this.

"I talked to him last week. He started rowing again and now he says he's in the greatest shape of his life. Hannah and Evan are OK too," I added, knowing the mention of his second wife and their child would hurt her. My dad started a second family after he and Mom divorced. I used to go once a year for a week to his new house in New York, spend seven days feeling weird and hating every second of my time with his new family. I blamed my mom for his leaving and she knew it.

"Good. I'm glad he's doing well." Silence for a moment. "Have you heard from Jamie?" My brother Jamie was four years older than me. He was so beautiful in both spirit and body it was hard to believe we had come from the same womb. "I talked to him yesterday and he said the weather out there has been gorgeous. He's already skiing. And he was chosen for the mountain rescue team!" She practically gushed when she said that. "I'm so proud of him. He's wanted this since he was a little kid."

"That's great Ma, I'm glad for you both." I rolled my eyes and lit a cigarette.

"Have you thought any more about going to school? You wouldn't have to quit work, just take a few classes. See what you like."

"How come you never nag Jamie about school? He didn't go to college either." I sounded whiney and regretted not controlling my voice better.

"Honey I don't care if you go to school or not. Jamie's living his passion, he knows what he loves and is doing it. I just want the same for you," she said.

"I'm fine doing exactly what I'm doing," I replied defensively.

"I just don't want you to miss out on anything. You know I love Dev, but you're so young to be all tied up with a man already."

"You were married at twenty three," I threw back, knowing her reply.

"But I had already been to India, and Thailand. And all over the States. You've never even been out the eastern US." She paused for effect. I lit another cigarette.

"You know how you got your name, don't you?"

I huffed a loud breath. I'd heard this story so many times I could tell it in her exact words. Sometimes I would mouth them silently as she said them.

"I tried for three years to have another baby after Jamie and I just couldn't conceive. Your father and I were teaching summer school at the mission in New Mexico and every day I would see Sister Guadalupe leaving the chapel as I was going into the schoolroom. She said, 'Miss Clair, I'm saying a novena for you that you have a daughter as beautiful as you, who helps people like you.' Nine days later I found out I was pregnant, and nine months later you came to us."

"I know. That's why you named me Novena. So I would always remember I had been prayed into the world for a purpose."

"Baby, I don't care what you decide to do. Just understand that when you know what your gifts are your whole life becomes a blessing, to others *and* yourself," she said softly.

"I'll think about it," I said. That would appease her till the next phone call. "When are you coming home?" I asked, unable to keep the longing out of the question. It galled me that I missed her so much.

"This semester ends in February and Richard and I are going to Costa Rica. Pittsburgh is no place to be in winter." She sounded apologetic. "Expect us sometime in April. I miss you so much!"

After we hung up I thought about what she said. It was true. All my life I had drifted along without direction or goals, waiting for someone else to let me tag along on their journey. I had no idea what interested me. It disturbed me for about ten seconds, then I grabbed the TV remote and clicked on some relief.

Chapter Five

"The new renter is moving in today. His name's Wayne." Dev said, nodding his head toward the window.

"What's he like? Did you ask Jon?" I wondered and went directly to look out the window Dev had vacated.

"You know Jon," Dev said with a smile, referring to the owner of the house next door. He rented out rooms in his giant renovated Victorian house and we were friendly with him and all his boarders, most of whom were flamboyant gay men, as was Jon himself. "All he wants to know is your name and do you have first month's rent and security deposit."

I sat in the window and eyed the grizzly, bushy bearded, beer-bellied biker with suspicion as he moved his few belongings in the building next door.

"He looks rough and scary to me," I mumbled from my post.

"Sounds like he'll fit right in," Dev said with a smile in his voice.

A few days later we accepted Jon's invitation to visit for afternoon tea. He liked to put out dainty pastries and fancy candies and have company over. Jon was a successful business man and the crowd at tea was an odd mix of people. No one was turned away. The tea was usually spiked with whiskey and the conversation was sometimes on the vulgar side, but it suited Jon's personality. He was a small, delicately built man with fragile features and a lilting voice. He was as hard as a brick wall however, and just as rough.

The other guests were milling around, sitting and standing in small groups enjoying the deserts and tea. We sat with Wayne at a small antique table, balancing tiny cups of strong tea on our knees and picking at petite fours from the bone china plates covering the table. Wayne was open and friendly, telling us he was just out of prison where he had spent three years for assault: he had pistol-whipped a guy who tried to steal his leather jacket. He told us with a big toothy smile that his jacket was worth killing for.

"It was my second time in jail. I've had my problems with drugs in the past, you know," he told us in a serious voice. Then his eyes twinkled as he continued. "Yup, picked up a nasty heroin habit in Viet Nam, along with every type of venereal disease ever heard of. One you get from stickin' someone else's needle in you, the other you get from stickin' your needle in someone else, can't win either way!" He threw his head back and laughed at his joke, delighted that he'd made me blush.

"Didn't you have to quit when you went to jail?" I asked.

"Hell, no, honey. It got a worse hold on me than ever while I was in there. Dope was just so easy to get in prison," Wayne said with a full-bellied laugh. "The guards sold it, the other inmates sold it. It was like being a kid locked in a candy store. And what the Hell did I care, I was already in jail!"

"Did you ever kick in lock-down?" Mick asked with a slight shudder. Wayne kept smiling and lit a cigarette.

"Sure did."

Dev swore softly and shook his head. I looked from one to the other in confusion.

"What? Is that bad?" I asked.

"Heroin withdrawal cold turkey won't kill you, it won't give you seizures and most times it won't even make you hallucinate. It'll make you really uncomfortable, though," Mick explained.

"It'll make you wish you were dead," Wayne offered.

"It feels like having a really bad flu: your joints hurt like they're on fire, you puke like crazy and you get delirious. It lasts for about a week," Mick told us.

"Doing it in a cold jail cell on a hard metal cot with bright fluorescent lights in your eyes is enough to make you never want to pick up that needle again," Wayne said.

"Till the next week when somebody's cookin' it next to you and your mouth starts waterin'," he added with a laugh.

"You clean now, Wayne?" Dev asked.

"I had my problems, like I said, on and off. My old lady don't like it one bit and now that I'm out where she can keep her beady eye on me better, I got to clean up. Or she'll cut off my allowance." He elbowed Mick and leered. "Yeah, I'm using the cut-down method this time. I'm only goin' to get high a few days a month, those bein' the ones directly followin' the arrival of my Vet's disability check and I'll stay clean all the rest of the time."

Dev clapped him on the back and smiled. Wayne was impossible to dislike in that way that sociopaths usually are.

"It sounds like a pretty good plan to me," Dev told him with a wink. Wayne smiled back at Dev and Mick and I knew I'd be seeing more of Wayne.

"I'm going over to Rachel's," I said one afternoon.

"What are you and Rachel doing?" Dev asked, looking up from his book. He was in the chair in the corner reading. The walls of the room glowed yellow from the old lamp on the dresser. "Try not to get in any trouble." He shook his finger at me before I could answer, frowning in mock disapproval.

"We're just having coffee," I told him, planting a kiss on his forehead before I danced out the door.

"How's Dev?" Rachel asked after I'd settled in. She pushed her short brown curls off her forehead. She was small although her muscular build made her seem taller. Her hair was cut boyishly short but her full red lips and the thick lashes framing her bright hazel eyes gave her a decidedly feminine appearance. We were sitting in the kitchen of the apartment she shared with her lover Amy and a couple of cats. Their table had only two legs and the end without legs was propped on the windowsill to hold it up, very thrift-shop-chic. As long as one didn't wiggle around too much, it was stable. The three of us considered it a work of creative genius and we figured in a few years all the designers would be charging big bucks for two-legged tables.

"Working, reading, nothing interesting," I said. "He was pissed off about someone at work making fun of a homeless guy and fumed about it all last evening. I kept telling him to let it go, but he was all worked up. I calmed him down, as usual, but it took a while. How he got along before me I'll never know." I made up the story just to have something positive to tell, feeling the need to make Dev a hero.

"Well, you two certainly fill in each other's blanks," Rachel said. "You're calm when he's angry, he's sensible when you're doing high drama. But no one can get along in this world unless they can stand alone." She looked at me from under her lashes, then busied herself pouring coffee. "Cock-sucking bastard!" she swore as hot coffee spilled onto her hand. "Honey, hand me that God-damned rag will you. This whore-son of a fucking pot has to go!" Words of wisdom and profanity, the two things I could always count on from Rachel.

She, Amy and I sat in the kitchen all afternoon drinking coffee and laughing. The shabby kitchen with its two-legged table was one of my favorite places. No matter where Rachel lived, how worn-out her furniture or run-down her apartment was, I always found a sense of peace in her space and I soaked it up like the first warm rays of spring sun after a long cold winter.

I started twice during our visit to tell her about the drugs and the new fear that had begun to follow me everywhere, casting a cold shadow on my thoughts. Instead of unburdening myself I made idle conversation. My fear sat next to me during the visit despite the warmth of her kitchen. I could feel its icy breath on the back of my neck each time I opened my mouth to begin the story. Rachel would never judge me if I made a mistake but I just couldn't tell her about our new habit. Not returning a library book is a mistake. Shooting heroin is more like hitting a large angry dog on the head and standing around to see his reaction then whining when he bites you in the ass. I knew she'd be shocked and scared and I didn't want a reminder of the fear I was trying to avoid thinking about, so I kept my secret. I was beginning to get accustomed to the weight of it.

"Tell Dev to get his ass over here and visit with us," Rachel called as I left. "And give him a big, sloppy, gooey heterosexual kiss for me!" She stood in the doorway with her arm around Amy, smiling and making loud kissing noises against her hand. I looked at them for a long minute before getting into my car. Rachel's compact form wedged against Amy's tall thin frame melded together and became a silhouette against the orange light behind them.

That night when I got home Dev and Mick were at their usual positions at the dresser, spoons and lighters ready. I flopped down on the bed and began to flip through a magazine and wait for my portion to be handed to me. Suddenly the door was flung open, hitting the wall behind it with a loud bang. They had apparently forgotten to lock it on the way in. Wayne slammed his back against the door and held a pistol in both shaking hands, pointing it at Dev and Mick. I always seemed to be a second behind everything and I stared dumbly at Wayne, my thoughts blank.

"Goddammit, you gotta give me some or I swear I'll shoot you both!" he yelled. Mick and Dev barely looked up from what they were doing.

"Jesus Wayne, put that thing down before you hurt someone," Dev mumbled, keeping his attention on the tiny bag of dope he was trying to get open. "All you had to do was ask." He reached into the dresser and pulled out another spoon.

"Apparently Wayne's had all he wants of the clean life," Mick said, continuing to heat two of the spoons.

"Well it's been four whole days," Dev countered evenly, also holding a lighter under two spoons. "Now he's got no money, which is why he was clean four days in the first place, a gun he's violating parole to keep," Dev paused to place the spoons carefully on the dresser, "and a powerful need to get high," he finished.

"I just need a little to take the sick off me," Wayne whimpered from behind his hands. He had dropped the gun on the floor and closed the door behind him before falling into the nearest chair. "I'm sorry about the gun but I wanted to be sure. I gotta have some. I can't stand the sick anymore," Wayne continued in a hushed voice, his chin on his chest.

"It'll test ya," Mick murmured as he drew the murky liquid into a needle. "In both body and mind. Some people just suffer better than others."

"Wayne is definitely one of the others," Dev pointed out. "I'd say this man needs a little medicine," he said as he crossed the room to Wayne's chair and handed him the syringe.

I tried to avoid having to look at Wayne's crumpled form. It embarrassed me to witness his weakness as he struggled to hold the needle. Wayne's hands were shaking too badly to hit his own arm.

"Novena, help him," Dev ordered without turning his attention from the spoon in front of him. He was busy fixing his own dope now. "He can't hold his fit," Dev said, using the street slang for syringe. I sighed, went over and pushed up the weathered sleeve of Wayne's leather jacket to reveal the blue veins on the back of his hand. I tied off above his wrist and took the syringe from him. He was an easy hit and my own mouth watered when I saw the blood mix with the heroin in the barrel of the syringe. I pushed it in and removed the belt. As I withdrew the needle, Wayne grabbed my hand. His face was inches from mine and his eyes were fierce.

"Novena, promise me you'll quit before you get like me. Promise me!" He had a death-grip on my hand, but it was the intensity of his voice that kept me from moving away. "Tell me you'll quit," he pleaded. Hitting someone else was an intimate, almost sensual act and this glimpse inside him shook me. I had never known him to do anything but laugh. I didn't think he was even aware of how messed up his life was and this sudden revelation was more of an ominous warning than his words. I could never get like him, I thought, providing a defense against the fear his intensity had aroused. I withdrew my hand slowly from his grasp and pulled my eyes from his. This was heavier stuff than I wanted deal with, especially when I had a hit of my own waiting.

"Sure, Wayne, don't worry about me," I mumbled. I turned away to get my fit and lose myself in the rush.

***

I looked up from the table as a gust of cold December wind followed Gilbert and Mick into the dim yellow kitchen. They trooped through the apartment single file after saying hi to me. I followed them to the bedroom where Dev was getting out the spoons. Once inside, the door was locked and the blinds were closed. Gilbert had copped before coming to the house so he collected money from everyone. The going rate was fifteen bucks a bag.

"They should sell half-bags of this stuff," I said. "I only need half to get high and I hate paying for more than I need," I said. Not that the other half went to waste with three other junkies in the room.

"I'll put in a request with the dope-man," Gilbert said, glancing at me sideways. He handed me a syringe. I took a seat on the end of the bed and went through the usual motions, anticipating the coming rush. As I withdrew the needle I began to feel sick, my head hurt, my muscles ached, I felt weak and my joints were on fire. Gilbert and Mick were on the opposite side of the bed from me and weren't looking so good either. They were both pale and the usual after-rush euphoria was absent. Dev looked pissed.

"We got beat. I don't feel a thing. Gilbert who'd you cop from? This isn't Wilbur's shit I bet." Dev's face was dark with anger as he rose from the corner chair and came to stand in front of Gilbert.

"Wilbur didn't have anything. I had to go through Sissy." Gilbert had been rubbing his aching legs and stopped, looking up at Dev's sharp tone of voice. "It's not like going to the A&P, you know," Gilbert said. "You have to take what you can get."

"Yeah, that's the problem with the free market these days, too many ass-holes out to rip people off," Dev fumed. "Where's their sense of integrity, don't they know this is bad for business?"

"They're drug dealers, not master-craftsman," Gilbert said. "You don't get a money-back guarantee. Hell, I've been beat as many times as I've been high. It's all part of the game." He held his hands out, palms up, as if to demonstrate that it was out of his control. Dev shook his head and cursed.

"I'll call Sissy," Mick said quickly, crossing the room toward the phone. "I want to know who she got this from. Maybe there's something else out there by now."

Sissy Moore was the local clearing-house for drugs in our neighborhood and possibly the whole city. She lived in a run-down row house a few blocks from us. Her living room was decorated in a sort of white-trash-does-Camelot theme: red carpet, purple velveteen sofa cover, wrought-iron-looking plastic light fixtures and Elvis right there over the mantle holding court.

From her dirty old Lazy-Boy, Sissy could smoke Camels, watch TV and conduct thousands of dollars in business by phone. She knew every dealer in the tristate area, every junkie and most of the police. She didn't have a regular job, didn't have to. She made her money copping for other people.

Some people didn't have the nerve, or hadn't gotten to the point yet of copping on the streets themselves. So they called Sissy and for a fee (usually at least half the price of a bag of dope, depending on how desperate they were) she obtained their drug of choice. Anyone with pills to sell could call her, she knew who was looking for what and would then contact a buyer. Sissy did a brisk business in the sale of pills. A person could go to the ER complaining of tooth pain and explain that their dentist was on vacation, get a prescription for pain killers and then fill the script for twenty or so Darvocet on their welfare card, paying only a dollar co-pay. Sissy would then call the buyer she found, someone willing to pay six dollars a pill for narcotics they didn't have to shoot or snort. She took a buck a pill, twenty dollars in this case, and the junkie pocketed the other five dollars Sissy got for each tablet, or used it to buy the drug of his or her choice. Not a bad profit. And the street prices for speed, Valium and Percocet were even higher.

Sissy wasn't everyone's idea of the modern business woman but she kept her bills paid, her child in shoes and her habit fed this way. Her husband had disappeared ten years ago leaving her with a two-year-old baby and a heroin habit. Just when she thought she would have to give in and go on Methadone she hooked up a desperate, new-in-town junkie with a dealer she knew and an idea was born. Ten years later business was booming.

"Sissy says she hears there's some better shit out there. She'll fix us up," Mick said as he hung up the phone. He hitched his baggy jeans up around his thin hips and pointed to himself. "You should have let me call her in the first place. Sissy has a crush on me, she always saves the best shit for Mickey." He smiled widely, trying to placate Dev. Dev threw a pillow at him as we all headed for the door, his face relaxing a little.

"That's a real catch, Mickey," he said, his anger mutating into sarcasm. "A dope-shooting welfare-queen with a twelve year old kid and a falling down house. When's the wedding?"

"We'll see who you call the next time you have to go through Sissy, wise-ass," Mick shot back.

"I hate going to Sissy's house. I always feel like I need to shower after we leave," I complained from the back seat as we drove to her house.

"Suck it up Novena. It's only for a few minutes," Dev said.

"I get to sit on the hard furniture then. God only knows what or who's been absorbed by the soft stuff. And it smells like dirty humans," I wrinkled my nose as I spoke and held my hands up as if they were already dirty.

"At least she keeps it nice and dark Novena. That way you don't have to see anything in detail," Dev chuckled. I shuddered on purpose, making him laugh out loud.

"And there's always a couple desperate scary cases in there coughing and sniffling, waiting for Queen Sissy to hook them up with some instant karma," I continued as if I hadn't heard him.

"Wait for us while we go in and talk to her then, if you're going to be a princess about it." The three of them slipped out of the car. I sat back in relief and put Dev's sunglasses on before closing my eyes to relax.

Mick, Dev and Gilbert came out and Sissy was with them. Her skinny body was clad in tight dark blue ankle-biting jeans, a cut off fringed-at-the-bottom pink t-shirt, white high-tops left untied and a stone-washed jean jacket. The height of fashion in 1983. Unfortunately it was 1993.

"Hi Vena," she crooned in a nasally voice as she crammed into the back seat of Dev's small Honda with Gilbert and me. It irritated me that she always shortened my name like she was a close friend. "This guy has some good shit but we have to go get it and he won't talk to you without me there," she explained. I pressed myself up against the door in an attempt not to touch her. Her long dirty brown hair whipped into my face and I hoped she didn't see me cringe. Her skinny legs leaned against mine. I looked out the window and tried to concentrate on the passing scenery as she sang to the radio in a high, off key voice. Sissy always seemed happy and she was so friendly I couldn't find any way to be a bitch without well, being a bitch.

She balanced a beer on her knee and cracked it open while we were stopped at a red light. She took a sip then tried to stabilize it between her legs before the car started moving. "Devvy honey, I got me a nice buzz goin'," she said. "Don't blow my high with your Goddamned fast driving." Dev grinned like a kid and squealed his tires as he pulled out.

"God almighty!" she shrieked, and grabbed at my thigh in fear.

"The more you let him know you're afraid the more he'll try to scare you," I muttered and placed her hand firmly back on her own leg. I then squished myself up against the door to keep from having too much of her leaning on me until we pulled into a driveway leading to a large well-kept house and parked.

Gilbert and I waited in the car while the other three went in to pick up our stuff. I hated having to pay more money the same day. Our paychecks seemed to dwindle at an alarming rate lately.

"You should be careful Novena," Gilbert said. "Dev's going to have a bad time, I can see it in his eyes. And convincing Mick to quit isn't going to be easy." He turned to look at me. "Who got you started doing this, anyway?"

"Mick," I said.

"Damn. He should know better," he swore softly and shook his head.

"Dev would have just found someone else to show him," I said. "At least Mick taught Dev to be safe. We're never out of bleach."

"It's a bad thing to lead someone into this, even if they ask for it," Gilbert told me.

"Maybe Mick was lonely." I thought about how I couldn't tell Rachel what we were doing and how nervous I felt around people without a drug habit.

"So he created his own little fucked-up family complete with skeletons rattling in the closet." Gilbert shook his head and looked out the window. "That's just great."

I sighed softly and picked at a fingernail in silence.

Dev, Mick and Sissy returned to the car and we dropped Sissy at her place. She had a no-fixing-at-her-house rule. It helped keep her from being busted. All she needed was some over-anxious chippy overdosing in her bathroom, she said. She waved at us from the sagging porch, the Christmas lights framing her windows blinking on and off chaotically behind her.

Back in our bedroom we closed the blinds, they cooked, I smoked and we each took our fit to shoot. The rush washed over me like a gentle wave of warm water. It always started just below my belly button like orgasm. They had gotten China White, a potent pain-killer legitimately known as fentanyl. It provided the same high as heroin.

Afterward we went next door to visit Jon and his roommates. We sat in the kitchen for a while talking with the third-floor occupant, Laurence. He was my favorite of the guys in the house. He was emotional, effeminate and soft hearted. His blue eyes would fill with tears when the lion in TV nature documentaries we watched together killed an antelope and he'd run one hand through his short, thick dark red hair in distress while reaching frantically for the remote with the other. Laurence was a middle-aged man who stood six foot five but you'd swear he was a simpering southern maiden with his swishy walk and South Carolina drawl. He did odd jobs to pay the rent, being an artist by profession and art being a fickle thing. He spent lots of time in the kitchen drinking pot after pot of thick coffee, smoking unfiltered cigarettes and planning his next creation. He loved to tell stories about when he was young and times were wild.

"The excitement of sex in back rooms with strange men was as much a draw as the cash," he said. "One time, in New York I dry-humped this guy on the subway from one end of the city to the other. I was only nineteen and he must have been forty, with a thick wedding band on that left finger. By the time we pulled into the station he was so worked up he dragged me into the bathroom to finish. I was scared, it was my first time getting paid but what a rush!" We all nodded in understanding, having just shared an adrenaline surge ourselves thanks to Sissy.

I awoke the next morning with a pounding headache, one of the side effects of fentanyl. I turned over in bed as Dev left for work. It was my day off and encouraged by the gray skies I pulled the covers over me and stayed in bed. Later I tried to get up but my head still ached so I allowed myself to drift in and out of light sleep. That afternoon I heard little pings at the window. I heaved an angry sigh when it didn't stop after a few minutes and dragged myself out of bed to see who was disturbing my sleep. Mick was on the sidewalk below, his hair blowing wildly around him as he clutched his worn brown jacket close against the cold wind.

"Novena the outside door's locked. You got any fits?" He called up to me, making syringe-like motions with his hand. I cursed and stomped down the stairs to let him in before anyone could see him.

"What are you, high!?" I asked angrily before I realized what I said. "You want someone to see you?" We headed up the steps to the apartment.

"Not high yet," he grinned, "but I aim to be soon! Who in this neighborhood would even care? Half the neighbors sell the stuff, the other ones use it themselves." He had a point. "You don't look so good Novena, what's wrong?"

"I have a pounding headache from that dope last night." I plopped back down on the bed and lit a cigarette. He was already at the dresser with the syringe I'd handed him.

"I got something that will fix you right up," he said, his back to me at the dresser. He cooked and filled two fits, focusing on the task like a priest consecrating Holy Communion. Mick sat next to me on the bed and reached for my arm but I held my hand out for the needle.

"I can do it myself," I said, feeling suddenly shy. He nodded solemnly and handed it to me then crossed the room to sit in the chair.

The needle was dull and I felt a pinch as it pierced my skin. Then the glow began, everything softened and my headache was instantly relieved. My mind relaxed. I felt renewed.

"Better, huh?" Mick smiled. I should have thought of him as evil, a 'pusher' like the bad guys on TV who were always convincing young girls to get high: 'Come on, honey, this will make you feel real good.' But I just couldn't. I had made a choice too.

Mick stayed long enough to shoot his dope and share my cigarette before scurrying back to work. He had been on lunch break. I was glad he left so soon, it was uncomfortable to be alone with him sometimes. The air seemed to get thick. After Mick left I was able to get out of bed and clean the room. Being high made dusting and vacuuming enjoyable tasks. I had a cup of coffee with Laurence next door, did laundry in the basement and had just picked up a book to read when Dev came home from work.

He sat on the edge of the bed and took my face between his hands, looking closely at my eyes.

"Dr. Mick must have been here huh Novena?" he said. "You have no pupils and I bet you don't have a headache anymore either!" he laughed. "That little imp. He was looking for a fit wasn't he? He left his here last night. I swear that boy would lose his ass if it didn't follow him around everywhere," Dev snorted. "I better call that weasel and see what's out there." I went back to my book.

***

"You know you're using more than once a day now instead of once a week like when we started," I pointed out to Dev one evening in December during a commercial break. I had gotten high after coming home from work and was enjoying my nightly TV re-runs. I noticed that the rush was becoming less intense and even though I felt good, that all-encompassing feeling of well being I'd experienced in the beginning seemed to elude me now.

"Relax Novena. I'm not doing that much," he murmured. He was sitting in our worn overstuffed chair with his feet propped on a stool, teacup at his elbow, newspaper in his hands.

"You're buying two, sometimes three bags a day," I said. "You get up and get high then get high again when you come home. Not a huge habit, maybe, but it's making a dent in our paychecks all the same. We can never afford to go to dinner or see movies anymore." I let my preoccupation with his growing habit completely eclipse guilt about my own use. I shot dope a few times a week, maybe every other day, dancing precariously close to the edge of trouble but not close enough to get sick when I went two or three days without using.

"I need the relief it gives me right now," he said, continuing to focus on the paper. His face was serious, his eyes hooded by the dark hair falling over his forehead.

"Relief from what?" I asked.

"Sometimes I just feel … I don't know, lost isn't really the right word. Driven, maybe. I can't explain it," he said, and looked up at me. "Don't worry Novena, it's under control. I can quit whenever I want. All I have to do is buy some Valium from Sissy to help me withdraw. If things get out of hand I'll stop," he said with a reassuring smile. And I believed him, because I wanted to.

"Come here Novena," Dev murmured as he pulled me against him in bed that night. I drew a deep involuntary breath and closed my eyes. His breath teased my shoulders with his nearness. He was lying on his side and the curve of my back fit perfectly into his chest. I moved against him trying to get closer, fitting us together like pieces of a puzzle. I moaned softly when his lips brushed the sensitive skin just under my ear. His arms were around me, one hand caressed in slow circles over my thighs, his fingertips barely brushing the waiting place between my legs, making promises. Dev supported my head so his lips could move down my neck and I brought his hand to my mouth, biting his calloused palm softly. I loved the cardamom and sandalwood smell of his skin, the sounds coming from his throat as he stroked his hips against me. My breathing was slow and heavy and every inch of my skin tingled. I let myself sink into the colors behind my eyes, magenta and royal blue sliding seductively into each other. Dev whispered my name and I turned toward him, loving the weight of his body against mine. I trembled as his lips and tongue moved to the curve of my waist then my belly and then began to travel below my navel, his hands cradling my hips. My mind pulsed in a gyration of deep red and rich purple and as I anticipated his next move I arched my back, crying out his name.

Suddenly an alien sound invaded my senses and the colors faded away like paint running down a white wall. I shivered as Dev moved away from me and sat up to answer the phone. He shook his head and cleared his throat.

"Yeah," his voice was still husky. "It's Dev … yeah Wilbur. OK, I'll be there in a minute." I gathered the covers around me and tried to clear my own fuzzy head.

"What's going on?" I asked. Dev was pulling his clothes on.

"Sorry Novena. I know the timing sucks, but I gotta meet Wilbur. He's got some new shit and if I don't get it now it'll be gone." He took my face in his hands and gave me a lingering kiss. "We'll pick up where we left off when I get back." He smiled. I crossed my arms over my chest, becoming angry, knowing better. After getting high neither of us could get aroused.

"I may not be here!" I said.

"Come on Novena, don't be mad. I'll make it up to you I promise," he said and let his eyes get dark and wet. I sighed and rearranged the blanket over me with angry motions as Dev went out the door.

On my way out the door to work a few mornings later I noticed Mick's beat-up black van parked outside our apartment house. I immediately felt a sinking in my stomach and a tightness growing in my limbs.

"Francesca kicked Mick out again. He's sleeping in the van," Dev replied when I asked him about it. He said it in an offhanded way, like he didn't know the details. Francesca put Mick out of the house every few months or so for little quarrels. She always let him come back after a few days and usually it was no big deal but this time I got worried. Did she know he was getting high, that he was doing it with us? Hearing about

Mick's bad luck fired up my paranoia, moving it from the slow-cooking back burner to the high heat at the front of the range. I knew that shooting heroin wasn't like alcoholism where you can go along drinking socially for years without trying to hide it before you realize you have a problem. We went to great lengths to hide it from the very beginning. I decided to pay Francesca a visit after work to see if I could find out how much she knew and do a little damage control.

Francesca's apartment was on the second floor and had a wide stair case leading to a pair of pocket doors that opened to an airy living space.

"Come *in*, dear." Francesca flung the doors open and held her arms wide to me. She grabbed me in a tight embrace, swayed me side to side and then planted a wet kiss on my cheek. I blushed at her familiarity. We didn't know each other well. She was in her forties, dusky skinned and beautiful. She wore colorful flowing clothes and smoked slim brown cigarettes. A long black holder wouldn't have seemed out of place between her fingers. Coming from a wealthy upper-class family she was used to expensive things and her apartment was an eclectic mix of valuable antiques and modern art. She herself was an artist but made her money marketing other people's creations. She had a knack for bringing dying businesses back to life and was helping Mick's carpentry work grow from odd jobs into a bona-fide contracting company. I was intimidated by her composure.

"We don't see enough of each other, you and me. How wonderful that you came to visit! I get so lonely here even with all my beautiful things." She sighed. Her pale pink silk blouse and blue silk harem pants gave her an exotic sophisticated appearance. Her shiny black hair was gathered neatly in a knot at the base of her neck.

I smoothed my own unruly hair and adjusted my shabby clothes, trying to feel presentable and becoming uncomfortable with my own style, which could only be described as intentional neglect. I liked to think I was spurning convention but in reality I looked like every other grunge-influenced slacker on the block. My closet was filled with worn-thin T-shirts bearing the names of old punk bands and dark baggy sweaters. My skinny legs were usually encased in black tights and beat-up black boots. At that moment I was wishing I'd chosen a different outfit. Something lighter and not bought for a buck at the thrift store.

Mick had been doing odd jobs around Simon's building when Francesca had noticed him. She began giving him lunch every day and soon she had his few belongings moved from the dim basement dormitory of the Salvation Army where he'd lived on and off for three years to her spacious apartment. She introduced him to opera, theater and the arts. Francesca would dress him up like a living doll in the male-model clothes she bought for him and take him out to galleries and coffee houses for 'cultural evenings'. He tolerated it all with the mellow pleasant nature he was known for and was a good sport when we teased him about his artsy-fartsy tastes. We thought Francesca had taken Mick in just so she wouldn't be alone and she either truly didn't know about his heroin use or chose to ignore it. She tended toward the dramatic in every thing she did so it wasn't out of character for her to rescue a scruffy street-urchin and transform him into a well-rounded successful man. Just like the businesses she turned around.

Francesca and I settled at the table, thin china cups of tea in our hands. Her bright eyes never left mine. She seemed to drink me in. I looked away from her intense gaze.

"So how are things?" I asked, not wanting to let on I knew about Mick. She sipped her tea, taking her time before speaking.

"Is that your real nose," she asked, "or did you have it fixed?" This was not going to go well, I thought.

"It's my nose," I replied. "Jesus, what a question."

"It's a beautiful nose. Do you know how many people pay for noses like that?" she asked. I was a little embarrassed. I hated my nose. It was small and pointy. Dev said I was 'waif-like', but I thought I looked like some kind of elf-gone-awry with my dyed black hair and well-cultivated death-like pallor. All I needed was pointy ears and I could have been a candidate for Santa's Workhouse for Delinquent Little People, where they send elves with a bad attitude.

"What have you and Mick been up to?" I tried again.

"Are those colored contacts or are your eyes really that green?" She leaned forward to look at me.

"Just for the record everything I have is mine, OK?" I said. I was losing patience.

"Ah, well." She sat back in her seat and waved her hand. "You'd be surprised how much of a person can be fake, you know?" She looked at me slyly over her cup. I gulped my tea and set my cup down.

"On to unhappier thoughts," she quipped. "Mick is banned from my house. He's been lying to me. And after all I've done for him in the past few years." She closed her eyes and looked pained. "Without me he'd still be living down at the Salvation Army. I plucked him out of the gutter, everything he has I've given him and still he does this to me." She let her head fall back and to the side, her eyes still closed dramatically.

"What was he lying about?" I asked, trying not to sound anxious.

"He's been skimming money off his jobs, spending it on that God-damned motorcycle I bet. I begged him to give that thing up but will he do anything for me, I ask you? No, not for Francesca. And when I think of all the sacrifices I've made for him ah, my heart aches." She clasped both hands at her breast. Mick had an old Triumph, a real junker that he was forever trying to keep running. Of course I knew that's not what the money was keeping running lately but I breathed a sigh of relief.

"I know he isn't in love with me," she continued, her hands now clasped together and pressed to her lips. "But he could at least show a little respect. Pretend once in a while. Oh I don't know why I put up with him." She paused. "I guess it's because the sex is so God-damned good." She sighed in resignation then grasped the edges of the table with her hands and looked at me from under her long lashes. "There's nothing like the stamina of a twenty five-year old man!"

I grabbed my cup and held it to my lips, avoiding her eyes and struggling not to blush. "Ah," she went on, "you wouldn't know anything about that. You're young and beautiful," she said wistfully. "You don't know how it is to be constantly afraid you'll lose your man to someone new and exciting."

You'd be surprised I thought, remembering how Dev had turned away from my embrace in bed when Gilbert called with news of Wilbur's latest batch of dope.

Chapter Six

When Dev came through the door bleeding I reacted like it was a scene I'd rehearsed. 'Lights, camera, action,' I thought as the room became a movie set in my mind, allowing me to detach from the scariness of the situation and function as if it weren't real:

The door opens and a dark haired man staggers in. His face is bleeding, his torn jacket is thrown around his shoulders and he is holding a blood soaked t-shirt over his upper right arm. He falls to the sofa.

"What the Hell happened?" the woman demands frantically, holding his face in her hands to assess his injuries.

"I got beat, went to get my money back from those ass-holes, only there were four of them. Then I really got beat," he jokes, his voice weak. "It's not as bad as it looks. I got away before I got shot in the chest, they only got my edge." He pulls away the t-shirt to show her a ragged tear in his upper arm.

"Jesus Christ," she whispers and falls onto the sofa beside him, pressing her hand to her lips.

"Clean shot," he says. "Just across the flesh of my arm, didn't even hit bone. I need something to put over it. It's bleeding a lot but it'll be OK." His voice is ragged and he coughs. "Novena?" He looks at her. The woman takes a deep breath, rises and storms to the closet in the hall. She is shaking.

"You need to go to the hospital, you probably have a concussion. You have a huge bruise on your chest, one on your forehead and behind your ear, not to mention that you've been shot!" she says. She is pulling gauze pads and alcohol from the closet. Her face is tight, her actions violent.

"And tell them what?" he asks. "That I was beat up and shot over a couple bags of dope? That'll get me a nice cot in the infirmary at the county jail. You

have to take care of this. Wash it off and patch it up. I'll heal. But call Mick first. I need something before I get sick."

I poured alcohol directly onto Dev's arm and he cursed loudly, pulling me back to reality.

"Where did this happen?" I asked, clenching my teeth as I prodded his bloody flesh.

"Over on B Street in Calbride." He flinched as I removed a shred of skin that was hanging from the edge of the wound. Calbride was the roughest section of the worst area of the Northside which was itself one of Pittsburgh's less desirable neighborhoods. I wrapped a wad of gauze around his arm.

"Where's Mick?" was my next question. I needed to have someone else there to break the weird sense of isolation I was feeling. Mick, Dev and I were rarely far apart these days. After Christmas Dev was always laid off his job until spring and this year he'd picked up work with Mick. This was convenient, as Mick had been living with us since Francesca kicked him out.

"He's at Sissy's, call him there." Dev closed his eyes and let his head fall onto the back of the sofa, his face pale. I called Mick at Sissy's house, washed as much blood off the rest of Dev as he would let me and balanced an ice pack on the bruise swelling from his chest. Then I went to bed, too exhausted to wait for Mick to come home with more dope. I fell asleep as soon as I laid down, the numbness in my mind spreading mercifully to my body.

Dev went to work in the morning, his bandaged arm and bruised face the only evidence of his misfortune the night before. Mick had come home that night with some 'medicine' and copped again in the morning before we went to work. I cleaned up, spraying half the house with bleach to wipe up the blood and maybe try to scour the incident from my mind. This was the first trouble he'd had in the street. I was used to Wilbur, a retiree who dealt drugs for extra money to spend on his grandchildren. I chose not to think about the other dealers, the ones who carried guns and traveled in groups.

I threw on the scrub-suit I wore to work, scraped my hair into a ponytail and dragged myself to the nursing home, wondering how I was going to get through the day feeling so raw. Although I couldn't say I loved my job, it had a few perks, one of them being access to medical supplies which came in handy when we needed clean needles. I liked the people I worked with and the patients seemed to appreciate the care we gave. This morning I was grateful for the easy diversion it provided

My first task that day was to admit a new patient, Mr. Long. I sighed heavily as I entered the room. Admissions were tedious and I felt so far removed from reality I wasn't sure I could do it. Lynnette was working the evening shift and I wouldn't even have the consolation of her company.

The room was cheerful in a contrived way, the walls a soothing blue and the bedspreads a complimentary color chosen to hide stains. The overhead lights were kept off and lamps lit instead to give the place a homey feel, but the antiseptic smell that hid other, more unpleasant odors was a constant reminder that it was an institution. Suddenly I felt sorry for this man who had been living alone until his family decided that he was a danger to himself and placed him here. His whole life was going to be disrupted and his final days spent among strangers.

"Hello Mr. Long. I'm Novena, one of the aides," I said and went into auto-pilot, thankful that it was a routine procedure.

Mr. Long sat in a high-backed chair, his tiny shriveled and hunched form gasping for each lungful of air. His face was ruddy and his lips almost purple from years of oxygen deprivation caused by the damage smoking had done. His feet were swollen and mottled. He used a walker to weakly shuffle along, stopping every few steps to try and catch his breath. His limbs were bent and disfigured with arthritis and he was legally blind behind the thick glasses that magnified and distorted his watery red eyes. The elderly man answered the questions to my assessment, speaking little in between and I completed the process quickly. I stood at the dresser across the room from him as I finished my paperwork, my back to him.

"Do you have any questions, Mr. Long?" I asked in my work-voice, eager to be done.

"Heh … what would you do … if I touched your breast, nursey?" he wheezed. Shocked, I whipped my head around to look at him struggling for breath and barely able to sit up on his own, a weak smile on his dry purple lips and thought to myself, 'mister, if you could get to it in your condition, I'd *let* you touch my breast.' But I maintained my professional lack of sense of humor and wagged my finger at him.

"That's not appropriate, sir. Now I just need to watch you use your walker to make sure you're safe and we'll be done."

"Hey … hey nurse, we could test my walker. You run down the hall … and we'll see if I can catch you … heh, heh," he said in his hoarse voice, leering comically at me and breathing hard with the effort of speech. I rolled my eyes.

"Now, Mr. Long, I have lots of other patients to see today," I said.

"If I catch you, sweetie … you won't care about all those other patients, heh, heh. They don't call me … Mr. Long for nothin'!" He finished in a fit of coughing and wheezing and I hid a laugh behind my hand, the tension in my face finally breaking. You had to give the guy credit, ninety-two years old and still chasing girls. My job was becoming a relief from the stresses of home-life, I realized in alarm.

After work I changed the bandages on Dev's wounds. We both prepared for the ordeal with a shot of dope so he had little pain as I pulled the dried blood off with the bandages. The bullet had torn the skin neatly. I could see the red meaty flesh inside the wound, healthy and alive and already producing new pink cells to begin knitting itself together. Life was amazing in its determination to continue.

Later I met Rachel at her house. Every week we treated ourselves to dinner out and then browsed the local Goodwill Thrift shop for affordable treasures other people had grown tired of. My pockets were almost empty. Dev and Mick spent most of their money on heroin before they even got home. We used my paychecks for rent and bills.

"Where do you want to go for dinner?" Rachel asked as we left her house. The bitter January wind bit sharply into my back and the dark clouds hanging low over us in the late afternoon sky matched my gray mood.

"I don't care as long as it's cheap and plentiful," I replied.

"You low on cash?" she asked. "Cause you know whatever I have you have."

"Just being careful. You know, rainy day stuff," I answered. We walked briskly through the cold, our breath freezing in puffy clouds as it left our lips.

"Well, you can't take it with you, might as well enjoy it now. Besides, money is the root of all evil, or is evil, or some shit like that." She shook her head, trying to remember the saying. Rachel had had twelve jobs in one year. She refused to work for anyone who was homophobic, racist, chauvinistic, or in general not a nice person. So her options were limited. As a result she could do poverty and not complain.

"It may be evil but it sure pays the rent," I said.

"Yeah. I guess money's like sex, huh? The only people saying it's over-rated are those who get enough." She grinned and held the car door open for me, chauffer-style.

Later we sat in her comfortable living room sharing a cigarette and cups of tea. The wind was rattling the windows in their old wooden frames. The springs in her second-hand sofa had broken years before we dragged it from the thrift shop down the street into her apartment and I felt myself thawing as I sunk deep into the soft cushions. We sat on either end of the sofa with our feet propped on the wooden chest that served as a coffee table. My body began to slowly relax as I drew strength from the presence of my friend. Her energy filled me with restorative warmth. I sipped my tea tentatively, not wanting to disturb the first peace I'd had all day.

"How's Dev?" Rachel asked.

"He's good," I said and leaned forward to stub out my cigarette in the ashtray on the coffee table. I let my long hair fall over my shoulder to hide the tension that bound my face when she said his name.

"Mr. Sunshine meets the Princess of Darkness. Who'd have thought you'd be able to put up with each other." She puffed out a perfect smoke ring. I was quiet for a second. When I thought of myself without him all I could visualize was my own cavernous abyss, dark and unexplored and terrifying.

"You know how you and I have never felt like we belonged anywhere, never fit in?" I asked carefully.

"Sure, like at that punk bar we used to hang out at. Even among misfits we were misfits!" She laughed.

"Well, he and I just fit." I turned to look at her. She held my eyes for a long minute as if trying to figure out why the conversation had gotten so heavy, trying to read my thoughts. Rachel pulled her gaze away and exhaled another smoke ring.

"Yeah, I had the same feeling about each of my last four lovers. I thought it was love but it always went to shit," she sighed. "In my case it turned out to be lust every time. Pure, unadulterated, take-me-on-the-kitchen-table lust. And now looking back at it all, you know what honey?" she asked in a low, serious voice. "It was worth it every time!" she yelled and leaned over to tickle my sides, making me shout with laughter and choke on my tea.

***

That Sunday I slipped into the back pew of a crowded church as the opening hymn was being sung. I had started going to church every couple of weeks, not because any religious up-bringing dictated that I should but because I found comfort in the solemn ritual and the dark quiet of the old Monastery where mass was celebrated. It allowed my mind time to be quiet. I had not been raised in any particular religion. My parents thought it was better for my brother and me to make the rounds, see different ways of worship and make our own decision. I couldn't really follow what was going on during Mass but I sat, stood and knelt according to the little book in the pew, thankful for the words of prayer that were provided in ink before me.

After Mass was over and everyone else had filed out I knelt uncertainly in prayer. I didn't know how to talk to God but I had heard Lynette preach about it so much I put aside how awkward I felt and began to form words in my mind. I asked God to take the burden of my worry from me and to save Dev and me from the trouble we were getting into. I crossed myself and lifted my head, trying to make myself believe I felt better but chewed my lip in anxiety anyway.

I looked up at Jesus on the cross, bloody and beaten, and wondered why we all had to suffer so much. I wished I could reach out my hand to Him and rest in his grasp as the hymn we'd sung suggested. Lynnette said she could call upon the Lord anytime she needed to for help. It sounded so real when she said it, like there was no doubt He would answer. My prayers came out sounding like I was pleading for God to help me but I was also pleading with myself to believe He could. I had grown up knowing about Buddha and Krishna along with Jesus since my mom was eclectic in her beliefs. She believed in everything. Maybe she had the right idea, covering all her bases in case one holy being was listening closer than the others. I sure felt like I needed all the divinities I could call upon for help.

"Dev we don't have enough money for another bag of dope," I told him one afternoon in late February. He and Mick had quit work early in the day due to frigid temperatures. I had just come home from work and found them sitting on the floor in front of the TV watching CNN. The phone rang and I picked it up, happy for the diversion.

"Hey Vena-honey, your old man home?" It was Sissy's nasal voice.

"No, Sissy, my dad doesn't live here but you can talk to Dev if you like," I used my snottiest better-than-thou voice. I hated it when she referred to Dev as my 'old man' and it was even worse when she called me 'Dev's old lady'. I was only twenty-three for Crissakes. He reached for the phone.

"Sis we don't have enough for three bags, can you get us a deal?" Dev asked smoothly into the receiver. Sometimes if you were a regular customer the dealer would give you three for the price of two. A sort of Druggy's Special. "You say you need a ride? Sure, I can give you a ride. My price for a lift to the welfare office just happens to be fifteen bucks." He held the phone away from his ear for a second and I could hear her screeching. "No? How bad do you need that check? That's what I thought. I'll pick you up in ten minutes." He smiled, winking at Mick and me. "Never underestimate the power of the Welfare Check," he said in mock seriousness as he and Mick bounded toward the door. If only he could channel that creativity into something productive, I thought with a sigh as I got out the fits and spoon and closed the blinds in preparation.

The next evening we went to visit Dev's father. He was a reformed alcoholic himself. They say the apple doesn't fall far from the tree and not only was Dev's father a drunk, his full-blooded Cherokee grandfather had been too. Combine that with the crazy alcoholic Irishmen from his mother's side of the family and the whole damned orchard was soggy with booze.

Simon welcomed us enthusiastically into the kitchen where we sat at his wooden table. He smiled and hugged us both then went back to preparing dinner. He loved to entertain.

"I was lookin' at C-Span t'other night. Did y'all catch any of the senate sub-committee hearin's?" Simon asked. He spoke Russian and German and had a Master's degree in linguistics, but you'd never guess it by his desecration of the English language. He had been a translator in the Army. With his faded work clothes and long gray hair gathered in a ponytail that hung to his waist he looked and sounded like a good old boy from the back woods of Tennessee, which is where he had been raised.

He was clomping around the kitchen cooking furiously and didn't seem to expect an answer to his question. Watching Simon cook was like watching a war movie where the GI's were trying to take an enemy hill.

"Goddammit, where the hell is my slotted spoon? That crazy woman was in here again and now I can't find anything!" he cursed, referring to Francesca who often had coffee with him. He seemed to think everyone who came in was after his utensils. "Holy Jesus!" he yelled as a pot of rice boiled over. He grabbed a towel and slammed the pot to another burner, sloshing hot water over the range and onto the floor. "Dern, now my stove's a mess!" he yelled, throwing the towel onto the counter which was littered with crumpled paper packages and spice bottles. He claimed cooking helped him relax.

Simon always had two or three stringy dogs around and in the midst of his spoon crisis they were at each other on the floor by his feet, growling and wrestling. Mumbling curses at the dogs he grabbed a heavy iron ladle out of another pot and rapped each dog sharply on the head with it. They yelped in surprise and beat a path to the next room where they resumed playing. He dropped the ladle back into the pot and grumbled something about dog-stew.

"Hey you two, you stayin' for dinner?" he asked without missing a beat. This commotion was regular fare at Simon's house. I was eyeing the pot with the dog-rapping ladle in it, to be sure I remembered not to take any of its contents.

"No Dad, we just stopped by to say hey," Dev said. "You need anything?" he asked.

"No I got everythin' I need, 'cept my damned slotted spoon," he said, banging drawers open and closed looking for it briefly again. "I made stir-fry, sure you don't want to stay? Mmm, with snow peas and baby corn, you like baby corn don't you Novena?" He turned to me and smiled enticingly. "Let me get you a plate," he said in a conspiratorial tone, eyebrows raised, knowing I wouldn't refuse.

I always felt particularly on edge at Simon's house. He was sharp as a tack and if anyone was going to catch onto us it was him. Dev claimed to have made his peace with Simon's poor effort at fatherhood and the two were close enough that Dev would let his guard down at Simon's so I worried that he would slip and say something incriminating. Simon however, doted on his only son and was so pleased to have a real relationship with him at last that he was as oblivious to the signs of our problem as everyone else.

Dev drifted into the other room while I ate in the kitchen. Simon sat across from me, eyeballing my every bite expectantly. Every couple of mouthfuls I would say, "Mmm, this is really good Simon, you say you used how much soy sauce?" and other bullshit of the kind he liked to hear. He gloated over the meal and I got a full belly with no dog aftertaste, so we were both satisfied.

Dev wandered back in.

"Did y'all read about the new tax-hikes those assholes in Congress are proposin'?" Simon asked.

Dev seemed preoccupied. He didn't respond to Simon's question.

"Hey Dad," Dev said. "You think you can lend me a couple bucks? Mick and I had to quit early today and we didn't get paid yet." He avoided looking at me. I tensed, my insides pulling together to make a tight ball in the center of my chest. I had been relieved earlier in the day when in response to my reply that I was out of money Dev simply said, "OK, no problem." I should have known he had an alternative plan.

"Sure twenty OK?" Simon reached for his wallet.

"That'd be great. I really appreciate this. I'll have it back to you tomorrow," Dev said as he pocketed the money. "You done Novena? We need to get home." He rested his hand on my head. "Got to get up early. We aren't living the retired life like you Dad. Were workin' folk." He grinned as he mimicked his father's accent. Having gotten what he wanted he was ready to leave so he could cop. I followed him out the door knowing I had been conned, but I didn't have the energy to fight about it.

That night he overdosed again. Before the needle was out of his arm he was curling up and falling off the edge of the sofa, his lips a pale shade of blue. I had already done my portion and my limbs were heavy as I crossed the room to where he lay on the floor. This time there was no one to help me get him in the shower so I rolled him onto his back and began breathing into him. I sat on the floor beside him and automatically reached for the TV remote, clicking through the channels. I leaned over to seal my lips over his and give him a breath every few seconds. His lips and face pinked up. After what seemed an eternity but was probably only a few minutes he began taking slow deep breaths. I spread a blanket over him and felt my muscles loosen in relief. He slept for an hour on the floor then opened his eyes and grinned at me fuzzily, like a kid waking up after an afternoon nap.

"Well this is a fine place to find myself," he said, sitting up slowly and stretching his arms. "I guess I underestimated that stuff." He smiled and shook his head to clear it. "Sorry Novena. Good thing you were here. What time is it anyway?"

Realization crept over me like frost feathering a window in time-lapse photography. I had been left behind. Heroin was the beautiful trapeze artist starring in our sick little circus and I was the poor slob who swept up the elephant shit after the show was over.

"You think this is funny!" I said, my anger bubbled over, the heat rushing of it melting the iciness of my skin. "You're not the one who has to deal with it! You just go out and come to and don't remember anything else! What if I have to call the medics or tell your father you died shooting heroin?" I was pacing and smoking furiously. "Don't you understand how scary that is for me? You can just go to Hell if you think I'm going to go through this every week! I'm going to Rachel's." I stormed to the bedroom and began to shove things in my backpack.

Dev appeared in the doorway and rubbed the back of his neck, avoiding my eyes.

"Don't get so upset Novena. I'll be more careful. I just want to make sure I get my money's worth and there's no sense getting just a little high. If you're going to do it, do it right." He was no longer smiling.

74

"Right doesn't mean turning blue every couple of weeks," I hissed. "This is getting to be too much for me. I can't handle the lifestyle. This is not who I want to be." I began to weep. "You are out of control." I covered my mouth with my hands. The fear of losing him came spilling out in hot fat tears.

"Novena," he said softy. He guided me to the bed, sat me down and dropped beside me. "I didn't know this upset you so much. All you had to do was say something," he said, tucking my hair behind my ears. He held my face in his hands. "I promise I'll be more careful. Now unpack your stuff. You know you don't want to leave." He kissed me on the forehead and I nodded, drying my face with the sleeve of my sweater. Truth be told, more than being angry I just wanted acknowledgement. I wanted some attention to show I was still as important to him as the drug. And he was right. I didn't want to go anywhere. Especially not to Rachel's where I'd have to come up with another string of lies. His apology would do, sincere or not. I unpacked my things.

***

Breathing spring's rain fresh air hopefully, I felt a new energy as I walked from the car to the house. Mick had moved back in with Francesca and Dev was back at his regular job. Of course his whole paycheck went directly into our veins and we were living on my wages but we were still keeping the bills paid. It'll get better, I thought as I watched a bird soar into the cool damp breeze. At least he hadn't overdosed or been shot in the last three weeks.

Inside I looked at the clock. Dev would be home soon. My mouth watered with thoughts of the needle. It didn't change my perception of reality or make me forget my problems but it did make me not care so much. It numbed the anxiety I awoke with every morning and softened the jagged edge I was balancing on. If only Dev would slow his use down I wouldn't need to get high. Sighing, I clicked on the TV to wait.

"Hey Novena, I need some money," Dev said as he came through the door and headed for the phone. I was slouched into the soft second-hand recliner in the living room. The days were getting longer and I had the blinds closed against the evening light like a vampire waiting for dusk to crowd the last light from the sky.

Anxiety began to twist my stomach as I clicked the remote and I looked around for my bottle of Maalox.

"I don't have any. I just paid the rent." I went back to watching TV. I found a lot of comfort in the glowing box. The first thing I reached for when I got home was the remote and as soon as that screen came to life I could feel my tension easing.

"I owe Gilbert twenty, Mick bought for me this morning and I need to get something for tonight," he whined.

"You just got paid," I said sharply.

"Well it's gone, OK." He was getting angry. "Just give me the money." I lit a cigarette, didn't move from the chair. "Look Novena," he said. "I need to get high or I can't go to work tomorrow, then where will we be?" He really knew me, knew just what would get the desired reaction. I heaved a great angry sigh and reached under the stereo to pull out the small stash of twenties I had hidden there. My birthday had just passed and I was spending my Dad's gift money on dope. I peeled off two of the three bills and threw them on the floor. He glared at me and picked them up then stalked to the phone.

"You better get enough for me," I said without looking at him.

After he left to meet the dealer I thought about my options. If he lost his job, he'd have no money then he couldn't get high. But then we'd have to deal with the shame of his unemployment. Or he'd use my paycheck to get high and we'd really be in deep debt. I thought about leaving Dev but that would mean telling people about our mistakes. And besides, I still loved him. I slouched lower into my seat. Maybe if I just hang on Dev will come to his senses and we can go on as if nothing had ever happened, I thought.

Laurence and I were sitting in the sunny yellow kitchen at Jon's house drinking coffee.

"You don't know the half of it Sweetie." Laurence waved his hand in front of his face and put down his cup. I had asked if his week was going OK and realized my mistake only after the words left my mouth. "Jon's cat was on the porch yesterday." He leaned towards me. "And the hussy had a little bird in her mouth and was just about to break its neck! I didn't know *what* to do. God, it was awful!" He closed his eyes and put his hands to his face in horror. "I grabbed that little bitch-cat and shook her and yelled, 'drop that bird, drop that bird!' And you know what? She did. Just opened her mouth and out it flew. I have never been so scared in my life! I had to go upstairs and take a nap after that. I just couldn't handle anything else that day," he said.

I nodded in sympathy. Handling stress was not one of Laurence's strong points. He needed a nap if the mail was late.

Wayne came pounding down the stairs and flew out the door. Must be check day I thought. In a minute he was back.

"Forgot my teeth," he mumbled sheepishly, his mouth all mushy. That's a true junkie, so anxious to get that check and spend it on dope he forgot to put his dentures in. I covered my mouth to smother a laugh. Faster than I thought possible, he was back down the steps and out the door.

"He moves fast for a big guy," Laurence said.

"That depends on what the motivation is," I replied.

"Hm. I had a lover like that. Slow as a June bug in August until it was time to do laundry. That man loved to wash clothes. He'd spend all day at the Suds-o-Matic over on Carson Street separating, pre-spraying, loading, drying ... I accused him of having an affair with the attendant until I met her. He said it was gratifying to put the dirty rumpled stuff in and at the end of the job have the clothes come out clean and folded." He had one arm crossed over his belly, the other elbow resting on his hand and he waved the cigarette between his fingers in time to the cadence of his story.

"That must have come in handy. What happened to him?" I asked, hoping for a happy ending but somehow knowing better.

"We grew apart then he died of AIDS years ago. Right after Bill died. Then my landlord died and I moved here. People were dropping like flies." He shook his head slowly. "Funerals had replaced parties for a while. Now most of the old gang is gone." His voice had gotten soft and his gaze was focused somewhere above my shoulder, lost in memory. I was silent for a minute, comparing his situation to mine.

"Watching so many people you love suffer and die, wondering if it's going to happen to you, how do you deal with that?" I asked. The dark threat of loss loomed over my own life like a heavy veil. There must be a secret to surviving the devastation if even Laurence could do it. Something to make bearing the pain easier.

He took a long drag on his cigarette and his face took on a hardness I had never seen before.

"Three words about life Sweetie," He looked at me pointedly as he exhaled his smoke. "It goes on."

Chapter Seven

"Could you just try not to spend every penny you make on dope?" I pleaded in my martyr voice. It was a cool spring evening and we had the windows open for the first time. The breeze floating in reminded me of the far-away places I had wanted to visit when I was young. I stretched, trying to shake off the restless energy trapped in my limbs. We were watching TV at our house and Mick was sitting on the floor strumming his guitar. "I mean, I know we pull together on the money thing but I feel like I'm supporting you and you're supporting your habit," I continued. "I'm sick of being poor. I want to travel, eat good food, there's just so much more to life." My voice held the slight whine that accompanied every discussion about the sacrifices I was making so we could feed our habit.

"Twenty-four and I want much more," Mick sang as he looked at me. Dev chuckled and reached out to give Mick's ponytail an appreciative tug when he saw my anger rise. I stomped out of the room in exasperation.

"I didn't hear you refuse when I cooked you a spoon this afternoon," Dev called as I went through the door. In the kitchen I eyed our dinner choices: mac and cheese from a box or ramen noodles. Oh good, I thought, I don't have to worry about over-dosing. We'll all die of sodium poisoning. I had been skimping on the groceries to pay the phone bill again this month.

I had been considering taking a second job at a car wash down the street but luck was with me and I developed two abscessed teeth instead. This provided me with multiple scripts for pain-pills which Sissy gladly converted into cash. I also had begun buying food-stamps from the guys standing outside the grocery store who sold them for half their worth. At fifty cents on the dollar I could buy sixty dollars worth of stamps for thirty bucks. That bought a lot of ramen and my initial shame in handing over food stamps at the checkout counter faded after I had done it a few times.

I got out a pot, banging it noisily on the stove in resentment at having to eat a sixteen cent meal again. Having decided on ramen I was weighing my next choice, chicken sesame or mushroom beef when the phone rang.

"Hey woman." It was Rachel. "We're having poor-dyke stew. Wanna come over?"

"See ya in ten," I said. I grabbed a can of vegetarian baked beans from the cupboard and ran out the door, grateful for the distraction Rachel and Amy were sure to provide. Mick and Dev seemed not to notice my leaving. I slammed the door behind me.

Rachel had the want-ads spread out on the table when I got there. Amy was stirring the big pot on the stove and dumped my beans into the mix without even reading the label.

"Did you walk out on another job?" I asked Rachel.

"No. They fired me this time," she said.

"Fired you?"

"That's what happens when you call the boss a 'cock-sucking bastard'," Amy said peevishly from the stove.

Rachel and I looked at each other and giggled.

"Well he was always talking down to me," she said. "And all the other employees too. *Some*body had to stand up to him, that ignorant bully. He was even mean to Mrs. Gorbowsky, the little old checkout lady. I couldn't stand it anymore." She crossed her arms over her chest and put her nose in the air.

"How is it you can show up to volunteer at the cat shelter every week for years without missing a day but you can't hold a job longer than a few months?" Amy sounded angry.

Rachel's eyebrows raised slightly as she answered.

"I don't know. Something about those two little words, time and clock, just take all the fun out of it."

"Well I wish you'd remember that they're connected to two other little words, pay and check," Amy shot back.

"Honey." Rachel got up and put her arms around Amy, who kept her back turned. "You know we always get by and I can't work for someone who doesn't value my work," she said.

"You were the stock girl in a family grocery, for Crissake," Amy growled, but I could see she was softening. She planted a quick kiss on Rachel's arm and went back to stirring.

"We'll just have to eat poor-dyke stew a little more often this month," Rachel said, and bounced back to sit at the table.

Poor-dyke stew was a combination of whatever was in the pantries of those invited to partake. Each participant would bring whatever they had on hand and the odds and ends would be magically transformed into a feast. Today was soup I guessed, since Amy was stirring something liquid in the pot. You never knew what you'd get to eat but the company was good.

"How's Dev?" Rachel inevitably asked.

"He's fine. Working a lot. He's picking up extra hours so maybe we can buy a house someday," I told her. The hallmark of a really good lie was that it was totally believable. It also helped if it could be built on. My lies these days were so good I almost believed them myself.

"You? A house? Don't tell me you want 2.5 babies and a dog to go with it?" She raised her eyebrows at me.

"We aren't rushing into any thing," I said, trying to cover myself. "But we are getting older and someday we might want a little stability." I couldn't keep the longing out of my voice as that last word flowed off my tongue.

"You're the last person I'd think would want a house full of responsibilities to tie her down. What happened to all that traveling you wanted to do?" Rachel asked.

"I still want to see the world. It just doesn't hurt to plan for the future that's all." She shook her head and went back to the newspaper, mumbling something to herself about straight people. The image of a warm safe house with a loving husband and happy children sounded more appealing to me at that moment than a free around-the-world travel ticket. It wasn't the house and kids I wanted, it was the security they symbolized.

I had thought many times about unburdening myself to Rachel, planned how to tell her about our habit. She in her wise caring way was sure to offer suggestions and support without belittling me, this I knew. But Rachel's house was the one place I still felt like my old self. I didn't want the disease of my drug use to infect the peace I felt at her house.

"Here, have a 'whore'-derve." Rachel smeared peanut-butter on an Oreo and handed it to me, putting emphasis on the word 'whore' as she said it.

"Wow, you sprung for brand-name. You expecting a call from your agent?" I joked, eyeing the name on the cookie.

"They were donated to the food bank. They're way past expiration date so us volunteers got to take them home," she explained, cramming another into her mouth. "Speaking of gettin' by, you been selling plasma?" She was eyeing my bruised and marked veins.

"Yeah," I lied easily. "Fifteen dollars the first time, twenty after that, up to twice a month," I recited as I rolled down the sleeve of my black sweater. I had seen the ad in the paper enough times to have it memorized but at 94 pounds I didn't weigh enough to take advantage of the offer. I relaxed as I realized she was seeing what she wanted to see and coming to her own conclusions.

"Wow," Rachel said. "That's a lucrative gig. I wish I wasn't such a chicken-shit. I'd be down there every two weeks. Oh well, I'll just have to rely on my good-looks to get by, huh Baby?" she blinked coquettishly at Amy who flung stew off the spoon at her.

***

The alarm clock buzzed loudly, startling me out of my sleep. I pushed Dev's shoulder to wake him for work. He rolled over and groaned.

"I'm not going to work today. I don't have any money to cop and I can't go to work without getting high," he grumbled. I sat on the side of the bed, feeling drained even though my day hadn't begun yet.

"You have to go to work," I stated. I reached for the ant-acids I now kept with me as a wave of queasiness hit my insides. Every morning I held my breath as I waited to see if Dev would go to work, terrified that he'd lose his job. Not only would that put more stress on our already stretched finances, but I'd have to construct new lies to cover the reason for his unemployment.

"No I don't. Give me some money or leave me alone," he said, hiding his face in the pillow. "I don't care if I lose my job. I'm just a damned house-painter anyway, it's not like I'm vice-president of IBM." He didn't even open his eyes.

"I can't support us both," my voice cracked as I tried not to cry. "I'm so tired of this. I can't do it anymore."

"Then don't. I don't give a fuck. I'm tired of fighting." He rolled over again and pulled the blankets over his ears. My throat quivered with frustration and tears. Crossing the room, I lifted the stereo and took three twenty-dollar bills from their hiding place. I held them out to Dev stiffly, my face tight. He grabbed the money, pulled on his clothes and stomped out of the house. I dug in my purse for the bottle of pain pills I had bought from Sissy the day before, downing a handful with my coffee. As I left for work I waited in anticipation for the dulling effects the medication would bring.

I clocked in one minute late, ran up the steps to my floor and slid into a seat in the staff lounge for report. Not much changed from day to day and I felt suddenly smothered by the monotony of my life. Lynette eyed me from across the table, shaking her head slowly.

"You late again," she said in an accusing voice as we headed out to start our rounds.

"I am so bored with this job. I can hardly get out of bed to come in." I avoided looking at her. Grabbing the water pitcher cart I banged it against the ice machine. The pain pills had kicked in, making me feel fuzzy but not happy. "Maybe I need to look for another job."

"Humph." Lynette pouched her lips and began filling pitchers. "You can run Baby, but you can't out run yourself."

"What's that supposed to mean?" I asked. She turned to me and drew herself up tall.

"You floundering, girl. You can count on me being around when you fall, that's all I have to say. Me and the Lord, we both be here. You remember that." I turned to study her serious face. I could feel her concern and it made me nervous.

"That's good to know Lynette, good to know. Are you and the Lord free for lunch today? Cause I can save a place for you both in the cafeteria." I said. Lynette's face twisted as she tried not to smile. She finally broke and grinned. The air became lighter. "And maybe He can buy, seeing how He is the Lord and all," I continued. Lynette looked at me, seeming a little relieved.

"You on a speed boat to Hell, girl," she tried to smother a laugh. "I got to pray for you."

The mood returned to normal and I relaxed into the subtle relief of my pain pills as I began work.

"Are you at least getting out of bed today?" I asked one afternoon a few weeks later. Dev had the blinds drawn and the covers around his shoulders. I had just come home from work.

"Sit with me for a second," he said instead of answering. I sank onto the side of the bed and Dev slid his hand over my knee. He had barely been out of bed in the three days since he'd been fired. He'd just stopped showing up for work and finally his employer had lost his patience. "I was thinking maybe I should get on Methadone," he said, referring to the controlled, medically prescribed way of cutting down and finally quitting heroin. He sighed and sat up, moving to slowly pull on a pair of dirty jeans.

"Methadone isn't the answer. You know that shit is as hard to kick as dope," I said. I stood up and hung my hands on my hips. The past few days I had stalked out of the room to go to work and returned at night to get high and go to bed, barely speaking to Dev.

"Well maybe rehab then. I don't know anymore." He pulled a cap over his long shaggy hair, the brim casting even more of a shadow over his gaunt features and went out the door to cop.

A short time later a loud knock sounded at the door just before Mick walked in. I looked up from the TV guide I was using to plan my evening's activities. Mick's face was drawn but the tension eased immediately as he smiled at me. He unzipped his ever-present sweatshirt and let it drop to the floor. The t-shirt beneath was thin and ragged. Strands of his fine hair were escaping the pony-tail he'd gathered at the nape of his neck and he looked tired.

"Hey Novena. I didn't know anyone was here. How's things?" He took his fit from his pocket and spit two bags of heroin from his mouth.

"Not good Mick. Dev lost his job a few days ago. I don't know how we're going to make it." My voice quavered and Mick was instantly at my side, kneeling beside the chair and taking me in his arms as my face crumpled into tears.

"It's OK, Novena, shh, it's OK." He rocked me back and forth, smoothing my hair. I pulled away abruptly and wiped the wetness from my cheeks, resentment preventing me from finding any comfort in his embrace. He was no better than Dev. Both of them being the root cause of my troubles. He sat back on his heels. "Dev's let this drug run away with his life. You can't do that with heroin. You have to stay detached, not fall in love with it," he said, seeming to sense my need for an explanation. "I didn't know this would happen." His shook his head and rubbed his hand over his eyes. He rose slowly to his feet and turned to the dresser to prepare his dope. "I don't know how to help him. He's become a different person, bitter and angry. Sometimes I'm afraid of him ..." his voice was husky with sorrow.

I watched his reflection in the mirror above the dresser as he shot the dope into his neck. His eyes closed and he took a deep breath in before opening them again. He blushed as he caught my stare.

"So if you're not in love with heroin, why do you do it?" I asked. He turned back around to face me.

"I don't know anything else, I guess," he said. A long moment of silence passed then he looked directly at me, his face both open and fearful, as if he were about to expose himself in some way. "It always accepts me, you know? I never have to worry about who I am, who I'm not, it just lets me be myself," he told me. I returned his gaze, not sure what to say.

Mick took a step toward me, his hand outstretched, his eyes questioning. I sunk reflexively back into the chair in avoidance of his advance and he stopped. His face fell with his hand and he left the room.

The tension dropped from my shoulders as I pulled the needle out of my arm and let the belt fall to the floor. This morning's dose was going to be my last but I really needed it tonight so I had stopped by Sissy's on the way home from work. I'll quit tomorrow, I told myself. Every shot was going to be my last until the next time when I needed it to dull the pain of my thoughts. Two bags got me high enough to make it through the day and night but didn't make me so strung out that I craved it as soon as I woke up. I could go without heroin for a few days, suffering the body aches and nausea almost gratefully, like a penance, knowing I would get high again as soon as I was able to come up with more cash. Dev had gone beyond the point where he could take a day or two off without becoming really sick and most times it was easier to go without myself to make sure he got high.

Rising slowly I walked into the small living room and looked around. Memories of my old friend Deb stirred, how she was trapped in Roy's house. I fantasized about leaving Dev, moving away where he couldn't find me. The pain that came with those fantasies was deep and cutting. I didn't really want to leave him, I just wanted things to be different. Sinking into my soft chair I let the white light of the TV engulf my already fuzzy mind.

***

"I signed up with Day Labor down the street," Dev said one evening. "You just show up in the morning and they get you work. Hauling bricks, mixing cement, that kind of stuff. They pay you every day. And," he said, looking very pleased with himself, "the 7-11 on the corner will cash the checks right there." He had just come in from working with Mick. I was watching television with the lights off, basking in the glow of the screen. My high from earlier in the afternoon was wearing off and I felt tired and edgy.

I didn't look up from the TV. M*A*S*H was on and I was fully engrossed in an episode I had only seen maybe forty-seven, forty-eight times.

"That's great," I said dead-pan. "You can go to work, get your check, cash it and give it to the dope man all in the same block." I instantly regretted the harshness of my words.

Dev looked as if I'd struck him.

"You could be a little supportive." His voice was stinging. "I never realized you could be such a bitch. I know I'm a fuck-up, I don't need you to keep reminding me." His face was dark as he left the room and I heard the door slam. I turned my attention back to the TV, my forehead aching at the knot between my brows. Anger was not an emotion we were accustomed to. In the past years we had rarely even raised our voices at each other, just never disagreed much. Now it was how we communicated. Not that I yelled. I didn't need to. My tone of voice spoke volumes. I used it to hurt him, as if he wasn't hurting enough already. As if increasing his pain would lessen mine.

"I need some money Novena," Dev said after coming in one night. He used the tone he had adopted lately when he said that phrase. It had a hard flatness to it, like he was stating a fact instead of begging. It was late and he had already copped twice that day. His work with the day labor place was sporadic. He would work a few days, not work a few days. All the money he made went to the dope-man just as I had predicted. He was getting high throughout the day and needing it in the morning to get out of bed.

"I don't have any," I said. "The well finally ran dry." My own voice had taken on a sharpness in the past weeks that was new, a product of the constant slow-burning resentment I cultivated. My gaze remained focused on the re-run I was watching.

"I have to get high even if I rob someone to do it," he said.

"Go ahead. You'll wind up in jail. It'll give me a rest."

"You can go without heroin, you damned chippy, I can't!" he yelled. He no more would rob someone than Mother Theresa. When he needed money he would threaten all kinds of things. He'd yell then plead and this would go on until I was finally worn down enough to give in and throw bills on the floor in front of him. Usually I let him demean himself enough to satisfy my need to make him hurt then gave him whatever money I had so he would leave me alone. I was taking advances on my credit cards to pay the rent and put gas in the cars. Tonight however, I had a new plan. I had decided not to bring home cash anymore. We only used it for dope and food anyway and I had enough ramen in the kitchen to sustain us for a good six months.

"I know you have money stashed here somewhere," he growled.

"I can live without money or dope if I have to. I'm good at suffering. You've given me lots of practice," I said. "So no, I don't have any money hidden. I'm having trouble keeping the bills paid and I'm not living like this anymore."

"I'll find someway to get what I need," he spit out and slammed the door behind him. Quickly I jumped up to deadbolt the door, knowing he didn't have his key. I stomped to the kitchen and dug in the freezer, to the little space I had chipped into the built-up ice earlier. Pulling out the small plastic bag, I ripped it open and swallowed the handful of pain pills I had stashed and washed them down with a bottle of beer from the back of the fridge. Then I turned back to the TV. As soon as the glow from the screen hit my face my muscles began to relax. My sanctuary: a locked door and a TV with remote control.

A few hours later I heard a pounding at the door. I turned the TV down. The pounding continued.

"Novena I lost my keys. I know you're in there, open the goddamned door!" Dev yelled. "Novena!"

I cursed softly as I crossed the room.

"Stop yelling," I hissed as I opened the door. "The neighbors will call the cops." I turned away as he staggered in. He was drunk. "I thought you didn't have any money," I sneered.

"I borrowed enough for a pint," he slurred. "Now I need to get high. Give me some money. I know you have it." He swayed towards me, his eyes bleary.

"I don't have any money! Keep your voice down," I said again. I was beginning to be afraid. Drunk was much different than high.

"I don't care what the fuck the neighbors think, I don't care if they know I'm a junkie," he shouted. "Now give me some money!" I shook my head no. "You're a cruel, cruel bitch," he slurred softly, giving me an evil look. "Give it to me!" he shouted. He picked up a lamp and threw it across the room. His breath was fast and deep as if he'd been running and his face was contorted with rage. Terrified, I ran past him and grabbed my keys with shaking hands. I bounded out of the apartment to the car. I could hear him yelling behind me and my hands continued to shake, making the car door hard to unlock. I was sure he was right behind me. Finally I slid into the cool seat and sped off into the dark, not sure where I was going.

As I drove, I was quaking, my breath coming in shallow gasps. I had never been afraid of him for any reason before. *This is so out of hand*, my thoughts raced. *OK, I need someplace to stay.* I made myself take stock of the situation. *I can't go to someone's house, then I'd have to explain. I'm not going to a shelter and I don't have money for a motel.* I just wanted to lay my head down and not have to think. Passing St. Paul's Monastery where I went to Mass, I remembered their secluded parking lot. I pulled the car under an overhanging tree where the dark of the branches would hide me, thankful that it was summer so at least I wouldn't have to worry about the temperature. I put the seat back and squirmed around trying to find a comfortable position in which to sleep and then squeezed my eyes closed.

My over-active imagination kept turning every noise into an ax-murderer coming to get me. I weighed the outcomes: being chased by a crazed murderer or explaining to someone why I couldn't go home. A psycho with an ax seemed easier to face. I drifted off into uneasy sleep.

After long uncomfortable hours the sky finally lightened. I went to work directly from the parking lot. The coffee from the cafeteria would keep me going and I changed into an emergency set of blues I kept in the staff lounge. My mind was as sensitive as an exposed nerve, and I wondered how I would make it through the day feeling that raw, that exhausted. Thoughts of the pain pills locked up tight in the nurse's medication cart made my mouth water with longing. I would have to make it till three thirty when I could stop by Sissy's and ease my pain. Lynette eyed me worriedly as she helped me with my patients.

When I dragged myself home that afternoon the door was open and the apartment was trashed. Dev had gone through everything, torn our house apart looking for money. Of course there was none to be found. Suddenly I noticed that the TV was gone. So were the VCR, stereo, microwave and all our CDs. Amazing that a guy so drunk carry all that down two flights of steps. Then it sunk in: *he took my TV!* Anger engulfed me like wildfire. My house, my stuff, my *TV*, for God's sake. That bastard!

I stormed to the bedroom. He was lying in bed with the blinds drawn when I flung the door open.

"Hmm, what?" he mumbled in a groggy voice and rolled over.

"You took my stuff and trashed the house!" I shouted as I rushed towards the bed. I tore the covers off him and he snatched them back, beginning to wake up.

"What? What are you yelling about?" He was still out of it, sitting up and rubbing his head.

"You broke my things, the house is a mess and you sold all our stuff!" My breath came in ragged gasps and I was shaking. I was so angry I was afraid of myself.

"I can't even remember," he tried weakly.

"Oh you remember! You weren't that drunk. You yelled and threatened me. After I left you wrecked the house and sold all our stuff! I slept in the car because I was so afraid of you," I beat the words out like they hurt. "I am beginning to hate you," I said, standing at the foot of the bed staring at him. My fists were tightly clenched and my muscles stiff, my face a mask of tension. Dev let himself fall back into the pillow and covered his eyes with his forearm.

"I'm sorry," he whispered. "I was desperate. I hate myself," He began to cry silently. My anger melted away as I realized its ineffectiveness. It was replaced by the cold emptiness of defeat. What could I say, 'Get my TV back'? With what? He had sold all his own possessions weeks ago. In place of his stacks of CDs was an empty space on the floor. His weight bench and plates were gone too and a book dealer had sucked up all those beautiful old books, salivating while he gave Dev half what they were worth. All the things he valued were gone along with his self-respect and dignity. Suddenly I just felt tired. Tired in my body and tired in my soul. I closed the door quietly behind me as I left.

I crossed the yard to Jon's house and let myself into the kitchen. I needed a quiet place to think and I couldn't stand the site of our apartment. Laurence was at the table having coffee. I bummed a cigarette.

"Hey, Sweetie," he murmured, turning the pages of the Sunday paper, "how's it going?"

"I don't know Laurence. I don't know anymore." I picked up the part of the newspaper he wasn't reading and pretended to scan it. "Things have gotten weird." I said, glancing briefly at him.

"Dev's shooting heroin isn't he," Laurence asked, looking over his reading glasses at me.

"How'd you know?"

"He spends all his time with Mick these days and sometimes his eyes are glassy. I'm up a lot at night and I see him running around in the wee hours. I been around awhile you know. I couldn't help but figure it out."

I nodded wearily. It was a relief to have someone know. He reached out for my hand, held it in his and slid my sleeve up. The eye of my elbow was bruised and red in various spots along my vein. "Aw Sweetie," he said softly, and pulled me into his arms. I allowed myself to be held but couldn't find the energy to cry.

I spent the night in Jon's spare room. Shame burned in my stomach as I snuck into the bathroom with my lighter and spoon, finally getting the relief I craved. The next morning I gathered my resolve and went home to assess the damage. Laurence came with me for support. Dev was nowhere to be found. We still had furniture and a phone, he hadn't sold those. The rest of the place looked as if a tornado had hit. My neat drawers had been emptied, clothes were scattered everywhere. The cushions of the sofa were on the floor, he'd torn the carpets up from the corners of the room. Dev had thrown all the papers off my desk, dumped my well-organized documents out of their shoe-boxes and ripped open all the envelopes I had ready to mail. In his haste to haul my things out he'd put a dent in the wall. Our sanctuary had been reduced to ruble. I picked up the plants Dev had knocked to the floor, the leaves broken and roots exposed. Slowly I began to put things back in their places. Like a robot, I worked to put my home in order. I hated him for destroying our house and hated myself for letting it happen. I dropped to my knees to pick up pieces of white glass, realizing that they were the broken shards of the Buddha my mom had given me, the only thing she'd brought back from San Francisco in 1964. Tears began to run down my cheeks finally. I sat amid the torn plant leaves and chaos and sobbed silently.

The next two days I stayed at Jon's. Dev knew I was there and on the third night he brought a syringe full of dope to Jon's house in apology. I hadn't gotten high in two days and I was beginning to feel just sick enough that I held the door open and wordlessly let him in. He took off his belt and held it out to me. I grabbed it without hesitation, cursing myself for my weakness. I was silent as I climbed the stairs to the spare room, silent as I injected the poison into my body. I watched hungrily as it entered my vein and sighed as my body absorbed it. Heroin wagged its skeletal finger in gentle disapproval for my having strayed and then welcomed me into its warm embrace, patting my back comfortingly as I clung to the feeling, almost weeping with relief. I succumbed to its seductive promise, letting it ease the pain in my body and chase away the chills and nausea I had been fighting all day. I hated that it felt so good.

"You're a fucking bastard," I said to Dev as I melted into the chair and lit a cigarette. He smiled, happy that I was talking to him, not caring what I said.

"I knew what you needed though, didn't I?" He was sitting on the worn bed drinking water from the glass I'd left on the nightstand.

"What I need is my TV," I spat. He blushed and shrugged his shoulders, putting down the glass. He fiddled with the ancient radio on the stand next to him.

"What does that old song say? 'Freedom is another word for nothing left to lose', well now we're truly free," he said in a strained voice.

"That singer goes on to say she'd trade all her tomorrows for one single yesterday," I countered darkly, remembering the rest of the haunting lyrics. He lowered his head and clasped his hands in front of him, his face dropping.

"What can I tell you, Novena? I did what I had to. I wouldn't blame you if you left me. This shit has a hold on me I can't break. You were right, Mick was right, I couldn't handle it." He continued to look at me intently. "I'm doing everything I can to survive. I know you are too." He paused, lacing his fingers together in front of his lips as if praying and focused his gaze on his hands. "I feel like I've been looking for something my entire life and heroin gives me the answer. Or at least makes the search seem less important ... getting high calms the hunger." His voice trailed off and he looked away as he seemed to hunt for words to explain what compelled his addiction.

"What hunger?" I whispered, afraid if I spoke too loud his difficult explanation would end. He looked at me again and his brief show of vulnerability disappeared.

"If we stick together we can beat this. Just give me a little more time to kick this thing." He dropped his hands into his lap. "I love you." The shades were pulled, making the room dim. He leaned forward trying to see under the long hair that fell over my face as I sat with my head lowered. "Novena?" he questioned softly. I looked up and nodded.

Chapter Eight

The scene opens. A painfully thin young woman with a sallow face and pinched features stands in line at a food bank set up in a church basement. She keeps her head down and shuffles forward, careful not to look at anyone around her. She moves down the line in front of a row of tables, reluctantly taking items from each pile of canned and boxed goods as if it hurts her to touch them. Slowly she puts each one in her plastic bag and walks out the door. As she gets into the passenger seat of a waiting car she shoots an angry look at the driver, a pale man with dark hair hunched behind the wheel. The man turns his head toward the window as if ashamed and drives away.

The camera flashes to a small table in a city kitchen. The same man and woman sit alone, not speaking. The food is spread out on the table in front of them. Two cans of meat, two cans of beets and potatoes, a package of crumbling cookies and some packages of chicken soup.

"Well they were out of caviar today. I guess we'll have to make do with out of date Spam for a week," the woman says. The man hangs his head.

I didn't even know meat came in cans, I thought, eyeing my bag with disgust. It wasn't really me standing in line at the food-bank. It was some actor playing a part in a movie. A movie in which the characters would learn hard lessons, come to reasonable conclusions and in the end everyone would live happily ever after.

"Here Novena I saved you some." Dev held out a full syringe like he was making an offering to an angry god. Every day after work he had a hit ready for me. I never got that happy feeling I had in the beginning or the rush we were always chasing but the drug gave me a dull feeling that made life tolerable for a while. I went to the bathroom and tied off, slid the needle into my vein, loosened the belt and pulled back on the plunger to enjoy the sight of the blood mixing with the heroin then pushed it in. In seconds everything began to soften, my body, my mind, my surroundings. My brain continued to function as usual but my emotions melted into dull fuzziness, numbing the pain and reducing the anger to a faint sense of emptiness. I slouched into a chair by the bed and occupied my self by trying to rub the blackness left from the lighter off the back of the spoon even though I knew only steel wool would take it off.

"I'm going to try to quit tomorrow," Dev said. He was reading the book I had just finished. I had become as voracious a reader as Dev since he had sold my TV. The library was free. "I bought some Valium from Sissy today," he continued. "So tomorrow I'm just going to hole up in here and lie in bed and shake." He grinned at me expectantly. I kept silent. I had heard this particular line of bullshit before. He talked about needing to quit but never did anything about it. "Honest Novena. I'm going to really do it this time," he said when he caught my skeptical look. He crossed the room to stand behind me and gently kneaded my shoulders. My head fell back at his warm touch. Then I shrugged his hands away and sat forward to take off my shoes. He moved reluctantly back to his seat and ran his hands over his face.

"I'm going to Erie," I said. Lake Erie was the closest thing we had to the ocean and my friends and I made yearly pilgrimages to its sandy shores to lie in the sun and pretend to be on vacation in some exotic location. I hadn't seen Rachel for weeks. My fear of being found out made me reluctant to spend much time with her. But she had begged me to go with them to the beach and I was craving the comfort of her company. Nothing was going to keep me from making the trip, least of all Dev's empty promises.

"You can't go. You have to stay with me, to keep me from trying to get high," he said in alarm.

"I'll keep you from getting high by not being here. You'll just change your mind and want me to get a cash advance on the Visa card if I'm here," I retorted. He sat back in disbelief, a look of shock on his face.

"What a time to pick for a day trip! I finally make the decision and you leave. That's just typical. You never support me," he said.

94

"I hate when you whine, which lately is all the time. You whine and I bitch. We probably get high just to tolerate each other." I told him.

"I went to the store and bought some good food, checked some books out of the library. I'm all set. It would just be helpful if you were here."

Staying clean even one day was going to be a big production. He expected me to hold his hand and comment on how well he was suffering. If someone really wanted to get clean, all they had to do was not get high, I thought to myself.

"I'm leaving at six in the morning." I went to the bedroom to pack my beach clothes.

It was a beautiful day. The sky was a deep cloudless blue when Rachel and Amy picked me up at six in the old clunker they shared. I had gotten high at my house when I woke up so I could enjoy the day. No sense in getting out of the city if I couldn't really relax. As we putted down the highway I sat in the back seat searching the newspaper for our horoscopes.

"What's our boy doing today?" Rachel asked, referring to Dev. She was driving and had one arm hanging out the open window.

"He's working," I said, not raising my eyes from the paper.

"Working again? Is that all the poor guy does?" Amy asked. Rachel sighed.

"God I hate to see this happening to you two." She shook her head. "Remember when you used to be fun? Now you always look stressed and he's always working. I hate to see my friends becoming slaves to their jobs," she said. I put down the newspaper and leaned toward the front seat.

"What do you mean I look stressed?" I asked. Rachel was quiet for a minute. Then she spoke, keeping her eyes on the road.

"You're just different now. You seem tired or scared or something" Rachel's face was serious and Amy turned to look at me. I sat back in the seat and picked up the paper again to buy myself some thinking time. Stay as close to the facts as possible, I reminded myself.

"My job's been unstable lately and Dev's had to work more to make up for that. It puts a strain on our relationship. I guess I should look for a new job but I really like the nursing home even if the hours aren't consistent. He's been pressuring me to go back to school. It's just been a hard time that's all." It sounded pretty good to me and I watched them both closely for their reactions.

"Yeah it's always tough on a couple when money's tight," Amy said. Rachel nodded her head in agreement.

"Don't get too hung up on it Novena. Things will work out, they always do. You two will be fine." She sounded like she was trying to convince us both. She caught me looking at her in the rear-view mirror and her face transformed from a mask of worry to an exaggerated look of satisfaction. "The lottery is thirty-six mil today and I bought ten tickets. When I win, you'll never have to think about money again bud," she said, and nodded to me. I eased against the hot plastic of the car seat and let out a soft sigh of relief as conversation drifted to what Rachel would do with her winnings.

After the two-hour drive we found an empty beach and hauled all our gear to the shore, having to make several trips. They had packed food and water, toys and lawn chairs, enough to keep us occupied for three days instead of one. Rachel then set up the umbrella, chairs and snacks, blew up all the water toys, spread out the towels and dug a pit for the little grill where we would later cook our hot dogs. She looked at where Amy and I sat at the edge of the water, brushed her hands off and smiled.

"Ain't it great to go away and relax?" she asked, holding her arms out to indicate the paradise she'd created.

We spent the morning sitting by the lake watching the sun glint off the waves. The day was warm enough to venture into the water but none of us made a move to get out of our chairs. A few families with children milled around, their voices carried away on the wind.

I was fidgeting in my chair, going from magazine to magazine trying to find something interesting to read, wondering how Dev was faring.

"We're on vacation dammit, would you settle down," Rachel chided. She was leaned back in her beach chair 'sunning' with her eyes closed. She had slathered oil over all her exposed skin trying to soak up as much sun as she could draw to herself.

"I'm having trouble sitting still," I grumbled.

"So I've noticed. And take off that stupid shirt, I feel like I'm at the beach with a vampire for crissakes. You're embarrassing me." I had a long sleeve blouse on over my halter to keep my bruised arms covered and was wearing dark black sunglasses to protect my heroin-sensitive eyes from the glaring rays. For good measure I had thrown an Indian-print towel over my legs up to my cut-off jean shorts and had on an old black wide brimmed straw hat with a long red scarf.

"When you're drinking through a straw sewn into your face because skin cancer ate it off, you'll think about me in my shirt on the beach," I said.

"You're sick," she complained, without looking up.

I took a deep breath and tried to relax. My body and mind were so tightly wound these days I was never comfortable. I needed to be looking over my shoulder to see what was coming next, so I could be prepared. Amy was snoring under the umbrella and Rachel had drifted off in the sun. I watched the waves come in and go out. The cry of sea gulls and rhythmic crash of the waves lulled me into a light sleep. I floated into a dream, the sound of the waves crossing the border into my subconscious. In my dream I was on a boat. It was old and creaky and a storm was blowing furiously. I was fighting through the wind and rain to get to a lifeboat as the waves consumed the ship, but every time I reached one an invisible force would wrap itself around me, pulling at me and not allow me to get in. This force was strong, alive, the same ghost I fought in my dreams on and off since the first day I had gotten high. I tried outrunning it, beating against it and out-smarting it but each time just as I held out my hand desperately for the lifeboat the specter would grab me and pull me back as the waves got higher and lapped at my chest.

"Hey wake up, you're disturbing the tourists." Rachel was shaking me. "You were moaning, but not a good kind of moan," She bit her lower lip and looked concerned.

"Bad dream," I said. My voice was shaky. "I'm not used to relaxing." I sat up straight and took a deep breath, trying to chase the feeling of drowning from my mind.

The rest of the day was ruined for me. I couldn't seem to shake the sense of dread my dream had left me with. When I got home that night Dev was pacing and cursing.

"I thought you'd never get home, what the hell could you do so long?" He spat. "I need some money. I borrowed some from Mick, but now we're both broke." He stood in front of me with his hands in his pockets, glowering with agitation and impatience.

"I thought you were quitting," I mumbled as I looked in my bag for money.

"Yeah so did I," he said.

Sitting in the car outside a store a few days later I felt the tiredness in my body double as I thought of the task ahead. Grocery shopping. I had so little money to spend, it was like torture. I would roam the aisles looking at the food I had no money to buy, my stomach rumbling and my mouth watering at the sight of the fresh fruit and meat. Then I would load up on ramen and mac and cheese, splurging on ninety-nine cent hotdogs when I was feeling particularly protein-deprived. My friends and family would never have let us starve, but what could I say? 'Hey, I just spent my last dollar on heroin, could you lend me some cash so I can eat?' Yeah, right. I took as much food as I could risk from work, unopened cartons of milk and juice, uneaten sandwiches and packets of crackers. It would all just get thrown away, I rationalized. It helped but I couldn't afford to get caught. I was also stealing bags of syringes, toilet paper, coffee filters, whatever I could pilfer and I didn't want to get too careless and arouse suspicion.

It all becomes normal so fast I thought as I climbed out into the parking lot. One day you're respectable well-liked people with plans for the future, next day you're a couple of junkies doing anything for money to get high. It happens like a fast-moving storm, the clouds rolling in to destroy someone's sunny picnic before anyone notices and suddenly the thunder is shaking the ground and the rain is sending everyone running for cover. Later, they'll come tentatively out of the shelter, trying to salvage what's left of the day. Once you're caught in it, it becomes too dark to see any way out. I stepped out of the car and scouted the supermarket parking lot for men selling food stamps. This is how people end up living in the streets with matted hair and filthy clothes, I reflected. The path they take to get there is so gradual they can't remember how to get back. Or even where they came from.

"Hi, Mom." I said into the phone. I hadn't returned her calls in weeks. I just couldn't bear to have to come up with more lies. It took too much energy. Finally I called her back in the effort to keep her from worrying.

"Hi, Baby, how are you? I miss you and you haven't called. I called you four or five times. What's going on?" I could hear worry in her voice.

"Just really busy. You know, the usual." I exhaled a breath of smoke.

"What's usual? Tell me. I want to know about your life."

"Are you coming home anytime soon?" I avoided answering her question. I craved her company, longed for the affection and comfort only my mother could give.

"What's wrong, something's wrong, I can hear it in your voice." She issued the line calmly as a statement, not a question. A moment passed as I fought with myself over what to tell her. My body was shaking slightly with the need to purge myself of the poisonous truth I held inside. It was like being imprisoned inside a glass box; it would be easy to break the walls that held me but I was afraid to reach out my hand in fear that it would be severed when the glass shattered into sharp edges.

"I'm thinking about leaving Dev," I said. It was as close as I could come to the truth. I could hear my mom expel a quiet breath.

"Well love, you were so young when you met. I don't think it's a bad thing to think about your options," she said softly after a moment. "You have so much potential. You can keep playing house with him or you can grow up and find out who you are. You as a person. All you know at this point is you as a couple." She was quiet. I had only heard a few words of what she said. My mind was racing, my heart pounding and my breath coming in shallow gasps. I wanted to blurt out to her that I was in trouble, I was hurting, please come home, Mom, please come to me. I steadied my voice before speaking.

"When are you coming home?"

"Honey I know this is hard for you, but unfortunately my plans changed. We have to go to England to see Richard's daughter who just had a baby. Her husband was transferred to Germany and she's alone right now. You can get through this. Let your heart guide you."

"I don't know what to do," my voice came out in a weak rasp.

"Look around you. There are so many people who love you. You have to know that. Let yourself feel it. Be open to the love that your friends and family have for you and draw upon it." Her voice was confident and steady. The vibration in her voice was thawing the numbing cold in my limbs. We were talking about two completely different things but her words seemed to fit anyway.

"My friends don't know what's really going on."

"They don't have to know the details. They just have to know you need them. You'll be fine. You are my blessing. Just let go and ask for help and things will take care of themselves." She was quiet for a moment. "We all take turns wearing the face of God for each other. When you can't rely on yourself, you can fall back on those who love you."

Slowly I let out my pent up breath, my body relaxed slightly. I clung to the unwavering belief I heard in her words like I was holding onto the only rock in a rushing torrent of whitewater.

"I love you," she said and I felt as if it were the answer to all questions.

"I love you too." It had been a long time since I had said that. It felt good.

***

"So what would you do if you stopped getting high?" I asked Gilbert. Gilbert, Wayne and I were sitting in our living room waiting for Dev and Mick to get back with our dope. They had to meet an unknown dealer in a neighborhood they were unfamiliar with and had gone together for safety. It was early evening but the days were getting slowly shorter as summer neared its end.

"Not gonna happen," he said without looking up from his newspaper. Wayne laughed and lit a cigarette. The smoke curled out from his bushy black beard blurring his rough features for a second, swirling in the wedge of light the light made from above his chair.

"I mean if it did," I said. "Just play along, would ya?"

Gilbert lowered the newspaper and sighed. He pushed his glasses to his head where they sat unevenly on his wild red hair.

"Alright. Let me think … well, I guess if I was granted the grace to stay clean I'd want to help other people do the same." He looked at a spot above my left shoulder for a minute. "Stand-up comedy. That's it. That's what I'd do." I wrinkled my eyebrows trying to understand.

"What does that have to do with helping people?" I asked.

"Everyone takes this whole 'life' thing way too seriously," he said with a wave of his thin arm before going back to his reading.

"That's easy for you to say. You fucked yours all up," Wayne pointed out with a snorting kind of laugh that made his belly shake under his black t-shirt. Gilbert laughed too, exposing even white teeth.

"If people would lighten up a little they wouldn't feel such a need to rely on drugs for relief. I'd make fun of all the things we think are so scary, all the painful, dramatic muck we roll around in when things don't go the way we think they should. That'd help them see that it's not such a big hairy deal. You've got to look at it all with some humor because in the end, how much really matters anyway?" Gilbert asked with a shrug of his shoulders.

"It matters when you're in a situation you don't like," Wayne said.

"But if you're able to make fun of yourself you'll be forced to smile. Then you'll realize that it's going to pass, probably quicker than you think. So it's not so bad after all." Gilbert rubbed his chin in reflection. "Yep. Stand Up Comedy. That'd be my service to humankind."

Dev and Mick came in before I could respond to Gilbert's words. Mick's face was stretched with tension, his lips pressed tight together with lingering anxiety from copping. Gilbert stood and embraced Mick lightly in greeting when he handed him the small bags of dope.

"Is that a syringe in your pocket or are you just glad to see me?" He wiggled his eyebrows suggestively and winked at me when Mick's face lightened into a laugh. "See what I mean?"

"So if you don't do drugs for relief why do you?" I asked.

"Because I like it," Gilbert told me as he popped his little bags of heroin under his tongue.

"Aren't you staying, Gilbert?" Dev asked in surprise, looking up from counting Wayne's money.

"Nope. I've got to be at work at eight pm. I've got a special job I'm doing on a public building."

"Too bad. We always enjoy that fucked up perspective of yours," Dev grinned as Gilbert headed toward the door. "You be careful out there."

"Hey," Gilbert said from the doorway, nodding his head at Dev. "See you on the dark side of the spoon." Gilbert winked and left. The closing of the door seemed to echo in the room.

"Hey boy." Wayne said, pulling Dev's attention away from the door. "I gotta pay you and run. I wanna call my ol' lady and check in before I get high." He handed Dev a few bills.

"Good luck," Dev told him with a smile.

"You don't need luck, Devvy, when you got the gift of bullshit like I do. Hell sometimes I lie so well I believe myself!" Wayne said, clapping Dev on the back as he passed him on the way to the door.

After he left we went into the bedroom and Dev attended to the business of cooking our drugs. Mick had opened the tiny plastic bags and emptied them into two separate spoons and Dev took over from there while Mick lit a cigarette.

"I got you some coke. It'll give you a nice high," Dev said as he handed me a syringe.

"I don't think I like coke," I said. He and Mick wanted something different for a change they had told me.

"Just try it. It's not that much different than dope," he said. Mick was already tying off in the chair. Taking the fit and Dev's belt I sat on the bed and shot its contents into my arm. My heart began beating loudly in my ears and my breathing became labored. The room narrowed in my vision and I looked in fright at Dev but he was ignoring me as he prepared his own syringe. I flew off the bed and grabbed his arm.

"Dev, I think I'm dying," I said with alarm in my voice. He turned immediately to me.

"What's wrong?" He held my shoulders as I stared into his face. I was breathing heavily and holding my chest in fright.

"I don't know! I feel like my heart is coming out of my chest." I broke away from him and started to pace back and forth, my hands holding my flushed cheeks. I felt a heightened awareness that scared me, like all my sensations were multiplied by a thousand. Mick put down his syringe and caught my hands. He made me sit on the bed and Dev sat next to me with his arm around me. "You have to get me some dope. I can't stand this," I told him. He and Mick exchanged glances.

"It'll pass Novena, just hang in there." Mick held my hands in his. I pulled them away and jumped up to pace again. My breath was coming in shallow gasps and I was shaking. Everything seemed to be in double-time, like watching a movie in fast-forward. I put my hands out to try to stop things from going so fast but the movement made my heart thump even harder against my rib cage until I thought it was going to burst.

"No, I need something to make this stop now! Please," I begged. "Just get me some heroin, I can't stand it!" I was almost crying.

"You stay with her. I'll be right back," Dev said to Mick as he headed out the door. I sat on the bed and held my sides, staring at my knees and willing my mind to slow down. I tried to ignore the hollow rapid pounding of the blood in my skull, the way normally undetectable air currents stirred the hairs on my arms, the sensation of my breath warming and cooling the membranes as it entered and left my lungs. After months of dulling my senses with heroin this sudden increase in sensitivity was a shock to my system. Mick sat beside me and patted my back.

"You'll be alright, you just need something to bring you down a little. Lots of people only shoot coke in speedballs, that's when you mix it with heroin to mellow it out a little. They call it chasing the dragon." Mick told me. "At least you're not hiding in the closet, all paranoid and shit," he tried to joke with me and tickled my side softly. I raised my tense face to his, sure that I was dying while he cracked jokes, and my breath caught involuntarily. His eyes were a vivid liquid blue, the blue of a clear summer sky, of thick winter ice. I felt a familiar tingle in my lower abdomen like when I first started shooting heroin. I wanted the comfort of the warm fullness to continue. This is what I missed. This is how it used to be every time I did heroin. I leaned eagerly towards Mick and touched my lips to his.

Lightning struck entering my lips and coursing through my chest and stomach. It ran down my arms and legs along my nerve endings until my hands, feet and the top of my head seemed to be illuminated. I grasped Mick's shirt and pulled him to me. His mouth was so warm and soft, so accommodating. I let my body melt into his, let my hands find their way under his shirt to the smooth skin of his back, let the heat exploding in my lower body eclipse any thought trying to surface in my mind. I pushed myself against him and ground my mouth into his.

"Novena stop," Mick's voice was shaky as he held me away from him. "This is wrong," he murmured just before his lips dropped to mine again. I wanted to devour him, to take his whole being inside me. The hardness of his muscles beneath his soft skin, the salty smell of him, the life in him, it incensed me! My actions were violent as I forced Mick's gentle hands away so I could drive myself into him. In the moment before we heard Dev's heavy tread on the stairs, I was reminded by Mick's attempted tenderness that he held me for deeper reasons and I knew I was using him, but didn't care. We broke from each other before Dev opened the door. Mick threw himself into a chair, gasping for air and running his hands through his hair. I was still panting as I shot the heroin that killed my desire, not noticing when Mick said a quiet goodbye to Dev and slipped out the door.

Chapter Nine

The glaring sun of summer had passed and as fall blew in on a cold wind I dug in and prepared for the long dark days to come, relieved that the hours of light were dwindling. The summer sun depressed me. It reminding me that other people were out riding bikes, going on vacation, playing tennis while I hid in a room with the blinds drawn shooting my life away. The darkness of winter fit my mood, I thought melodramatically as I stared out the bedroom window one evening in October. The cold rain pounding the pavement and running in streams down the glass provided a nice backdrop for my misery. I touched my fingertips to the pane and lowered my head for dramatic effect. I could be in the movies, I sighed, enjoying the dark image I pictured myself casting against the window.

"Wayne's in jail." Dev interrupted my daydream as he strode heavily into the room. He closed the blinds and went through the ritual that had become as casual to me as washing my hands. "He beat this guy up outside some bar across the state line in West Virginia, way out of line of the conditions of his parole. His old lady doesn't even think they'll let him post bail." He handed me a filled syringe and took his to a chair across the room.

"So he's in for good?" I asked. I liked Wayne and felt bad he was going to waste more of his life behind bars. I shot my heroin while he continued the conversation, the familiar relief spreading through me as I pulled the needle from my skin.

"Yeah I think when you violate parole like that it's an excuse to throw your ass back in for a good long while. As claustrophobic as I am I'd hate jail. That would put me right over the edge." He smiled and looked up at me. "It's not the smallness of the cells I wouldn't like. It's just knowing you can't leave if you want to, knowing someone else has total control over all your actions. Your freedom's gone," he said incredulously.

I watched him cleaning up, putting his belt back on and preparing to go to work with Mick that evening to make extra money. They were going to work in the cold wet weather clearing someone's blocked drain of a whole summer's worth of dog shit and rotting grass clippings for a few measly bucks.

"It's not like he had freedom out here anyway," I said. "He had to chase dope every day, his life depended on it. He couldn't do anything without being high, he scammed all the time to get enough money and groveled in front of the welfare office on a regular basis. Maybe prison's easier than life on heroin. Or the same at least, but with regular meals." He looked at me curiously as he rubbed Vasoline into his raw hands.

"You might have a point there Novena, but at least out here we've chosen our jailer." He kissed the top of my head before I could duck away and put his jacket on. "I'll bring you a treat later," he said as he went to work.

My rubber-soled shoes squeaked rhythmically as I walked down the polished floor of the nursing home. I glanced at my clip-board, taking comfort in its neat rows of red and blue ink, each color designating a different shift's report. I was methodical about my job and the report I would add to the list at the end of the day would be in neat black writing when I handed it to the nurse at the end of my shift.

"Ah, excuse me, nurse." I turned to look at the elderly woman who sat in a wheelchair, her hands folded primly in her lap. "I really think this should be taken off." She showed me the belt that kept her restrained to the wheelchair. "In case of disaster I would need to be free to walk out with my cane." She held the cane up for me to see. She had fallen twice while using it, but hated the restraining seat-strap that kept her safe from injury.

"Mrs. Opay we have to leave that on so you don't try to get up and walk and then fall," I explained. In the past Mrs. Opay had wriggled out of the restraint, conned a new aide into releasing her and finally cut the belt with scissors she stole from the nurses' station.

"Ah. And what will we do in event of disaster or tragedy? How will I get out?" Her voice was calm and business-like. I smiled at her.

"I don't foresee any disasters or tragedies right now, but if something would happen, you'll be safer with the belt on, ma'am."

"You may think I'm safer but don't you think I should be left to make that decision myself?"

What could I say that wouldn't sound condescending? I just wanted to go about my morning routine as usual. The rest of the day would provide enough of a challenge.

"I don't know, ma'am." I took the coward's way out.

"When can you release me?" she demanded.

"I'd have to ask the nurse, I'm not sure. And she'll have to ask the doctor." I was focusing on my clipboard, hoping she'd go away.

"Well, what time is the doctor coming in?" She was blocking my path with her wheelchair.

"I don't know, Mrs. Opay." I answered. She stared at me with a look of growing annoyance.

"You don't know much, do you?" she asked, cocking her head sideways at me and rapping the arm of her wheelchair with her cane. "You young workers here with your safety belts, feeding us low-fat diets and treating us like fragile invalids, why can't you just let us have a little fun in our last days?" Her voice was harsh.

"It's our job to keep you from getting hurt," I said.

"No, you're just trying to keep us quiet. I buried two husbands and had two affairs. Three of my children died before they walked and the one who lived was killed in battle. I've lived through four wars and the depression, not to mention the Carter administration and you're trying to keep me from getting hurt?" She practically spat on the floor. "What I've learned in my eighty-nine years is that freedom is always sacrificed for security and it's not usually a good bargain!" She thumped her cane on the floor and wheeled off angrily. "You think about that for a while." I watched her for a minute before feeling a tug at my uniform.

"Nurse, take this, would you." Another resident carefully poured a handful of tiny shredded pieces of paper into my cupped palm. I threw it into a near-by trashcan.

"Goddammit I worked on that for hours!" she exclaimed, turning her walker quickly from me and clomping off. I sighed. It was going to be a long day. Lynette was watching from down the hall, smiling and shaking her head.

"Some days it just ain't worth gettin' outta bed, huh Baby?" she said to me as I passed.

Later that evening I lay on the bed reading. Outside the window the setting sun cast the sky in dark purple and orange stripes. A steaming cup of tea was on the floor beside me and I planned to spend the cold February evening reading the book Laurence had loaned me. I swore when I heard pounding and ran down the steps to answer.

"Hey Novena," Mick murmured as he came through the doorway and stood stiffly in the foyer. "Can I do my shit here? Francesca has some artist coming over tonight." I nodded and let him in, giving him a wide berth as he passed by me. Upstairs in the apartment he prepared two syringes full of heroin in awkward silence, then handed me one. I had already gotten high, but I didn't want to refuse the offer. He shot his dope in front of the mirror and came hesitantly to sit next to me on the bed, folding his hands in his lap and looking straight ahead. I held the syringe up to the light, checking the tip for sharpness. Mick looked sideways at me.

"Let me do it," he said softly, taking my arm and tying off with his belt. The warm rush hit me before I even realized the needle was in, my shyness and guilt floated to the back of my numbed mind. I lit a cigarette and Mick lit one off mine, then sat back against the wall and blew a stream of smoke into the air.

"So how're things going Novena?" He looked at me for a fraction of a second, his face serious.

"You know how Mick. I'm barely getting by," I answered. "I hate myself. I hate my life and most days I hate Dev." My gaze drifted to the window. "I've done stuff I never thought I'd ever do." I exhaled smoke in a deep sigh. "I just want things to be how they used to be."

He was quiet for minute.

"You know I never meant for things to get like this," he murmured. "Dev just kept insisting I let him try it. He kept saying we could get clean together, share the suffering so it would be easier. I finally gave in. He had me so convinced that everything would be OK I didn't think about it enough." Another silence. "I love Dev. He's the only one who's ever stood up for me. I just didn't want to lose him, you know?" He looked so forlorn. Tears stung my eyes and I wished I could comfort him. I touched his arm.

"I don't blame you for this and neither does Dev." A little silence followed. I listened to the crackling my cigarette made as I inhaled deeply. "I wish things were different. I want a new life, just be able to start over again. This one broken and I'm tired." The sun had set and the room was dim. Mick was silent again. He sat forward on the bed, putting his cigarette out. He glanced at me once then away then back at me again.

"You know," he said in a tentative voice, "we could go away together. You and I. We could just load up the van, take off, go west. I hear the job market is booming in Colorado. We could make a whole new start ..." How easy it would be to just leave everything and everyone.

"Mick," I began, but he cut me off.

"That night when you kissed me, if Dev hadn't come home, what would have happened?" His voice was soft as he let his blue eyes find mine. My chin fell to my chest in shame at the thought of my behavior that night.

"I don't know. I just needed someone that night ... anyone," I tried to explain without hurting him.

"I could take care of you. I'm a good worker. We wouldn't be rich but I control my habit better than Dev and you'd be free of this mess." He took my hand. "I know you don't love me but it would be enough just to be with you," he said. I thought about it. Free of all this, with the security of knowing Mick loved me. Halfway across the country from our dope connections. My stomach fluttered. Thousands of miles from Dev. My chest tightened and my throat began to close.

"It would never work Mick," I said, my voice catching. "We'd be like refugees, clinging to each other in our misery over missing Dev." I shook my head and raised my eyes to his. "Thank you for wanting to help me but I have to save myself." He leaned over after a moment and kissed my cheek.

"I've always loved you," he said and smiled. I nodded, afraid to trust my voice as I watched him get up to go.

Mick held me in a long embrace in the doorway before he left. He caressed my face with his hand, his eyes telling me goodbye.

Once he was gone I fell on the bed crying like a child having a temper tantrum. Why, why couldn't things be like they were before? Why did this all have to happen, why? I almost got up and ran after Mick. I could love him I thought. If I could forget Dev who knows what would happen? Maybe this was the answer to my problem, we could go west and just forget. As I curled up on the bed hiccupping with the last of my sobs I knew I would have neither freedom nor security no matter how far away I was.

***

"Sissy had a run on speed. I cooked you some," Dev said one evening. I took the syringe eagerly, not caring what was in it. Anything would do right now. As the substance hit my bloodstream I felt instantly energized, as if a switch had been flipped. I drew a deep breath in surprise and Dev chuckled. I smiled at him in wonder.

"I actually feel really high! Like I used to from dope. How much of this can we get?" I demanded.

"Whoa, don't get hooked on this. It'll kill you faster than anything out there," Dev warned.

"Just a few days won't hurt. Make sure Sissy saves us some," I told him. Ten hours later I could hardly tell any time had passed. I was singing to the radio and cleaning the kitchen, moving the mop in time to the music and swinging my hips. Dev came in, opened the refrigerator and stood studying its contents. The rhythmic sway of my body aroused a pleasant heat that I rarely felt anymore and I wrapped my arms around Dev's waist. My bitterness and anger towards him were replaced by an overwhelming feeling of happiness that I wanted to share. He chuckled and closed the appliance door. I kept my hands locked behind him when he turned to face me.

"Remember this?" I murmured, stretching up to run my lips along his neck. I felt his hands settle lightly on the small of my back. Rosy hues of pink and lavender blossomed as I closed my eyes. I pressed my body into him, expecting to feel the hardness of his response against me, but was disappointed. He kissed me quickly on the lips. I tried to hold him there but he backed away and attempted to remove my arms from around his neck.

"I gotta go Novena, I have to be at work in half an hour," he said.

"What time is it?" I asked, still hanging on to him.

"Seven in the morning. You've been awake all night." I continued to lean against him, paying little attention to his words. "You better lay off the speed today," he warned, swatting my behind lightly and slipped out of my grasp. I followed him to the door reluctant to let him leave now that I didn't have that stiff curtain of anger drawn between us.

"Don't you like me better this way?" I asked. "I feel almost like before. Like I used to when we were happy …" I hadn't meant to say it that way, but the words came out before I could catch them. His face fell, became sad. He laid his hand to my cheek in a gentle movement.

"You know I love you no matter what Novena," he said. Then he ducked out the door.

I started taking speed like it was medicine for an acute illness, popping a few little red Dexedrine anytime I began to feel down between hits of heroin. The joyful excitement it gave me was like being reborn and it was such a break from my usual feelings of depression and anger that I didn't want to stop.

At work I was happy and joked with the residents and other staff. My concentration was intense and in a single day I flew through my tasks and helped everyone else with theirs. I cleaned my house then cleaned Jon's three story home, buzzing with energy and singing to the radio. My mom and Rachel sounded puzzled by my exuberance when I spoke to them on the phone but I didn't take time to think about that. I felt like I was in another world, above all my worries.

"I get so much done and I feel *good*! I love this stuff!" I told Dev in a rush of words.

"I'm glad you're feeling better, just be careful," he said. The brightness in his face was proof that I was easier to live with this way and after a few days he stopped flinching when I looked at him. It was a relief not to want to cause him pain. The week flew by in a rush of bright colors and perkiness. After being up for five days without eating or sleeping, my body and mind suddenly just shut down, like a toy whose battery has finally run out. My arms and legs felt like lead. I swallowed and my throat was scratchy with dryness. I couldn't make even the simple decision of whether or not to turn on the light so I sat in the dark kitchen, my head lying on the table because I was unable to hold up its weight, and waited for Dev to get home from work. I was dehydrated and too weak to get from the kitchen to the bedroom. I wasn't sure what time or even what day it was.

"This is why they call it crashing," Dev said as he scooped me off the chair and carried me to the bed. I remembered hearing stories of speed freaks from the seventies using the word to describe what happened when their bodies gave in after too many days of amphetamine use. The bed was soft and it molded to my body as I melted into it.

"Novena, Novena," he murmured. "I should have been keeping an eye on you. It should have never gotten this far." He put me in bed and held a cup of water to my cracked lips. Then he reached for the phone and called my supervisor explaining that I had "a really bad upper respiratory infection and wouldn't be in for a few days," sounding just like a caring spouse. My supervisor gave me the week off and sent me a get-well card. I hadn't missed a day's work in three years and she was very supportive of my taking my time to recover 'so as not to infect the patients.'

All week Dev cooked my meals, picked out books from the library for me, helped me to the bathroom and kept my heroin habit fed so I wouldn't be doubly sick. He curled his body around mine and held me at night when I cried with the depression speed withdrawal brings. I found myself clinging to his strong arms and whispering words of desperation into his chest, begging him not to leave me and promising to stay with him always.

By the next week I could walk by myself, but was still weak. The shakiness of my hands resolved, the depression abated a little, leaving me with the disgusted bitterness I carried before my speed use and Dev was once again the object of my anger. I went tentatively back to work that first day, feeling uneasy about my absence. Although Lynette looked at me suspiciously she didn't ask any questions. I faked a few coughs anyway, just for good measure.

I shifted uncomfortably as the hard top of Sissy's coffee table bit into the bones of my thin behind. We were at Sissy's not only to cop but to find out what had happened to Gilbert. He'd not been seen for a few weeks and Dev was starting to worry.

Gilbert's girlfriend Viv, with whom he lived, had been evicted from her apartment and had moved in with Sissy. Viv said she hadn't seen Gilbert since she had taken up with a disgusting 76-year-old wrinkly smelly junkie whom she introduced as "my sugar-daddy Ed".

The old man was sitting on the dirty sofa skin-popping with a dull insulin needle full of heroin. He had been getting high so long he had no veins left that would take the needle and had to just inject the heroin under the skin and wait for it to absorb. You didn't get the rush that way but he was way past being able to feel the rush. He was dressed in a dirty bathrobe, ratty tennis shoes and filthy socks. His boxer shorts under the robe were stained with urine and other stuff I didn't want to think about. He was renting Sissy's spare room and Viv told us he paid her to do "odd jobs" for him. I'll bet they're odd, I thought as I eyed the old man.

Sissy was sitting on her throne, the phone in one hand and her black book of contacts in the other. She was working a guy new to the drug-selling business, trying to convince him that *everyone* gives two for one deals to regular customers if they hook you up with other clients. It was how business was done she explained loudly, taking long drags on her cigarette and rolling her eyes at us. Viv was talking over Sissy's voice, telling us about her bad luck.

"Gilbert took it real bad, my movin' in with Sissy'n' Ed," Viv said through her black speed-rotted teeth when we asked her how Gilbert was or if she'd seen him. She shook her bleached head and rolled her black ringed eyes skyward. Viv's mutilation of the English language grated on my nerves and added to my dislike of her. She was sitting all squished up against Ed, who had just tucked his fit behind his ear. His greasy yellow-gray hair hid the syringe.

"Me'n Ed's been together for two weeks now," she gushed and rubbed his skinny thigh. He was ignoring her and trying to get his shriveled penis into the milk carton between his shaking hands, unable to make the steps to the bathroom and oblivious to the other people in the room. I turned my head away so as not to gag.

"I ain't seen Gilbert since I tole him I was movin' in here with Sis. Ed's been stay'n here since that senior's apartment building kicked him out for having dealers deliver to his place. He gets a big pension check and Sissy likes the money so I figured maybe I could get me some of it," she explained. She smoothed her faded orange T-shirt over her saggy breasts uncertainly. "What was I 'sposed to do, I was bein' kicked outa my place.

I gotta make money some way, n' my ass is too old to put it on the street anymore."

When we'd first entered, I had planted my butt on Sissy's coffee table before Dev could, like a kid rushing for the last seat in a game of musical chairs. It was the only hard surface available and I had gloated as he remained standing behind me, not willing to sit on the soft furniture. It led to the misfortune, however, of also being closest to Viv. She leaned toward me from the sofa, throwing a sideways glance at Ed who was still struggling with his penis. "I tole Gilbert it was just business, me'n Ed, I mean," she whispered wetly into my face. I pulled back reflexively as her breath hit me and I heard Dev smother a laugh. "But he was all pissed off. I don't know where he went. I been worried for him. Its cold out and he ain't got nowhere to go. If you see 'im, tell 'im to call me here." She looked sad and desperate for a minute and her thickly made-up face fell, making her look older than I had initially guessed her to be. Then her attention went back to Ed. She grabbed his withered thing and pushed it into the milk carton for him. Then she kissed his cheek enthusiastically and he slapped her arm hard.

"Leave me the fuck alone, I'll call you when I want something you godamm whore. I ain't payin' you to kiss me," he said meanly. His voice sounding like he had swallowed gravel. Viv giggled nervously and waved her thin hand at us in a dismissive gesture.

"He gets ornery sometimes but he loves me," she said, trying to screw her face into a smile. Jesus, what was I doing here I wondered, somewhere between despising and pitying Viv.

"Tell Gilbert to call me." She licked her dry lips and leaned forward again as if to speak but just then Sissy slammed the phone receiver down triumphantly.

"Let's go kids. I just got us the deal of the century," she said, slipping her shoes on. Viv jumped up to go with us, all thoughts of Gilbert vanishing from our minds.

Two days later Sissy called Dev, Mick and I to her house to tell us that Gilbert's body had been found by the city police. He'd frozen to death while sleeping beneath a highway overpass. We greeted the news with solemn acceptance as if it were to be expected. I saw a muscle flinch in Dev's jaw then he embraced Viv and held her tight. Sissy was weeping into a crumpled tissue as she told us that Ed was paying for a small memorial service. Mick sat shaking his head sadly. He looked like he was trying not to cry. When Dev and Viv parted Viv said in a tired voice that she had loved Gilbert, but at least with him gone, she didn't have to worry about him. I saw Dev wipe away tears that had been hidden by the thick locks of dark hair falling over his eyes. I wanted to cry and mourn like the others but no tears would come. The emptiness in my heart made me afraid. It was so easy to lose someone, maybe numbness was a blessing.

At work a few days later I sat on the floor in the staff lounge cleaning the small refrigerator. It was a slow day and I had already made rounds to change people, helped Lynette with her patients and wiped down every counter behind the nurses' station. One of the new nurses came in and sat at the table in the middle of the room. I was eating the remains of a sandwich one of the residents had left on her lunch tray and I crammed the last bites into my mouth guiltily while she took out her food. She smiled shyly at me.

"You're Novena, right?" She asked.

"Yeah, that's me." I looked up only briefly to be polite. Because the scheduling at the home was so unpredictable and the pay low, nurses and aides came and went so frequently and stayed for such a short time it was hardly worth it to get to know them. I figured this one would be no different. She would work for a few weeks, maybe a few months, become bitter and go somewhere else, only to find it the same.

"How long have you worked here?" she asked.

"About 5 years. Ever since I graduated from high school," I replied. She finished chewing a bite of food.

"Do you like it?"

"It pays the rent. I like the patients and it's an easy job," I said. Was she just making conversation, I wondered, or was there a purpose to her questions?

"Are you married?"

"No," I told her. *Here it comes. She's going to ask me if I have a boyfriend, then she'll want to know what he does, how long we've been together. All those questions that make me have to lie. I'll tell her my usual fibs about his job as a painter, how he works a lot and we don't go out much because we're saving to get married and buy a house, how well we get along, all those fantasies I tell until I start to believe them myself.* Then I'll go home and he'll be high and I'll have to scrounge some pennies to buy food for dinner and get high myself and my lies will come back to torture me because I want them so badly to be true. Suddenly my energy level plummeted. It's all getting so hard I sighed to myself.

"Do you have a boyfriend?" She asked. People were so predictable I thought in annoyance. I hesitated a minute, sorting through my collection of stories to pick out the ones that would seem to win her particular approval. Then my mind calmed and a cool blankness settled into my heart.

Work was the one place I could control what was happening. I could immerse myself in the trivialities of a small nursing home and pretend the rest of my life was normal. I could be whoever I wanted.

"No," I answered. "I don't."

***

Dev and I were sitting in the dim living room when we heard Mick's heavy footsteps coming up the stairs. He knocked and walked in, then stood at the door with a frightened look.

"I'm quitting," he said without preamble and dropped into the nearest chair to light a cigarette. Dev and I stared at him without saying anything. He looked at Dev and continued. "I want to marry Francesca and I can't unless I really stay clean." Avoiding my gaze, he fidgeted uncomfortably and told us Francesca loved him and wanted a commitment and he felt he owed her that.

"It's easy. I just take myself down to the clinic at seven every morning, drink my cherry-flavored methadone and I'm good for the day," he said, his face pale and uncertain. His eyes were focused on the cigarette between his fingers.

"How long till you're really clean?" Dev asked.

"They'll gradually cut down my dose over about two years till I'm off all together. They say the relapse rate is pretty low." He smiled but the shakiness of his voice betrayed his feelings. Dev shifted in his chair, leaned forward and clasped his hands in front of him, his elbows resting on his knees.

"You know you need to stay away from us if you really want to do this don't you?" Dev's eyes were dark and intense. "You can't be coming up here seeing us high, or you'll be runnin' the street again in no time." Mick nodded, keeping his eyes on the floor.

"I just wanted to come tell you, so you know why I'm not going to be around," Mick said and got up to leave. Dev joined him at the door. His hand slid softly around the back of Mick's neck, not allowing Mick to avoid his gaze as he held the smaller man's eyes captive for a long moment. Then Dev bent to rest his forehead against Mick's, his eyes closed tightly. When Dev pulled away, his hand still cradling his friend's neck, Mick's face was flushed and broken with tears.

"Do this right my friend," Dev said softly to Mick and pushed him out the door. I watched their good-bye from my seat in the corner, furiously trying to keep from crying. Dev's face was serene as he passed me. He rested his hand on my head for a second before picking up the phone to punch in a pager number.

Chapter Ten

"Novena. It's Simon. What's goin' on with that son 'a mine? He's been over here bummin' money every other day. He lose his job?" I had known it would only be a matter of time until Dev's father knew something was wrong. For an old farm boy, he was pretty quick.

"He lost his regular job Simon. I'm not sure why. Something about having to cut staff or something," I evaded, thankful we were having this conversation over the phone so he couldn't see me.

"He ain't drinkin' bad, is he? Or doin' drugs? I seen him sneakin' around with Mick all winter, not sittin' and talking like they use to but all quiet and secretive. What's he up to?" Simon demanded. I coughed weakly, trying to buy myself some time. "You might as well tell me Novena," he said in a gentler tone. "I'll find out one way or another. I'm a wily old bastard."

"He's shooting heroin. It started as an experiment and now he's hooked," I blurted out, then held my breath for the explosion. None came.

"Well, damn," he sighed. "I figger'd as much." His voice held sadness and resignation. "Sweetheart you got a long haul ahead of you. I got to cut him off. If he gets too rowdy you come to me. I'll put you up. You got to get away from him, he'll kill himself and take you with him." Tears of relief and gratitude came to my eyes. He continued, "I see a lot of my father in him, damned wild Indian. My father fought liquor till it killed him. Forty years he suffered with that demon until it finally got him." Simon was quiet for a minute but it was the kind of silence you can hear and I swallowed the discomfort growing in my throat. When he began talking again his voice was heavy. "It was bad the way Dev grew up, his momma leavin', me too damned drunk to take care of him. He likes to make it out to be nothin', but I remember how he cried when she left. I remember … how quiet he got after a while. Then I dropped him at my sister's house and didn't see him until years later. I wanted to dry out and make it up to him but he was grown by then and I didn't even know where he was."

I could hear Simon's breath on the other end of the phone.

"Dev told me once that he thought by saving me he'd save himself," I told Simon. "It was when we first met and I was sad all the time. He never told me why he needed saved. I don't want to lose him Simon."

"Dev's gonna make it but we got to be tough with him," Simon's voice held the conviction I needed at that moment. "You get out while you can. Without you he'll have to sink or swim. You hear? By savin' yourself this time you might just save him."

"I know. Thanks Simon. I'll get by." No commitment. Jesus I thought, I can barely get through the day without having a nervous breakdown as it is. Leaving Dev was too much to ask right now.

"You keep in touch darlin'. We need each other now," he said before hanging up. Damn. I wiped my eyes on my sleeve marveling at how well he took it. He must have suspected for a long time.

Dev came home pissed off that night.

"Did you tell my dad anything?" he demanded, striding into my living room and filling it with his wide shoulders.

"I didn't have to. He guessed. He knew for a long time. I guess you aren't as good a liar as you thought," I said. I started heating water for mac and cheese.

"He won't lend me any money even for food," Dev complained.

"Like you'd spend it on food anyway. And lend is a bad choice of words. You haven't ever paid him back. He's doing you a favor, the same favor I should be doing you," I said. "He's trying to save you from yourself."

"Well don't do me any favors. If you want to be Mother Theresa go find a beggar to feed. I don't want to be saved. I just want dope. I gave Sissy a ride to the store for a couple of bags. I'll cook you some," he said as he headed for the bedroom to fix.

Ten minutes later I was digging in my arm trying to get the dull needle into my vein. My skin was toughened and my veins bruised. Both arms were in the same bad shape. We used sharp new fits as much as possible but I couldn't risk taking too many from work so we reused them often.

The thin needles were made for single use only, as each package proclaimed and the tips became burred quickly. I was getting high every day and the frequent poking had done serious damage to my vessels.

"Fuck," I whispered. I fastened the belt around the other arm. No hit there either. When I could get the needle in no blood came back when I pulled on the plunger, just air, telling me the dull point was rolling off my scarred vein.

"God*dammit*," I cursed as I jabbed the needle in for the fifth time and missed again.

"Let me," Dev said softly, sliding onto the bed beside me. He took the syringe, tied me off, patted a vein on the back of my hand and hit me without trouble. The warmth flowed over my body, relaxing me and dulling my frustration. I sighed heavily. The stress of trying to get the needle into my abused vessels melted into pleasant apathy.

"This is the most intimate we've been in six months," I said, looking at him.

He took the belt off my arm and got up from the bed.

"You know as well as I do heroin knocks out the sex drive. I couldn't get it up now for anything. They should give it to convicted sex offenders to keep them from repeating their crimes," he said with a forced smile.

"I've not exactly been in the mood lately anyway," I said, looking away. I missed the sharing, the physical closeness that was an expression of my trust in him. I used to love the light scratchiness of his calloused hands on my bare skin, would beg for the gingery taste of his mouth and had welcomed the secure feeling the weight of him gave me when he moved his body onto mine. Now I could hardly bear to look at him. We had become like two lepers forced to live together in our isolation, each abhorring the other for the mirror image they reflect.

Laurence and I were sitting in the kitchen. I stopped by every week or so to visit. I felt I should be ashamed but Laurence was the one person who knew about my habit and I needed him. Jon passed through on his way to his own apartment on the third floor. I knew he had told the other guys in the house about Dev's use incase I needed a place to stay but I wasn't sure what he had reveled about my habit. I averted my eyes from his but he clamped his bony hand on my shoulder.

"You know I have to say my piece Novena. I love Dev," Jon began. "But I can't stand to watch him killing himself day by slow day while I'm fighting to stay alive," he said, referring to the positive HIV diagnosis he lived with. He shook his head. "I'm sorry. Seeing such intelligence and potential going down the fucking toilet is too much for me. You should come stay here with us and let him fend for himself. He'd be better off in the street. Maybe he'd be forced to make a change. You just pack your stuff and come over anytime you're ready." He patted my arm and went upstairs.

"Sweetie, are you off that poison yet?" Laurence asked. He lit a cigarette for me and one for himself and squinted at me through the smoke.

"I won't lie to you Laurence. It's the only good part of my day. I don't do much. One bag a day. It gets me a little high, but nothing earth-shattering." I minimized my use by a small bit. In reality my habit had grown.

"When you're ready to stop I'll help you any way I can," he said.

"I don't know why I put up with Dev. I'm so ashamed of myself. I never thought I'd ever do anything like this," my voice quavered. "I just don't know how to leave. It's all so fucked up. I don't know where to begin putting it right." I twisted my hands together. This was the most I'd spoken about it ever. I looked at Laurence from under my lashes, testing his response.

"When you're done, you'll find a way out," he said and poured me a cup of coffee.

"I just want it all to go away," I said. "Something must be wrong with me to let this happen." Laurence's face softened and he shook his head slowly.

"There's nothing wrong with you, Sweetie. You must have something to learn or you'd have quit by now." He looked at me gravely and I rolled my eyes.

"Thanks for the words of wisdom Buddha, but if this is what it takes then I don't want to be wise. I'd just as soon stay ignorant and be happy," I said then sighed. "I can't quit. I'd have to leave Dev to quit. What would I tell people? He'll make scene and I'll be evicted. I could lose my job. I'd have to change everything. How can I live without Dev?" I paused for a second. "See how hard it would be? How can I quit?" My voice sounded whiney to me and I felt exhausted.

"Sweetie, the answer to your question is in your question," he said.

***

Dev and I were sitting at the table in my small kitchen, eating our box of mac and cheese. Rain was pounding on the window outside and I pulled my worn sweater close around me. I was so hungry all the time I was having dreams about food every night and spent my days fantasizing about what food I would eat first if I had enough money to buy it. Dev was reading the empty mac and cheese box. He had made a chunk of money the day before by helping someone in the neighborhood tear down an old brick wall. He then spent the money on dope and shot it all before I got home and I was holding a grudge.

"Hey look Novena," he pointed to the box, "not only do we get carbohydrate-packed nourishment for twenty-three cents a day, if we save twelve box-tops we can send away for a plastic yellow-cheese-colored rain jacket. At the rate we eat this stuff we could have matching outfits in a remarkably short time. We'd be the cheesiest couple in the food-bank line." He looked up at me and smiled at his own humor. I stared back at him.

"Go ahead, make jokes. The heroin use I can hide but when my belly is sticking out with starvation like those kids on TV people are going to suspect something is wrong," I said. Dev's face flushed with anger.

"Forgive my ignorance, not having been raised Catholic, but do you contact the Vatican to apply for sainthood or does John Paul call you directly? 'Cause to hear you tell it you're up for the martyr-of-the-year award," he said in an even tone, tossing the box away.

"Do you care at all what I need?" I asked in a hard voice. He looked at me and his face was serious.

"Of course I care. I don't do this because I want to anymore. I can't stop. When I stop I have too much pain. Not just in my body." His eyes were compelling me to understand, pleading with me.

"Every junkie has an excuse," I said, carefully licking the last of the fake-cheese from my spoon which was bent to sit evenly on the table holding heroin, its bowl blackened like every other spoon in our house. "You could slow down if you wanted to. That was the idea in the beginning, remember? You were going to quit after a few weeks." My face stretched into a sneer as I taunted him. A small jab of guilt stung my heart as I realized he never mentioned my use, which seemed insignificant compared to his. Dev slammed his hand flat onto the table with a loud smack.

"You know I've tried," he said, his eyebrows raised and hand held out to me, begging me to understand. I didn't move. He hung his head and shook it side to side clenching his outstretched hand into a fist before dropping it. When he looked up he had a look I'd never seen before-a terminal weariness, like a man waiting to die. "I'm so tired," he said in a hushed voice. "I hate myself. I'm ashamed. Not a minute goes by I don't regret my choice to do this. I've hurt everyone I love, you most of all." There was a silence. He was looking out the window. "If I had the courage, I'd kill myself and get it over with. I just can't seem to do it. I'm sorry Novena." He shook his head again and got up from the table.

Dev was trying to get clean. He told me he was going to quit then I watched him become silent and withdrawn during the day until finally he was sweating and shaking in bed, fighting the urge to use as the drug's withdrawal wracked his body. The room was dark and I sat in bed reading by dim lamp-light. He lay next to me, seemingly unaware of his surroundings. His face was ashen and dark circles hung heavily under his closed eyes. Sweat rolled off of him dampening the sheets.

"Can I have some water," he whispered from between chattering teeth. I handed him a glass as he pushed himself painfully to a sitting position. Dev's teeth clattered against the glass and the water spilled as his hand quaked with the effort of holding it. I reached out reflexively to steady the glass then stopped, unsure if I wanted to touch him. I shook off the feeling, took the glass and smoothed the damp hair from his forehead.

"I'm so sorry Novena." His voice was a raspy whisper and his face contorted as he tried not to cry. "I never meant to hurt you. You're the only good thing left in my life. I've got to get off this poison then I'll make it up to you I promise." I gathered him against me and rocked him as tears rolled silently down my cheeks.

I looked into Dev's slack face after he fell into a deep sleep that night. He lay in my arms quiet and pale. His usually neatly trimmed hair had become long and shaggy in the last few months. His face was thin and drawn. His skin felt cool but he was damp with sweat. Memories of him two years before came to me unbidden and I ached for him to be the strong laughing man I knew in the past. I loved who he used to be and I believed could be again, but my angry wall protected me from the pain of seeing what we'd become.

While he was unaware I felt free to stroked his face, my hand lingering on his high cheekbone. I picked up his hand, hard and thick from years of physical work. Such a strong hand. It was so soft when he touched me. I held it against my cheek then slowly moved it down my neck, let the back of his fingers brush against my breast, felt my nipple tingle and harden and my breath become deep. The breath became a sob and I turned my head to the side as my face crumpled into tears of longing. I held his palm flat against my chest, hoping the feel of my beating heart would speak to some unconscious part of his being, convincing him to save himself. And maybe I could also be redeemed.

Dev's first real attempt to get clean ended the next day when he couldn't take the pain in his body and torture in his mind any more. I watched him shoot his heroin, taking what was left from his spoon and putting it in my own veins to supplement the pain pills I had downed. My face was an angry accusatory mask and he refused to meet my eyes. He shouldered the blame I continued to heap on his shoulders, never mentioning my own responsibility in our situation. I let him accept the load. It added one more item to the long list of things I hated about myself.

Dev wrecked my car while high and I drove it with a huge dent in the side, thankful that it was still running. He got beat up again, brought dope dealers and other addicts to the house. I never knew what was going to be waiting for me when I walked in. Maybe this was the punishment I deserved for getting high but I couldn't fathom living through my days without the blunting effects of heroin.

My footsteps echoed hollowly as I climbed the three steep flights of steps to Laurence's attic apartment. I was breathing hard by the time he answered my knock. I flopped onto his brass day bed and hugged a tasseled satin pillow.

"You're painting again, huh?" I asked as I eyed the figure in charcoal on the large canvass by the window. His tall lanky form was standing back from it, concentrating on the drawing from a distance.

"I'm trying. Motivation has never been one of my strong points." He wrinkled his forehead in a frown. "Discipline eludes the artist in me." He picked up his pencil and went back to the canvass, continuing to chatter on about 'the artist's heart' and what he needed to help him 'focus'. I sat up and looked around his small room. The roof was slanted and two dormer windows let in the cloudy day. Thick brocade drapes hung from the ceiling and if pulled closed would separate the bed from the rest of the room. His dark heavy old furniture added to the claustrophobic feeling building in me. The early summer heat seemed to be concentrating in the attic and I removed my sweater.

"Remember when you used to model for me?" Laurence asked and turned around to study me objectively, as if sizing me up for the canvass. "My God. You've gotten so thin …" His voice trailed away and his face became concerned. He stared at me, as if noticing the changes in my appearance for the first time. Laurence put down the pencil and pulled me up off the bed, guiding me to the oval full-length mirror in the corner. He stood behind me with his hands on my shoulders, forcing me to look at my reflection.

My hair was limp and hanging down my back in a stringy mess, my skin looked sallow below huge frightened-looking dark-ringed eyes. My arms hung like pale sticks from the frayed sleeves of my ragged t-shirt. Old yellow and green bruises and new purple and red welts stained the skin of my forearms. I stood looking at myself, the shock of my appearance barely registering in my brain.

"What do you weigh now, about eighty-five pounds?" he asked, meeting my eyes in the mirror. I didn't answer. "Look at what you've done to yourself. What could possibly be worth this?" It was a statement, not a question. I wiggled out of his grasp and flung myself back on the bed, pulling my shapeless black sweater back on, conscious of the safety pins holding the gaping hole in the shoulder together.

"This is what junkies look like, I guess." I kept my face turned away as I lit a cigarette. Laurence sat heavily on the windowsill.

"Sweetie don't call yourself that," he said.

"Why not? That's what I am. A skinny worn-out white-trash heroin addict. I'm one step away from losing everything. I just try to blend in with the scenery and keep things quiet, that way maybe no one will find out and I won't lose my job." I bit my lip to keep from rambling on and avoided his eyes as I picked at a broken fingernail. "I know how I look." I hated to leave the house. I felt like I should step aside when I passed regular people, apologetic that they even had to tolerate the sorry sight of me.

Laurence shifted, making the windowsill creak.

"Novena let me help you. At least let me give you some money for food and clothes," he said.

"I'll just spend it on dope anyway, Laurence." I hadn't stooped to taking money from my friends. I had shot away most of my self-respect and credibility but I didn't want to lie to Laurence.

"I can't believe it got so bad without my noticing." He shook his head and covered his mouth with his hand, his eyes squeezed shut.

"Don't blame yourself," I reassured him. "I've gotten to be really good at keeping a low profile so no one suspects." I tried to flash him a smile but it felt more like a grimace.

"What does Dev say about all this? He's always taken care of you. How could he let this happen?" Laurence asked.

"Dev's so caught up in his own use he can't help me." I lit a cigarette at the same time as Laurence and the mingled light of the flames illuminated the dim room for an instant. "He's hanging on to life so tenuously. Every day he seems closer to just letting go." My voice had become deep and quiet. "I keep a black dress in the closet for his funeral all the time," I said. I was trying to joke again but sounded like I was on the verge of crying. I took a deep breath and gathered up all my unshed tears, putting them away. Sacrifices had been made and I'd deal with them later.

"Do you still love him?"

I paused for a second to think about it.

"I love who he used to be and I can't let go of that. It's all I have left." I bit my lower lip and raised my eyes to his.

"Why don't you take some time away from Dev?" Laurence's voice was a pleading whisper.

"I'm trying to hold on to the bits of myself that are still me. And I guess Dev is a big part of who that is." I said honestly.

***

"I just got a couple bags of really good shit," Dev said as he came in the door and headed for the bedroom. "You want some?"

"No I got high when I got home. I'm going to Rachel's later," I told him as he passed through the living room. He locked the bedroom door and minutes later I heard the familiar thud that meant he had gone out. I jiggled the doorknob lock with a butter knife to get in. Sure enough he was on the floor turning blue. I looked at him for a second, moved toward him and stopped. I turned and left the house. The door closed behind me with a soft click. What would be would be. I struggled to unlock the car door with shaky fingers.

At Rachel's apartment I slid into a chair in the kitchen and accepted a cup of tea. I felt numb. Was he alive or dead? If he were dead, wouldn't it be a relief? I sat quietly for a second, wondering if I would feel some kind of rift in my heart when he died, if I would know the exact moment his soul left his body, tearing him from me for the rest of this lifetime. We had always been so close, surely there would be some sign, at least a chest pain warning me of his death. I held my breath but I felt nothing. The weight of my action settled into my mind. Realization washed through me like a cold wave leaving me so tired I wanted to lie my head on the shabby table. My mom's advice came back to me. Trust those around me even if I couldn't trust myself. I opened my mouth and words came rushing past my lips before the conscious decision was made to stop them.

"Dev's been doing drugs," I told Rachel. Having begun I needed to finish. "He's passed out in the bedroom now. He may be dead. I just left him there." Rachel fell into the chair across the table, staring at me.

"Can you repeat that?" she asked, blinking.

I smiled in weary resignation.

"I know it's a shock. I just couldn't bring myself to tell you till now. Sorry." My face was blank, my heart standing still for her reaction. She reached out and grasped my wrist, holding on as though she needed to steady herself as she sat.

"Honey don't apologize. When did this all start? What can I do? Can I help? Are you OK? How did this happen? Do you want to call the police and have him arrested?" She was all action, wanting to fix things. She's not going to leave me, I thought with disbelieving gratitude and my heart began beating again.

"No, no, just leave it alone. He'll either be OK or not at this point. This is something he has to work out himself. You know what they say. Till you can admit you have a problem, you can't start to fix it. He needs to want to get clean first." I looked at her, hoping she'd understand my reluctance to jump into making major changes.

"So what are you going to do?" She asked. I shrugged.

"Wait it out. See what happens, same as I've been doing. If I kick him out he'll just bang the door down and I'll get evicted. I try to just give him money and keep him quiet so no one in my apartment building complains to the landlord. I'm so afraid of being thrown out. I can't leave the city, I have to work. I can't not give him money, he'll cause a fuss. I'm caught. That's why I didn't tell you before. I didn't want to complain about something I was doing nothing about," I said. It was mostly true.

"What are you doing about money?"

"We've been getting advances on the credit cards to pay the rent and bills. They'll let you dig a hole deep enough to bury a bus," I said, trying to force a smile from my stiff face. I kept my eyes on her as I revealed little pieces of the truth.

"So the bastard's bringing drugs into the house. I still think you should have him arrested. He'll think about what he's doing if his pretty ass is sitting in jail," she said, shaking her head and crossing her arms over her chest.

"That won't do any good Rachel. He just has to get through this," I said softly.

"Well you tell him if he hurts you he'll have worse to worry about than drugs," she stuck out her skinny chest and tapped it threateningly. "I've loved him because you do but that won't stop me from coming after him if something happens to you." I nodded in appreciation and smiled faintly.

"The only person he's hurting is himself."

"You're not doing that shit too, are you?" A look of alarm crossed her face and she grasped my upper arm tightly. I shook my head side to side.

"You know me better than that," is all I said, keeping my eyes locked on hers. Rachel let her hand drop and she nodded.

"You're right, you'd never do that to yourself. Good thing too, cause I'd have to kick your ass from here to the moon if you were putting that shit in your body."

"Even if I wanted to, we don't have enough money to support two habits," I explained, just to be sure. She nodded again, looking almost as relieved as I felt.

"Is he working?"

"He lost his old job painting a long time ago. He just stopped going. Now he picks up work at that day-labor place but that's sporadic. We live on my paycheck and credit cards."

She nodded.

"That's why you've gotten so thin, all the worry. I wish you would have told me sooner. At least talking about it would've helped you not feel so alone," she sighed. "You're such a hard-ass. You never want anyone to know if you're having a rough time. I knew something was wrong. You've changed over the last six months but I'd have never guessed *this*. I should take you out and whoop your ass for not calling your friends. I've called you enough in the past, I'd say you were overdue some support." She touched my hand and I grasped her fingers in mine.

"Now you know. From here I just wait until he gets clean or until I can't stand it anymore." I held my hands out, palms up then clasped them together in a symbol of closure.

We tried to go about the rest of our visit as normal but Rachel stared at me throughout the evening when she thought I wasn't looking. Amy wasn't home and we were slouched into the soft couch watching their fuzzy old TV and eating popcorn. The vulnerability of my exposure made me self-conscious and awkward. Later I would feel relieved I knew but right now I was working hard at acting as if nothing was any different.

"I'm not going to have a breakdown right here in your living room or anything, so stop looking at me like my head is going to explode," I finally said.

She sighed and leaned toward me, her hands clasped together as if in prayer.

"Sorry, I can't help it. You never have problems. It's always been me who's in trouble. I'm just trying to be here for you and help. I won't do anything. I just don't want to miss an opportunity to be, you know, supportive," she said, bobbing her head like an over-eager chipmunk.

"I promise I'll call you no matter what I need. Even if it's a ride to the loony bin," I said.

"Well, that I don't know about. They may decide to keep both of us," she said.

"You want me to go home with you?" she asked later in concern as I prepared to leave.

"No. I'll be fine. I'll call you." I smiled to show her I was OK. She hugged me as I left and I squeezed her hard in unspoken thanks. I had told her most of the truth anyway and I sighed in relief, grateful that it was over. At least I didn't have to lie to her about Dev anymore.

My hands felt stiff on the steering wheel during short drive home and I chewed my lip painfully. My legs felt like lead as I trod up the two flights of steps to our apartment door. It was dark and quiet. My heart was pounding. Would I find him blue and cold on the floor? How was I going to tell people it happened? God forgive me but I wanted him to die some days, only I wanted him to go respectfully so I didn't have to hang my head in shame at the funeral. So I could remember him as the hero he'd been to me in the beginning. I dropped my backpack on the floor and went into the dark bedroom, swallowing the lump in my throat and steeling myself for the worst. My hands trembled as I fumbled for the light, listening for any sound from the room. The silence clung to me, making my movements slow and weighted.

"Novena, that you?" Dev's groggy voice called out from the bed. Relief flooded through me, caught me off guard and almost knocked me over like a warm unexpected wave. My knees went soft and I hugged the wall for support. I breathed a deep sigh and whispered a prayer of thanks, forgetting for the moment how I'd left him to die earlier in the day. Exhaustion washed over me and I dropped my clothes to the floor, wanting to feel Dev's warmth next to my skin.

"I'm here," I said as I crossed the room and fell into bed beside him. Dev slid his arm around me, pulling me against his chest and for the first time in months I didn't push him away in anger. I relaxed into him inhaling the warm scent of his skin, knowing it would linger on mine in the morning. I slid my leg between his and let my hand grasp his fingers as I drifted into sleep.

A week later Dev went into rehab. He packed carefully, taking lots of books. He'd been in the Army so all his health care came free from the VA. They were one of the few remaining detox facilities in town. The plan was to do seven days of detoxification, where they would slowly wean him off narcotics then twenty eight days of rehabilitation, during which they would teach him how to live clean. I planned to get clean at home myself while he was doing it in the hospital so when he came home we could start our lives over. I fluttered around that morning doing last minute checks of what he'd packed, making my lunch, anything to keep my mind occupied. I wanted him so badly to go and was afraid he would change his mind at the last minute.

I dropped him off at the hospital on my way to work. We kissed good-bye, our lips lingering like in the old days. I had dinner with Simon that night and we celebrated Dev's decision with a big meal of his 'famous' meatloaf. On the way home I stopped at Sissy's and bought a handful of pain pills so I could relax then went home and spent a peaceful evening and night, sleeping better than I expected to. And at six am the next morning Dev called asking me to pick him up. He was done.

"You couldn't even last two days?" I shouted, flinging my arms up in exasperation as I stormed across the VA's parking lot towards him. He didn't break his stride as he walked to the car I'd just parked. I fell into step beside him, trying to make him face me, my breath quick with anger.

"They weren't giving me enough downers to stay comfortable. I'm having cravings and feeling sick," he complained. His pace was almost leisurely but I could see that his knuckles were white where his fingers grasped the suitcase handle. He avoided my eyes and his face remained blank as we got into the car. I slammed my door closed.

"Well guess what? It's not fucking Club Med, its detox and it isn't supposed to be comfortable! If it was no one would be a junkie!" I wheeled the car around and stepped hard on the brake for emphasis.

"Whoa, pull over and let me drive OK?" he said as he braced himself against the dash.

"No fucking way, you wrecked my car remember? I'm driving or you can walk." I didn't look at him. He continued to hold on and point out my poor driving habits. I stayed quiet, my face becoming a smooth stone of determination.

When we pulled in front of the house I shut the car off and stayed in the seat.

"You need to quit or get out of the house," I stated without turning to look at him. "I won't live like this anymore. I'll call the police to get you out of here. If I have to I'll move." I continued to stare straight ahead.

He was quiet.

"You know I don't mean to mess everything up all the time," he said.

"Well you do and I want you out and that's what I know."

He cursed under his breath as he got out. I slid out of the car and headed for the door. He came around the car and blocked my path.

"Why don't you quit?" he said to me, his face hard. "You've never really tried have you? What do you think, that if I quit your habit will magically disappear?" he spit at me. "You need to step away from my problem and take a look at your own." His voice was harsh as he hunched his shoulders and stalked past me. I stood quietly in the street for a moment and blinked against the sunlight. Behind a tightly closed door in my mind lurked a fear that he was right. So much energy was spent in anger at his actions and use that I had none left over to apply to my own. I made my way upstairs and accepted the syringe he handed me with slightly shaky hands.

Chapter Eleven

Rachel and I sat on her back porch drinking tall glasses of ice water to keep cool in the sticky evening heat. Amy fanned herself in a beach chair and three cats sat at the screened window watching us lazily from inside the apartment. We hadn't spent much time together. It felt too scary to me. She was bound to guess my secret sooner or later. How she hadn't yet was a mystery to me.

"How's Dev," Rachel asked. She hadn't pushed the subject of his use since I'd told her about it a few months before. Instead she inquired after him carefully and listened to the few details I provided with concern but didn't offer advice or lecture. I mostly avoided talking about it. The less I said the smaller the chance I'd slip and expose my own use.

"You mean the Black Hole of Financial Burden?" I asked. "He's using a lot more and drinking," I replied in a deceptively calm voice, refusing to let myself acknowledge that those words could describe my habit as well. My throat began to ache with the lump of swallowed sorrow that arose when I spoke of Dev these days. I was playing idly with a strand of lavender plucked from the planter beside me. "He's not working at all now. We just spiral closer to disaster all the time."

"Why do you stay?" she asked.

"I don't know." I sighed and let my shoulders sink forward. "It feeds the illusion that things will be OK someday, I guess."

"Illusion is what got you here in the first place," she said, touching my shoulder to soften her words. "Do you still love him?"

"I love him but I hate him," I said in a rush of words, my face flushing with emotion.

Rachel's face was pained as she nodded.

"You could always get a restraining order to keep him away from you, if that's what you want," she said after a minute of silence. Her voice was serious and low. I could see that she struggled with the idea herself; she loved Dev because I did and she too hated to see him hurting. I twisted the lavender stem.

"I don't know what I want anymore."

"If you get a restraining order he can't come within five feet of you. Anyone can call the cops if they know you have an order and see him around your house. You could tell your neighbors and tell them at work," Rachel said. This was becoming more complicated as we spoke.

"Oh yeah, tell the nuns at work to call the cops on my junkie boyfriend. That sounds like a good way to get a few month's unpaid vacation," I said. "Next I'll be on daytime TV slugging it out with Dev in front of a million viewers. Maybe I should bleach my hair and knock out a tooth so I really look the part." I shredded the lavender, my fingers tearing the soft purple flower buds from the stem.

"I'm just making suggestions," Rachel shrugged and looked away. "You'll know when you're ready." I threw down the ravaged flower remnants.

"Everyone seem to think this is my responsibility? Why the Hell do I have to be the one to change my whole life? Dev had started this, why does everyone think ending it is my call?" I narrowed my eyes at Rachel and shook my head, reaching for another piece of lavender to destroy.

"No one's saying this is your responsibility Novena. It doesn't matter who started it. If you want out you have to be the one to finish it," Rachel said. Her face was earnest, as if she were begging me to understand.

I sat still and quiet, the lavender limp in my fingers. If Dev would just quit then my use would stop too. We'd go back to how we were and things would be fine. I nodded at Rachel, and lit a cigarette, thinking in longing of the colorful little bundle of relief I would pick up at Sissy's back door on my way home.

That night I walked into a mess as I opened the door. Dev had gone through all my drawers looking for money and my clothes and papers were scattered on the floor. He wasn't home and I put the house back together and went to bed, the familiar weight of resentment lying heavily on my chest.

A few hours later Dev woke me up as he came in. A thin young man, little more than a boy really, followed him warily into our living room and stood where he could see the door. Dev ignored me when I peered out from the darkness of the bedroom.

"Here's the keys Tay. Have it back by morning. If it's not in front of the house I'll page you and I know where you live. Anything happens to that car and I'll come find you," Dev told him in a deep voice, forcing him to make eye contact.

"Hey Dee, its cool. I'll be careful." The kid nodded at Dev and slouched out the door. Dev brushed by me like he didn't see me as he went into the bedroom to fix.

"So what was all that about *Dee*?" I asked, my arms crossed in front of my chest.

"Nothin'," Dev replied. He slipped into street slang seemingly without realizing it, but to me it was a glaring departure from his usually impeccable English. It was a reminder of the increasing time he spent chasing dope. We used to keep a dictionary by the bed because we argued so much over correct word use and pronunciation and here he was sounding like a street kid.

"Did you give that boy your car?" I asked in disbelief, knitting my brows together. His car was an older Honda but he had always kept it clean and in good shape until recently. He said a car was like insulation from the world: warm in the winter and cool in the summer, you could listen to music and most importantly, it could take you away from your usual surroundings even if was just a drive around the block. His car to him was freedom. And he had just given it to some drug-dealing boy for a few bags of heroin.

"I need dope, I got no money. Tay needs a ride, so we made a fair exchange. He's a good kid, he'll be true to his word and have it back tomorrow." Dev didn't look up from the bubbling contents of his spoon. His face was flushed with vodka.

"You're way too trusting. He could sell it in ten minutes and then what would you do? You don't have insurance to cover theft. You'll lose your car." I reached for the antacid I kept in my purse and drank the chalky white liquid straight from the bottle to calm my burning stomach.

"He's afraid of me. That's how I know he'll bring it back. They only respect you in the street if people fear you. And I'm desperate enough to be scary," he said, looking displeased at his revelation.

I tried to focus on a magazine during the evening, ignoring him and hoping he'd stay quiet. Finally I got into bed with my clothes on in case I had to leave in a hurry and fell asleep. Later that night I felt his weight on the bed beside me and opened my eyes.

"I need some money," he stated. He was sitting on the side of the bed staring straight ahead. His eyes were blood shot and wild. His face was a rock hard mask of impassivity. I sighed and sat up, reaching for the last twenty in my bag. "I need your keys too," he said. I reached under the mattress where I'd hidden them from him, having foreseen this very situation before falling asleep. I dropped them on the floor; he picked them up and was out the door. I knew I'd be up the rest of the night, waiting for him to bring my car home and wondering who would be with him and what shape he'd be in. I rolled over onto my back, lit a cigarette and inhaled deeply, staring into the dark as I felt the smoke burn my throat. The streetlamp outside threw a gray light on the wall. The light was broken by the blinds into straight neat lines, evenly spaced, not touching, just running parallel into the blackness.

Dev stumbled in at five am and fell into bed fully clothed. The next morning I left the house at six as if I was going to work. It was my day off but I didn't want to be home with Dev. The sky was clear and a slight wind ruffled through my hair as I stepped out. I bowed my head and searched frantically in my bag for my sunglasses, pulling them out and sliding them on before lifting my sensitive eyes to the sun. I looked up and down the street as I stood on the corner, trying to decide which direction to take.

Gathering my courage I got in the car and raced downtown to the courthouse to get a restraining order before I changed my mind. I parked the car, a heavy knot of dread growing in my chest as I crossed the busy street and ran up the granite steps into the old building. The guard pointed me to the right room and my heart seemed to thump in time with the echoes of my footsteps in the cavernous lobby. I detoured into the bathroom to dig in my purse for my stash of pain pills and dug out five. I swallowed them dry and continued on.

The room I entered was large, with high ceilings and huge open windows. Obviously the building's old wiring wasn't supporting the air conditioning and the wind that blew into the room relieved the humidity and ruffled the faded posters thumb-tacked to a bulletin board on the wall. There were three other women there. One had two black eyes and a broken nose. The other was deaf from a blow to her head delivered by her husband during a fight, I was informed by the third, who was hovering protectively over her deaf friend. She appeared to be on the verge of tears. I took a seat uncertainly at the large wooden table and we all waited in silence for someone to tell us what to do next.

The woman with the broken nose sniffed once or twice, wincing with the pain and the two others remained quiet. I stared out the window wondering if I was doing the right thing. At least maybe this would demonstrate to Dev how bad things had gotten, and the sacrifice I was making by coming down here had to count for something. The door opened and a neatly dressed, anxious woman bustled in and handed us each a packet of forms.

"Hi, I'm from the woman's shelter. Fill in these forms and someone will be in to talk to you," she said, then disappeared. I flipped through the papers, eleven pages of questions and some spaces for signature. The other women finished before me and each left, gripping her papers, until I was alone with the scratching of my pen.

A tiny nun in a black habit and veil glided in as I finished the last page. Her skin was so pale it was almost translucent. Her eyes were deep blue like the day's sky and seemed to shine with compassion and humor. I couldn't guess her age, she could have been twenty-five or fifty. The nun, her nametag said Sister Raphael, sat next to me and took my completed forms. She read them in silence then met my gaze.

"I'm so glad you're here." Her voice was as soft as the breeze drifting in the window. "We see many women at the shelter who still love their husbands and don't want to take this step," she said, as if she could see into my heart. "But we have to take care of ourselves too. Loving someone doesn't mean you should sacrifice your own safety." Something about her eyes made me want to trust her. I swallowed and opened my mouth to speak. My voice squeaked as I spoke.

"He's not the only one who's been wrong Sister. I've been as bad as him," I confessed. She waited until I looked at her before she spoke. Her face held no surprise or disappointment. She broke into a slight smile.

"Sometimes the best way to show someone the right path is to find it yourself first," she said.

I let her words give me strength as she took me by the hand like a child and led me to the courtroom where the judge would see us. The room was almost empty and she gave me a slip of paper from a machine, like the ones at the bakery.

"This is your number dear," she said. "When the bailiff calls it, go up to the table and the judge will look over your forms. Then she'll decide what to do." She patted my hand and smiled then went to find the next lost soul. Her presence made me feel invincible, like I had an angel standing beside me. I sat up straight, my back aching a little at the unaccustomed position.

The room filled quickly. I glanced at my ticket, number five. Most of the occupants of the room jumped as the door banged open.

"All rise, court is in session, the honorable judge Ellen Courney presiding." The bailiff marched in, the judge close behind her. My stomach tightened. What if she wouldn't grant the order, what if she questioned me, what if all those people look at me while I'm up there, questions tumbled in my mind and I had trouble focusing for a minute.

The judge was a refined black woman of about sixty. She banged her gavel and called the first number. I watched closely as the cases before mine were heard. The judge asked almost no questions, giving out restraining orders to the deaf woman, the woman with black eyes and two more women, both of whom were holding small children. The judge listened to each woman's story told in a soft voice, some with tears, and nodded in compassionate understanding. She then granted the orders for restraint.

"Number five," the bailiff called. My legs shook as I stood up and walked to the bench. Sister Raphael smiled encouragingly at me from the corner and my muscles steadied. The judge looked at me over her glasses and then her eyes darted back to my forms.

"So you're afraid of him?" she asked.

"Yes, m'am," I replied hoarsely. She signed the order and handed it back to me.

"That's it?" I asked, blinking at her.

"That's it. You have to present that to him yourself sweetheart. You can ask the local police for an escort if you want." She banged her gavel and I stepped back. As I passed Sister Raphael she smiled and made the sign of the cross, blessing me. Suddenly I wished there was some way I could express the gratitude I felt. Maybe getting my life in order would be enough, I thought. I walked out of the room with my chest lifted, proud that I had taken some action.

It was quiet in the apartment when I got home. The lightness with which I had left the courtroom was replaced by a heavy feeling of dread. I gripped the paper in my hands firmly and pulled open the bedroom door. It seemed dim despite the bright sun outside. Dev leaned forward from his chair, startled until his eyes recognized me in the dark of the room with the light behind me.

"Hey Novena, what's up?" he asked over the book in his hands. I stood in front of him and handed him the restraining order. He began to read it then glanced up at me.

"What's this?" he demanded.

"A restraining order," I started, my resolve crumbling. "I didn't know what else to do. I don't want you in the house anymore. I'm afraid the landlord will evict us. I'm afraid of you and the people you bring to the house. I'm just so scared … I didn't know what else to do!" The words gushed out of my mouth, not at all the cool-headed delivery I'd planned and I felt my face twist with growing sorrow. Dev's cheeks flushed and tears flooded his eyes. He ran a rough hand over his gaunt features, banishing any evidence of his tears but leaving him looking stricken.

A hard painful lump had formed in my throat as I watched him struggle to maintain composure and my own eyes filled. I sniffed loudly and took a deep ragged breath. I fell to my knees in from of him and clenched the edge of his thin t-shirt as I tried to look into his wet eyes and fathom what was happening behind them.

"I'm afraid to be without you but I'm afraid of you too. You bring those people from the street with you, you've been drinking a lot and I just can't live that way anymore. It's killing me!" My quavering voice was high, strained with the effort of holding back tears and my chest ached with the breaking of my heart for the thousandth time.

"I don't blame you for feeling like this," Dev said in a quiet steady voice. "I don't trust myself anymore either." He looked like a desperate animal. "Just don't leave me. I'll start staying at the Salvation Army tomorrow. Let me stay here with you tonight, I can't stand to lose you too right now. I don't have anything else left." His voice was hoarse and emotionless and he continued to stare out above my head like a shock victim.

Dev left the apartment we had shared for five years the next morning with a packed bag. He mumbled something about staying at the Salvation Army or in Mick's van. I swallowed hard and nodded. He slipped two balloons full of heroin wrapped in a crumpled piece of newspaper into my pocket before he left.

I punched my timecard at work, began gathering the water pitchers after hearing report, greeted the patients, but all I could think about was that small round bundle in my pocket. I was tired, my joints ached, my head pounded and my stomach was churning. Maybe just a little shot would help me get through the next eight hours. I parked my linen cart and went directly to the supply room, slipped a bag of the tiny orange capped insulin syringes into my pocket and told Lynette I was going to the bathroom.

The bathroom in the staff lounge had a good lock on the door and no smoke detector anywhere close. I pulled out my lighter, cooked my dope and shot it quickly. Instantly I felt better. I cleaned up carefully and then slid into a seat on the couch in the lounge to rest for a second.

Someone was shaking me, I heard Lynette yelling. Lifting my heavy lids I could see her come into focus, her face in mine, worried.

"What in sweet Jesus' name is wrong with you," she hissed, gripping my upper arm tightly.

I struggled upright from my slouch on the sofa, wiping my face with my hand.

"I just sat down for a second and fell asleep," I defended myself. I could feel the droop in my face, the lethargy in my limbs.

Lynette rested her massive weight on the couch beside me, folded her hands in her lap and tilted her stricken face toward mine.

"I know more than you think. You think you goin' un-noticed around here, all pasty faced and skinny, pupils pin-point, your hair unwashed. I see you stealing food from the patients' trays, missin' work, comin' in late. You think you can say you just tired and get away with that. But I know better. I got eyes. I got knowledge, too. You see dope in the face of someone you love and you never forget it. And I see dope in your eyes."

I stared at her, my mind hardly registering her words. "Now," she continued, "I could take hold your hand, roll up your sleeve and see for myself. But I don't need to. Cause you goin' to tell me what's going on." She sat back and waited, her hands clasped in her lap. God, I am so tired, I thought. I wanted so badly to spill my secret but the same fear that made me pick up the needle in the first place kept me from asking for help to stop. I sat up straight and looked right into Lynette's big brown eyes.

"I have no idea what you're talking about." My voice was full of indignation. "Can't a person even be sick around here with out getting accused of something?" I shook my head in mock disgust. "Really, Lynette," I said, getting up from the sofa, "what do you think, that I'm shooting something up right here in the staff lounge?" I stood in front of her and held my arms out, palms up in exasperation. "I had the flu, I still feel weak and washed out. My stomach was queasy and I came in here, sat down to rest and fell asleep. Now can we get back to work?" I stomped out, giving her no chance to reply.

I could feel Lynette eye-balling me all day. I pushed myself to keep a steady pace, wiping the sweat from my face and drinking coffee to keep the eyelid droop to a minimum. Lynette laid her hand on my shoulder as we punched out at the time clock to go home.

"You know you can always come to me if you need something, girl," she said quietly. "I tease you about calling on the Lord, but that's because it helps me. It can help you too."

I felt a sneer coming to my lips.

"And which Lord do I call on Lynette? Buddha, Allah, God, who?" I tried to provoke her, wanting to spread my bitterness. I expected a heated Jesus-lecture, but her face softened.

"It don't matter by what name you call Him, baby, He'll always answer."

"I'm going home to lay down." I said quietly without looking at her.

"You take care of yourself," she said. "See you tomorrow."

I wanted to feel ashamed of the lies I told her but I just felt empty. Gathering my resolve I made a silent promise to myself and to Lynette to quit soon. As a symbol of my commitment I pulled the stolen bag of syringes from my pocket, opened the car window and tossed them out.

***

"You know Novena he's goin' to die if we don't do somethin'," Simon said to me as we worked in his yard. He had a huge fenced-in garden, like an oasis in the middle of the city and we were picking the last of the summer crop of tomatoes and peppers for our dinner that night. Despite my promise to Lynette I had downed a small handful of pain pills upon coming home from work. They took the edge off my misery and pills didn't really count anyway, as long as I stayed away from the needle. When Simon called to ask me to dinner I couldn't think fast enough to formulate a good excuse. I hadn't realized I'd be working for my dinner.

I wiped a trickle of sweat from under the neck of the long sleeved cotton shirt I wore; the late August evening sun was warm and heavy, casting an orange glow over Simon's yard. The sounds of boom-box car stereos and friends calling to each other snuck over the high wooden fence and mingled with bird songs and the tinkling of Simon's wind chimes.

"I got a restraining order to keep him out of the house," I told Simon, and threw a pepper into the bag at his feet.

"You still give him money, though, don't you?" Simon asked. "I understand, I'm not judgin' you, just askin'. I know what it's like to be in love." He threw a rotten tomato over the fence.

"He has nothing left, Simon. It breaks my heart to think of leaving him," my voice trembled. I couldn't stand the image of Dev alone; it was like leaving a small child to fend for him self.

"He's already more alone than you can imagine honey. He can't love you back, he can just feed his habit and wait to die. Dev's not livin' in our world anymore," he said. We continued to pick and weed, pulling the plants out of the ground root and all and throwing them into a bucket to be dumped into his compost. They had given their produce and were now used up and useless, time to be plucked out so the soil could be fertilized for the next year's crop.

"I wish we could lock him up and tie him down until he was clean and it was all out of his system. That way he'd have no choice but to get clean. We could untie him when the hard part was over and he would be past it. It's just that initial suffering he has to do to get it out of his system that he can't get past." I said.

"If he's not careful he'll wind up in jail and then he'll get clean under lock and key," Simon said, pulling hard at a wilting tomato plant. He sat back on his heels in the dirt as if an idea had suddenly occurred to him. "That might be the best thing that could happen to him," he said. He rested his garden-gloved hands on his thighs and looked hard at me. "Novena next time he comes home will you be able to call the cops and have him arrested for disobeyin' the restrainin' order?" he asked in an encouraging voice.

I shrunk inside at the mere mention of actually using that order. It had taken so much out of me to obtain it and then serve it to Dev I knew there was no way I would ever invoke it. In a fit of desperation I had wrongly seen that order as a symbolic step in the right direction, but hadn't foreseen the price my heart would pay. He was still staying at the apartment most nights, only occasionally resorting to the Salvation Army.

"I know I won't," I replied. I dug my fingers into the cool dirt, grasping handfuls of it and feeling it mold inside my clenched fists. "The reason I got the order was more to scare him into seeing how serious things have gotten. He knows how bad things are, it's not like he really needs a reminder. I see that now. I guess I just needed to take a step in the right direction." I sighed and avoided Simon's gaze. He leaned over again and pulled a weed, tossing it over his shoulder.

"Yeah, it would be better for you to stay away from pressin' charges aginst him anyway. That kind of thing is touchy. It makes for future resentments," he said. "I'll have to be the bad guy." He winked at me almost imperceptibly and I didn't ask what he meant. I just went back to picking and weeding.

That evening as I returned home Dev was sitting on the steps of the porch, face puffy and flushed with booze and cocaine.

"I need some money and your keys," he said, his eyes empty. "Tay has my car, I'll bring yours back in twenty minutes." I could smell alcohol on his breath as he grabbed the keys from my cold hand and took off.

I jumped out of bed as the phone rang, feeling like I flew clear off the mattress and into the air with the violence of my waking. Dev had been banging on the door earlier that night and had been too drunk for me to remind him of the restraining order. Now he was lying fully clothed on the bed, smelling of alcohol and breathing raggedly. I fell into a troubled sleep with my own clothes still on and I was awake immediately to the loud ringing of the phone. I felt as if I were in shock, my ears ringing and my eyes wide as I groped for the receiver. Squinting, I read the clock. It was 1:20 am but it seemed like no time had passed since I'd come home from dinner at Simon's house. I slid off the bed to sit on the floor with my back against the side of the mattress and held the phone to my ear.

"Novena its Simon. I'm givin' y'all a heads up. The cops are on their way to your house. I'm havin' Dev arrested for B&E," he said. It took me a minute to collect myself enough to speak. I reached under the bed, feeling in the dark for my cigarettes.

"B&E?" What was he talking about?

"That's what the cops call breakin' and enterin'," he informed me, pronouncing the two words loudly. Simon watched way too much TV. "He came up here reekin' a booze and demanding twenty bucks. I sent him packin' and went out to visit someone. Came home'n my door was busted open, my drawers turned over and forty bucks gone. Now who do you figer took it?" he asked, not expecting a reply. "This is our chance Novena, we got him on this and can send him to jail where he'll have to get clean. I called the cops and filed a complaint, they know about him, been watching him last few months they say. So they're on their way down to your place. Get him ready," Simon stated. My heart jumped at his words and I gripped the receiver.

"Do you think they'll really arrest him for forty dollars? With all the over crowding in jail what if they just release him to himself, or what ever they do these days," I whispered. I rubbed my eyes and lit a cigarette, glancing up sideways at Dev who was still passed out beside me.

"Oh they'll take him. If I'm pressin' charges they have to. I explained about his heroin habit too and they're always wantin' to get junkies off the street. You better go, they'll be there any minute. I'll call you tomorrow. Get some sleep," he said the last three words kindly and hung up. Before I could think there was a pounding at the door. I replaced the receiver and scrambled off the floor to answer the knock. Three Pittsburgh Policemen filled the doorway: tall, big muscled men with imposing black uniforms and grim faces

"Hello m'am, is there a DeValera Roan on the premises? We have a warrant for his arrest," the largest officer stated, tipping his hat to me.

"He's in the bedroom. I'll get him," I said in a weak voice. I motioned them in the door and rushed into the bedroom, my ears ringing and my mind blank. How do you wake someone up to send him to jail? I shook Dev hard, hissing at him to get out of bed.

"What, huh? What are you doin'?" he mumbled, trying to push me away.

"The cops are here to take you to jail." My voice shook slightly as I said the words. His bloodshot eyes flew open at the insistence in my tone and he sat up, rubbing his hands through his hair, seemingly trying to orient himself to what was happening. He stood from the bed and strode into the living room with no sign of a stagger even though he was obviously still drunk. I followed behind him, my arms crossed protectively over my chest and stood in the door, out of the circle of men who filled my small living room with their size and authority.

"Is there a problem, sir?" Dev asked the in-charge-cop, his voice strong but polite, without even the hint of a drunken slur.

"Mr. Roan were you at 349 Vineland Street tonight?" the officer asked. Dev looked at me questioningly then back at the cop.

"Yes, I was there earlier but I …" his voice trailed off as he appeared to be recalling the events of the evening. Sudden realization crept over his face and he closed his mouth, accepting the charges without protest.

The cops read him the warrant, listing him as suspect in the theft of forty dollars and informed him that he'd been identified by a resident of the building while leaving the scene of the crime. They read him his rights, hand cuffed him and led him out. Dev stood unspeaking through the whole thing, nodding his head, looking disgusted. As he was lead out he instructed me to call his father in the morning and to use his black book to page the kid who had his car. Then they were gone and my house was empty and quiet. Not sure what to do, I sighed and ran my hand through my hair. I lit another cigarette, exhaled and felt a strange calm settle over me. I had developed the habit of taking each stressful occurrence as it came and since this one had been survived I went to bed and fell asleep immediately, resting better than I had in weeks.

By six o'clock the next morning I was wide-awake and crying. Dev's arrest the previous night had seemed so easy and fast and I had slept so well, but in the light of day my outlook was dark. Dev was in jail, some kid had his car and I was alone. The stress of the past few weeks must be getting to me, I thought as I wept. He was safe and locked up, just what we had wanted. So why was I crying, I chastised myself, refusing to admit it was because I missed him already. Before I could pick up the phone to call Simon it rang and Sissy's straggly voice was on the other end.

"Novena honey! I heard Devvy got busted last night," she said. "You gotta need somthin' and I got fresh stuff here. Com'on up." I was reaching for my car keys before I even answered her, not stopping to wonder how she knew already about Dev's arrest.

Sitting on the coffee table in her dusty living room, I was the center of attention as she and Viv related their own jail-time stories to me, reassuring me that Dev was safe and things weren't so bad. Sissy had even broken her own rule and let me fix in her bedroom. She was slouched in her recliner wearing worn-thin Winnie the Pooh pajamas and taking deep morning drags off her unfiltered Camel. Viv perched on the arm of the sofa where her filthy old sugar-daddy Ed sat spitting into his milk-carton.

"Don't fret," Ed said, his rough voice garbling around the cigarette dangling from his pale lips. "Every junkie gets clean in lock up at least once. Hell, I done it five times. They take care 'a ya. Wipe the puke away an' all. He'll be OK. It's only bad the first time, when ya don't know what to expect." Ed made it sound like a right of passage.

"Sis how'd you know he was in jail already?" I asked, remembering my puzzlement from earlier in the morning.

"Honey nothin' happens in my neighborhood that I don't know about. It's my job to know who's gettin' clean, who's in jail, and who's lookin' for what. That's how I stay in business," she stated, nodding her head at me. She passed me a lit cigarette which I accepted gratefully. "You may think we're all just a bunch of degenerates but we take care of each other." She looked over her glasses at me and I blushed.

"If we don't look out for each other no one else will." Viv finished for her. "This is no life to be alone in, that's how people die." She blinked at me starkly then let her face warm with a smile. "Dev's in the best place he can be. He's been wantin' to quit, you know. It's just so hard when you're really hooked." she looked at Sissy for conformation and Sissy nodded.

"Some people aren't really meant for this life. It's just a detour the wrong way down a one-way street," Sissy said. "Once you realize you're headed in the wrong direction and turn around, you never look back." She leaned over and stubbed out her cigarette then lit another, meeting my eyes over the ashtray. "You and Dev, you ain't meant for it. You just need to get turned back around and you'll be OK." She smiled at me through her cloud of smoke like some other-worldly creature.

Ed spat into his milk carton and Viv giggled. Sissy sat back in her chair and picked up the phone.

"Now go wait for Dev to call. He'll be wanting to know you're alright. I got business to attend to," Sissy said and held out her hand to me. She pressed a wad of dope into my hand for later, giving it a squeeze of affection.

I entered the apartment just as the phone rang and I ran to answer it, kneeling on the floor in front of the low phone table like it was an alter.

"This is a collect call from the Allegheny County Jail," a cheerful recorded voice stated.

"Press one to accept the call," the voice continued in an upbeat tone. With shaking hands I held the phone away from me and pressed the first button then placed the receiver back against my ear.

"Hello?" I managed to get out, my voice practically a whisper.

"Novena?" Dev sounded better than I expected him to. In fact he sounded better than I did. "You doin' OK?"

"Yeah, I'm fine," I said, and dug in my bag for my smokes.

"I guess I really did it this time. My memory of what happened is a little foggy …" his voice trailed off.

"You got drunk and broke into your dad's house and stole forty dollars. He called the cops and they came to my house to arrest you," I explained in a rush of words. My mind was brimming with anxiety like a glass too full of water, the surface tension all that holds it from making a mess. "Are you alright?" my voice broke.

"Novena I'm OK," Dev said in a soothing voice. "It'll be all right. I got roughed up by the cops a little and my head needed stapled but I'm OK. I guess they thought I resisted arrest when I stumbled on my way out to the car." He paused. "My dad finally found a way to get me locked up, huh? His way of showing me he loves me." Dev sounded chagrinned.

"So what happens now? Do you post bail or do you have to stay there. I don't know anything about this," I tried to sound calm for his sake but my voice was hollow and I lit a cigarette with shaky hands.

"They set my bail at five hundred dollars but I'm betting no one will post it so here I sit till my hearing. That'll be when ever my number is up on the list, probably a couple of weeks." He paused for a second before continuing. "In a day or so I'll be dope sick. That's something to look forward to," he said sarcastically, but his voice held a touch of fear. "At least this time I won't have an excuse. I'll have to bear it. This is probably the best place for me to be." There was a silence as I tried to think of something encouraging to say. "I gotta go, there's other people in line to use the phone. Don't worry about me Novena. I won't be able to call for a while but I'm OK, just take care of yourself ... I love you," he said and hung up before I could respond. I replaced the receiver and let a few tears of gratitude escape. It had been a relief just to hear his voice. I took a deep breath and faced the next challenge. I had to get his car back.

Picking up the phone again I punched in the beeper number of the boy who had his car, Tay. Within seconds the phone rang. I explained who I was that Dev was in jail and I needed the car back. The boy clucked his tongue in sympathy and told me not to worry about Dev. He'd been in jail twice himself and it wasn't so bad. He'd made some nice friends while he was there, he said. Ten minutes later Tay was outside my house in Dev's car.

"See Miss Novena, I even got a air fresh'ner to cheer you," he said and pointed to the smiley face hanging from the rear view mirror. He told me to call him if I needed anything then pulled a bicycle from the hatchback of Dev's car. I watched as he rode off, feeling humbled that everyone was being so helpful.

For the third time I ran for the phone as I entered my door.

"Well, hi, darlin', ain't it a nice day?" Simon's voice boomed at me sounding more cheerful than I could remember hearing him in months. "You com'on over. I'm makin' pancakes and bacon for brunch. I talked to Dev this mornin', he's stayin' in there till his hearin', then I'll drop the charges if he'll agree to a twenty-one day rehab. By then he'll have two weeks clean under his belt and be ready. We got to celebrate." I could hear his smile through the receiver and I began to feel better. It seemed like the heavy storm clouds were finally lifting and the sun was peeking through. This is what I'd wanted for so long, a chance at a new start.

Chapter Twelve

"Novena, get your ass down here," Rachel called to where I lay in a sunny spot on the porch of my apartment building, nodding after my post-work dose of heroin. I had been waiting for her to pick me up for an evening of trash picking. She and Amy sat in the car as I ran down the steps and got into the backseat. Rachel took off before I even had the door closed. "Ha, tonight's going to be a lucky night, I can feel it!" She shouted to me, taking her eyes off the road for a long moment to lean into the back seat. I laughed, enjoying myself for the first time in too long.

"How's Jailbird?" Rachel asked.

"I talked to Simon yesterday. Dev's been in jail four days and he's in the infirmary being sick and getting clean," I replied. I felt light as air. Finally I was getting a rest. I was still getting high every day but I planned to quit altogether before Dev got out. The cut-down method was the most logical, I rationalized.

"Hey, maybe we can go visit him before he gets out. I always wanted to see the jail," Rachel looked back at me hopefully.

"He should be about done detoxing in a few days. I'll call you when I'm going to visit," I said.

"Cool! Maybe we'll have lunch and make a day-trip of it," she suggested. "Honey I'm getting to see the jail!" She reached over and pinched Amy's thigh just to make sure Amy understood the excitement of the moment.

"At least you'll be seeing it as a visitor, that's more than I expected," Amy sighed.

It was the second week of September and the mild temperatures and clear sunny days of early fall had arrived. I was sleeping well, eating better, getting high less and was hopeful about the future for the first time in two years. Rachel and Amy and had been hauling items out of people's trash all summer and "refinishing" them in preparation for a big flea market over the weekend.

"What a great idea, take stuff out of people's garbage, tighten the screws, slap on a coat of bright paint, call it art and resell it to the same suckers who tossed it out in the first place. No over-head, all profit!" Rachel proclaimed when we had stopped to investigate an intricately carved wooden end table sitting by the curb a few months prior. All it needed was a good sanding and a coat of varnish and it would be a gorgeous antique. Amy and I agreed, seeing the beauty of the piece. Rachel saw only money. *"If it doesn't make dollars, it doesn't make cents,"* she chanted, quoting the line of graffiti scrawled on a crumbling wall near their apartment. "Don't get too attached to that old thing," she had told us as we pushed the table into the back seat. And so by September they had filled their living room with "Objects D'Art" that would soon be for sale. Rachel rubbed her hands together in anticipation as we eyed the treasures. "Soon the trash will be cash," Rachel sighed in satisfaction, spreading her arms wide to indicate the expansiveness of their booty. They could hardly walk through the living room due to the clutter waiting to be refinished and sold.

Our haul at the end of the evening was an interesting old lamp that needed a shade, a fifties era solid-state radio that still worked when tested in Rachel's kitchen, a small bed-side table that would look great stripped and varnished, it's dark red cherry wood visible under the peeling paint, and our greatest find, a heavy old bicycle with two flat tires which we inflated at a gas station on our way back to Amy and Rachel's apartment. After hauling in everything but the bike we sat on the front stoop enjoying the last rays of the sinking sun.

I jumped up suddenly and grabbed the bicycle, wondering if I could still balance like when I was a kid. Rachel and Amy giggled as I wobbled down the alley next to their building, screeching with fear when I hit a bump. The smothering anxiety of the past few months was left behind as I gained speed, feeling like I was flying. My confidence soared with my spirits and I let go of the handlebars, holding my arms out to balance as I laughed breathlessly at my own daring, oblivious of the looks I got from strangers. Finally spent, I huffed and puffed with the effort of peddling the heavy thing and I turned around. My legs felt like noodles as I pulled up in front of Amy and Rachel, shaking and laughing uncertainly at the same time. This was how most people feel all the time, I thought in wonder; this is how I want to feel from now on.

As the second week of Dev's incarceration approached, Rachel and I made plans to visit him. I called to find out what we had to do.

"Just come down and wait in line. It's first come, first served and if you don't get here early you won't get to see him," the officer told me gruffly over the phone.

"You mean I have to make an appointment or something?" I asked.

"No," he snorted. "I mean we only got eight visiting phones and if you're number nine in line you don't get to visit."

Rachel and I packed lunches, prepared thermoses of hot tea, made a 7-11 run to buy magazines and set off to the jail. The Allegheny County Jail, located in the middle of downtown Pittsburgh, was a huge stone fort of a building with an arched entrance and parapets that make me think of a medieval castle. The day of our visit was cool and rainy and by afternoon a fine mist hung in the air, heightening the eerie quality of the surroundings.

"Wow, how cool," Rachel breathed as we passed under the arched door and walked up the stone steps to the guard's window. We were the only ones there and the door to the guard's office was closed. At least we would be first in line.

"I always fantasized about going to jail," Rachel said, gazing around the dank entrance way. It definitely felt like a dungeon. "Of course, I'd be a political prisoner. It's not like I plan to be locked up for grand-theft-auto or anything. I could go on a hunger strike to protest my unfair incarceration and write my memoirs on toilet paper and smuggle them out to be published. And then people would start rallying around my cause and demand my release and when they finally let me out I'd be interviewed on TV …" She gazed off into space, enjoying her daydream.

"All right Norma Ray, come back to reality. You're way too spoiled to go to jail. You think they'll bring your coffee to you in bed like Amy does every morning?" I asked.

"Yeah, I guess you're right. Things always seem more romantic than they turn out to be. I'd hate having someone tell me what to do all the time." She poured tea from a thermos and opened a magazine. A few other visitors were beginning to show up, mostly young women with small children. They didn't look nervous like I felt. But they all looked tired. An older woman with a haggard face sat on the step below us and Rachel offered her a magazine. She was gripping her fake-leather purse tightly and shook her head no at the offer. Voices, footsteps and kids' laughter began to echo across the stone walls and off the worn granite steps of the entranceway. The cool damp air was odd for early September and many of the women were still dressed for summer. They shivered in their light clothes as the breeze whipped into the hall from outside.

Suddenly the window to the guard's office flew up with a crack and all the women stood. We were first in line and the guard motioned us forward.

"I have a change of clothes for him," I said, holding up the bag I'd packed for Dev. The guard looked at Dev's name I had written on the ledger handed to me.

"He can't have anything," he said.

"What will he wear to his hearing? He's going to be in here at least two weeks," I said in dismay.

"He can do laundry here. He'll wear what he came in wearing." The guard was busy writing, and his voice was impatient.

"But what will he wear while he washes his clothes?" I asked in confusion.

"His underwear," the guard said rudely, like we were ignorant children.

"Excuse me sir," Rachel broke in. "But isn't that a little, well, dangerous?" She asked in a polite voice, raising her eyebrows meaningfully. The guard looked up at us for the first time.

"Lady this ain't Alcatraz, it's county jail. Now move along, I don't got all day." He dismissed us and I realized how truly powerless you become once you're in the grasp of the legal system.

"I have half a mind to remind him that our tax dollars pay his fucking salary and he should show a little courtesy!" Rachel fumed as we were herded into another waiting room.

"Relax, or your prison fantasy is gonna come true faster than you'll like." I took a seat on a wooden bench against the stone wall in a round room that seemed to be at the base of one of the parapets. Seven other groups of people sat around us. Long slim windows with iron bars on them were open above and the cold wind continued to plague us. My legs began to cramp. Rachel sighed and reached for another magazine.

Finally after another hour of waiting they opened a door and called for visitors. Rachel stayed on the bench as I shuffled along with seven other women to the row of scratched Plexiglas-covered windows. Each window had its own little plastic cubical built around it with a phone attached. I walked along the row of windows looking for Dev's face but didn't see him.

"Excuse me, I'm waiting for DeValera Roan," I said to the guard at the desk. He looked at his list.

"Not available. He's in the infirmary," he told me then went back to shuffling his papers.

"Is he sick?" I asked, furrowing my brow in concern, trying not to give in to the intimidation I felt.

"They don't tell me, they just give me the list," he informed me. My patience was waning. I had waited three hours in the cold to see Dev; they had plenty of time to tell me he wasn't available. I wasn't leaving unless I knew why. I took a deep breath and gathered my nerve.

"Could you please find out why he's there?" He made no move to answer my request. "Please, it would just help me not to worry if I knew." My stomach twisted with the nausea I felt at hearing my high, begging tone of voice. The guard sighed and picked up the phone. After a short conversation he hung up and looked at me, a faint sneer on his face.

"Seems he had a rough withdrawal," he emphasized the word, making sure I heard his disdain. "They want to check his blood pressure one more time." He raised his eyebrows and tossed his papers to the desk. "Satisfied?" My cheeks burned with shame and I lowered my face.

"Thank you," I said and walked away.

"What's the matter? Why can't you see him?" Rachel asked, scrambling to pick up the magazines and thermos she had spread out in front of her. I stormed towards the door, my shame turning into anger.

"He's not available," I quoted the guard in a hard voice.

"Why didn't they tell you that from the beginning?"

I didn't break my stride as we hit the street and followed the sidewalk to the parking lot.

"Because they don't care if we wait three hours, they don't care if we're cold, they don't care if we're disappointed, that's why," I said. "We're just trash. I need to get used to it. That's what I am, unsightly garbage." I paid the parking lot attendant five precious dollars and sped away, Rachel cursing beside me.

At home that evening I turned on the little solid state radio we had salvaged from the curbside. It hadn't sold at the yard sale and neither had the bike, so I had taken both home the evening after the sale. The radio crackled as I turned the knob until I found a tolerable station. Slowly I began to relax as the soft music floated into the air. I had forgotten how good music could sound, even from a thrown-away old radio. The light began to fade from the room and with it my bitterness. I lit a candle instead of turning on the lamp and sat on the floor with my back against the wall. I took a deep breath, held it and released it slowly. My muscles began to relax and I felt the lines of tension smooth from my face. The candle sputtered, distracting me for a second from the sound of the radio. Its glow cast a gold light on my closed eyelids. A vaguely familiar feeling crept over me, something that teased the edge of my memory, just out of reach: peace. It hit my system like a lungful of pure oxygen after being in the thin air at high altitude and I reacted to it the same way, with a heavy feeling of nausea.

I lit a cigarette and watched the smoke curl in the air, retreating from my first taste of serenity in two years like a frightened pilgrim running from a vision of holiness. The smell of the lighter reminded me of cooking dope. My mouth watered as I thought about getting high, surprised at how strong the craving for oblivion was. I still have a couple weeks till Dev is home; I might as well have a few more hits before then I thought as I reached for the phone to call Sissy.

My seat in the back of the courtroom gave me full view of the activities. People bustled around me, oblivious to my keen interest. The metal folding chairs filled up with anxious family members, bored-looking cops and harried public defenders carrying Styrofoam cups full of coffee and briefcases bursting with papers. A policeman led three people into the room from a side door and directed them to stand in front of the judge's bench.

The door opened again and a cop led Dev in, shuffling around his chained ankles. His hands were cuffed in front of him and he was dressed in a hazard-orange prison jumpsuit. Under both dark eyes were purple-fading-to-green bruises and staples gleamed from a jagged cut on his forehead. He turned and found me in the crowd, his eyes lighting when he saw me, his smile exposing a space in his lower jaw where there used to be a tooth. 'Hi Novena', he mouthed to me, continuing to smile.

I followed the court proceedings numbly, Simon sitting at my side. It was just like a movie except the attorneys weren't dressed as well as on TV. The scene was very dramatic, with the judge giving Dev a stern talking-to before releasing him into Simon's custody.

Dev's arms closed around me in a strong embrace and I clasped my hands together behind his waist.

"God it's good to see you Novena," Dev said into my ear. We stood like that for a long time in front of the cashier's window at the courthouse. I was so glad to hold him again I didn't even feel self-conscious that our display of affection might be witnessed. Dev had been released to Simon on grounds that he go directly to the Vet's hospital for twenty-one days of drug rehabilitation.

"Hey you two let's go. Dev has to be at the VA by two pm." Simon had a hand on each of our backs and he spoke quietly, as if he hated to interrupt. We parted and Dev took my hand as we walked toward the elevator.

"So that's all there is to it," Dev said. "I stood there for ten minutes and the judge sentenced me to what I had already decided to on my own anyway and probably cost the taxpayers a couple hundred dollars in the process."

"Well you only stole forty bucks, what do you want, hard-time?" Simon asked with a laugh.

"No, I just think it was a waste of time for me to sit in there on the peoples' dime for so long when I could have been bailed out two weeks ago," Dev said.

"On my dime," Simon finished. Dev's face flushed.

"I guess it was worth it to finally get clean," he said and I caught the split-second of uncertainty that passed over his thin face. Then he smiled as if stepping back into character. "Too bad it's not closer to Halloween. I'm all ready to play a monster with my stapled head and missing tooth." He flashed me a grin, showing off the space in his lower jaw. He squinted painfully as we stepped out side into the sun, like a night-creature unused to light.

"How did that happen again?" I asked. We were crowding into the cab of Simon's pickup truck and Dev's hand came to rest comfortably on my thigh. My skin got warm where he touched and a pleasant tingle traveled up my legs, making me grow hot all over. I had to concentrate hard on what he was saying.

"Well, you know I was high as Hell and drunk too that night," he began, smiling and sounding like he was going to enjoy telling the story. "I remember tripping off the curb. It's hard to walk in that condition under the best of circumstances but with my hands cuffed behind my back it was a real trick. I think I cussed and tried to twist my arms loose from the cops so I could get my balance and they thought I was trying to escape. With handcuffs on. Resisting arrest they called it right before they beat the tar out of me," he finished. I touched his head where the staples held his puckered skin closed. They had shaved a bald patch to put them in.

"Jesus," I swore. I didn't feel sorry for him exactly, but I felt like I should say something.

"The cops were real nice to me in the infirmary, apologizing for the misunderstanding and everything. I guess they're so tightly wound that any excuse to blow off some steam by roughing up a junkie is a good one. No hard feelings. I was wrong in the first place. I never should have let things get so out of control," Dev said, his eyes on the road as Simon swerved back and forth over the yellow line while trying to light a cigarette. Dev grabbed the steering wheel, steadying it until Simon put his attention back on his driving.

"Christ, Dad! Your driving is going to kill me just when I'm starting to put my life back together," he said.

"Don't you worry about my drivin'. I may look like I'm not payin' attention, but I got all my faculties focused right on that road," Simon answered, waving his cigarette forward. "You just better worry about focusin' all your faculties on stayin' clean." The truck swerved again as he glanced pointedly at Dev.

"I'm grateful for the chance to start over." His voice shook with sincerity. "I'm sorry I caused you both so much trouble and I'm sorry for my attitude back at the courthouse. It's all been a little overwhelming that's all." He tightened his grip on my thigh. "I know you were doing what you thought was best Dad. I doubt I'd have been able to quit otherwise."

"Was jail really bad? You know Rachel will want details," I said, trying to mask my concern. He chuckled.

"Jail was no worse than being in the Army: bad food, tight quarters and people telling you when to eat and when to shit," he smiled. "It's not bad at all. For the short term, that is. I wouldn't want to go to prison but county jail was almost a relief after a couple years of chasing dope. I knew I couldn't get any so I was able to just relax and get clean. I met a couple of nice guys in there too. We may hook up at meetings when they get out," he said.

"What meetings?" I wondered.

"These meetings people with drug problems go to. I'll have to go to a few every week after I get out of rehab, it's part of the conditions of my release. I went to some in jail and they were interesting. Someone gets up and tells their story, we all clap and shake hands and everyone drinks a lot of coffee," he explained in a light voice. "You might want to go with me." He finished. I looked at Simon out of the corner of my eye but he didn't seem to notice what Dev had said.

We parked next to the institutional yellow brick buildings of the Veteran's Administration Hospital compound and Simon clasped Dev to him in a short hug then walked toward the door to find a cup of coffee and give us some privacy.

Dev had both hands in the pockets of his jeans; he was leaning against the side of Simon's truck. I leaned beside him, the sun-warmed metal heating my back. I was suddenly, inexplicably uncomfortable with the man I had spent the last five years with. I captured a strand of hair from blowing across my face and tucked it behind my ear. My eyes crinkled against the grit in the breeze.

"I wish we had more time together," Dev said, kicking at the ground a little. "I know the past few years have been hard for us Novena." His vision was focused out across the tree-lined drive. "I can't tell you too many times how much I love you." He chewed his lower lip and looked down. "Thank you for staying with me. I promise we'll make it through this." He turned to me and his fingers on my chin brought my head around to his dark gaze. Slowly I brought my eyes up to meet his. He pulled me to him and I hung on, to him and to the hope I read in his face.

***

A week into Dev's twenty-one days of rehab and I was enjoying myself. He was safe, doing well, happy and hopeful. I felt like I was on vacation. A light breeze blew in the big open window of my bedroom making the sheer curtains flow. I had developed a comfortable routine. I got up, read from my little book of prayers that Lynette had given me, making sure to say please for the future and thank you for the present at her suggestion. Then I had breakfast went to work, came home to my peaceful house or went out visiting in the evening. I read while I ate my meals, listening to the little old radio and wondering why I needed that TV so badly. My heroin use was staying at a couple bags every other day and I was proud of my ability to cut down, although the pills I bought from Sissy were helping control the craving for dope.

"Hey Novena," Dev purred over the phone to me. He was allowed to call once a week to let me know how he was doing. "I miss you," he said. My heart fluttered a little.

"I miss you too," I answered. I was still getting used to being able to love him again.

"Things are good for me here," he said, his voice more excited than I'd heard it in months. "I'm learning a lot about addiction and about myself. This program has some really good people in it. The dental office fixed my missing tooth so I don't look like a derelict, I been working out every day and eating a lot so I put some weight back on. I feel a lot better about myself already. They are helping me get an efficiency apartment around the corner from you. It's furnished and I'll share the kitchen and bathroom with some other guys from the program. So you and I can start over, from the beginning."

"That's great," I said.

"You know, I've been talking to one of the councilors and I'm thinking about going back to school when I get out. He says with my street-sense and my intellect I could do well in the business world." My heart quickened at his encouraging words. "I feel really good about this," he said again before he hung up.

I fantasized about our life together in the future: two professionals who had been through the hell of heroin addiction but were now clean, living in a large brownstone home in the city, a few children in the yard. I could see us mingling with our affluent neighbors, exchanging loving looks with each other, never forgetting where we had been and appreciating how far we had come.

The breeze sang threw the window making the light cotton shirt I wore flutter across my abdomen. Soon Dev's hands will touch me like that again, I thought, and enjoyed the thrill that caused my eyes to close. I remembered the whisper of his breath on my lips, the softness of his hair when I clasped my hands behind his neck, the strength of him when I wrapped my legs around his waist and let him rock slowly into me. My eyes opened. It had been a day since I'd gotten high. I'd call Sissy tomorrow I thought and get something to make the waiting easier.

As the days passed I began to worry that Dev's coming home would disturb my pleasant routine. I liked having him locked up somewhere safe. I could do my own thing while knowing he was OK. Fantasy has always been so much easier for me than reality. When he got out I would have to worry about him all over again. I'd have to worry that my daydreams would remain just that.

"I've read every book in my house," I told Laurence during a visit to his house. "I'm trying to occupy myself while Dev is away but I don't know what to do. I come home after work some days and just wander around the apartment."

Laurence looked at me for a long minute.

"I may have something to help you," he said, and left the room. I could hear him pulling down the foldable steps that led to the attic crawl space. Then I listened curiously as he rummaged around, rustling and banging in the small area where he stored things.

"These are a little old but oils never go bad or dry up. I bought new paints recently. You might as well take the old ones," he said. In his hands was a worn brown leather trunk. He set it on the table and I flipped it open. Inside were small misshapen tubes of paint, a little glass bottle of turpentine, brushes and pallet knives, a rag and charcoal pencils. He ducked out of the room and upon return presented me with a small hand-stretched canvass and tabletop easel.

"What am I going to do with these?" I asked in wonder.

"Paint," Laurence replied. "Just give it a try."

"I don't know how to paint," I protested. I loved the colors on the tubes, the silkiness of the brush-tips against my fingers. I wanted the case and its contents even if I never put brush to canvass.

"There's no such thing as not knowing how. Just let go and see what appears on the canvass."

I took the paints home and set the canvass on the table-top easel she gave me, got out all the paints, poured a little cup of turpentine and sat in front of the blank canvass waiting for inspiration to strike. Two days passed without any ideas of what to paint and finally in frustration I drew a matched set of mountains that looked like pointy boobs and a lake at the base of the mountains with a childishly simple boat floating in it. I left the canvass propped on the table just in case that bolt of inspiration hit while I wasn't expecting it.

Next I dragged the big old heavy bike out of the basement of my building. When it hadn't sold at Rachel's flea market, I silently rejoiced and crammed it into the back seat of my car. It had sat idle in the basement since then.

I oiled the chain, put on the used helmet I had bought at the second-hand sports equipment store and heaved my leg over the bar onto the pedal. If I do six times around the block this week then I can gradually increase until I'm really in shape, I planned enthusiastically. I rode around my block, waving to the kids on the sidewalk. After one lap my lungs were burning and my legs were reduced to wet noodles. I wiped the sweat from my face in irritation and dragged the bike back into the basement. So much for getting in shape, I thought.

As pitiful as they were, I was proud of my attempts to branch out and try new activities. There was something about that bike that I absolutely loved, if only it wasn't so painful. And I craved the feel of the pencils and paint brushes in my hand, savored the smell of the turpentine, if only I had some ideas of what to paint.

"What have you been up to Novena?" Dev asked over the phone a week later.

"Painting," I said, trying to sound nonchalant. "And biking." I heard him chuckle on the other end.

"When I get home I'll give you something to do," he said suggestively, "so you won't have to make stuff up to keep busy."

"I'm not making stuff up. I like to paint and bike." I defended myself. "Since when?"

"Since last week. There's a lot of things I've never done and now I have the opportunity to try so I am," I explained. I lit a cigarette, suddenly feeling a little angry but not sure why.

"OK, OK. So I'm coming home to a painting cyclist. That's great, it's good to explore new things," he said in a patronizing voice.

I blew a stream of smoke into the air.

"Do you still like being clean?" I wanted to change the subject.

"Yeah, everything is great." He sounded less excited than during our last conversation.

"You said you really enjoyed the program," I reminded him.

"Oh I do. It's just that they expect everyone to think the same way. There's no room for questions. Every time I ask about something they tell me to just not get high and keep coming back. What kind of answer is that?" He sounded skeptical. "It seems like brain-washing to me."

"Well maybe you need your brain washed. After all, that's better than running the street." I began to get that sick, gnawing ache in my stomach again. I hurriedly lit another cigarette and looked around for my bottle of ant-acid.

"You're smoking an awful lot. How much heroin are you shooting?" Dev asked, in an apparent attempt to distract me.

"You just worry about yourself, this is supposed to be about you. You should listen to what they say and try to follow the rules. If they're managing to stay clean then they're doing something right." I tried not to sound like I was lecturing.

"I gotta go Novena, it's time for dinner. I'll call you next week and let you know when I'll be home," he hung up. The conversation had completely unsettled me. I could hear a subtle change in his tone of voice, a less positive than last week kind of change, like he was over the initial rush of sobriety and was realizing that he'd have to change his whole life.

***

Dev's hand caressed down the back of my hair and came to rest heavily on my shoulder as we walked from the VA hospital's entrance to my car. The autumn sky was dull and windless and the air dried my throat as I breathed. He was finally coming home and I was trying to conjure up some excited. Instead my stomach was clenched in the familiar grip of anxiety.

"You been doing OK Novena?" He asked in a quiet tone. He was subdued. I had pictured us embracing, him swinging me around, kissing me, celebrating that he was out of rehab and ready to start a new life. Instead he seemed withdrawn and preoccupied.

"I'm fine. Your dad is making dinner for us tonight," I told him. I wasn't sure how to act. Should I be the one to set an example and grab him to me or should I follow his lead? Watching him out of the corner of my eye I decided to remain quiet like him.

"I don't know if I'll be up to dinner at Dad's house," Dev said. "I really just feel like staying home alone and reading. It's been tiring, all this thinking and learning. My body isn't used to functioning clean yet and I take a lot of naps." He avoided my gaze as he got in the car. I tried to drive and study him at the same time. Dev stared out the window.

"So are you going to a meeting tonight?" I asked.

"I might. We'll see. It's not like I haven't been to a meeting every damn day in there. I think I might need a night off." His voice was even, almost cool and we rode in silence the rest of the way to his new apartment. We walked slowly through the small room. It had a bed, a table and chairs, dresser and desk. All obviously from thrift stores or donations, but the place was clean and bright, with a high ceiling and big windows.

"I'll need some cash to buy groceries," he told me as we opened drawers and looked in the closet and small fridge. "There's nothing here."

"We can go to the store together later. I'll be done with work at three o'clock like usual then I'll come by here. I need to get stuff too," I said. I had picked him up while on my lunch break and still had two hours till I could punch out for the day.

"But I'm pretty hungry now, I missed lunch at the VA. I eat a lot now that I'm clean." He smiled briefly. "Just give me some money and tell me what you need. I'll get everything." I heard something unnerving in his voice, a familiar edge of desperation that made me reluctant to leave him alone. I had no choice, I had to go back to work. Sighing to relieve the tension that had begun to build between my shoulder blades, I handed him forty dollars and left. I had to trust him sooner or later, might as well get it over with now, I thought as I drove back to the nursing home.

My stomach twisted in and out of knots the rest of the afternoon and I raced back to Dev's apartment after work. He answered my knock but held the door so I couldn't walk in.

"Novena I'm just tired. I need to crawl in bed and sleep for twelve hours or so. I'll call you tomorrow." He gave me a half-smile and avoided looking directly at me.

"Last week you couldn't wait to see me and we haven't had any real time together in months," I protested hotly, my knees going weak.

"I just need some time alone, to adjust." His jaw was set and I whirled away angrily then stomped down the porch steps outside to my car. I slammed the car door shut and let my tires squeal as I pulled away from the curb, incase he hadn't gotten the point.

At home I paced the floor on shaky legs. He must have already gotten high, not even four hours after coming home. How could I be sure, though? I didn't want to accuse him and I wasn't able to see his pupils in the shadow of the entranceway. My skin was cold and my limbs restless. I lifted my shirt and peeled off the clear plastic patch of narcotic painkiller I had bought from Sissy the day before. I had stuck it to my side thinking it was better to cut down from shooting heroin to taking pills, then to wearing a narcotic patch for a few days, then stop completely. These patches were the same kind used in the hospital for pain control. They were a slow time-released dose of narcotic that was absorbed through the skin and were usually worn for two or three days at a time. I flushed it down the toilet angrily and lit a cigarette, reaching for the phone to call Sissy and get some real dope.

The pink bicycle helmet I used the few times I rode was hanging from my bedroom door-handle and my eyes landed on it mid-dial. I put the phone down. I smashed my cigarette into the ashtray half-smoked before running down to the basement. Maybe I could stay clean today even if Dev didn't. I dragged the old bike out and began peddling furiously around the block.

There were no traffic lights in my neighborhood and the wide streets were lined up neatly in square blocks, allowing me to ride without having to think too much about traffic laws and right-of-way. I struggled at first to turn the stiff pedals, my breath coming in sucking gulps. I stood and shifted from side to side, using my body weight to push the pedal down for each revolution. The bike picked up speed and I sat in the saddle, feeling it bite into my bones. Soon my peddling settled into a steady cadence and my thoughts were focused on the rhythm of my breathing. Sweat began to roll down the sides of my face and my lungs were burning but I kept peddling. My anger diminished as exhaustion took over until I pulled slowly in front of my apartment house, legs shaking and chest heaving. I dragged the bike back into the basement, climbed the stairs and locked the apartment door behind me.

Chapter Thirteen

The next morning I was banging on Dev's door early. It was Saturday and I didn't have to work, but I had been awake since four in the morning, drinking coffee and waiting for a reasonable hour to confront Dev. I needed to find out if my fears were true.

"Jesus Novena, what time is it?" he yawned and stretched after opening the door then shuffled back to the bed and fell onto it. He fluffed his pillows and settled his back against the headboard.

"Are you using again?" I stood facing him and put my hands on my hips. Dev hugged his arms to his chest and appeared to hunch down into himself. His face became stiff and set, his eyes focused defiantly on the wall across the room.

"Look, I don't need a lecture," he said.

"Are you getting high?" I asked again, not moving. He was silent for a second.

"Coming home to an empty apartment and a pocketful of money was a bad idea," he said, instead of answering my question directly. I began shaking.

"That's why I wanted to pick you up after I was done with work. You're the one who insisted I come to the VA early in the day," I spat, completely exasperated. "I can't stand this, you couldn't even get through the first fucking day and after all that trouble!" I shouted. I threw a coffee cup against the wall, stomped furiously on the broken pieces that fell to the floor and then I sank onto the side of the bed and cried. Dev remained in the bed, face dark, eyes hooded beneath his brows.

"Don't cry Novena," he reached out his hand to me but I jumped up and ran out of the apartment. I went directly to Sissy's house, wiping my eyes on the sleeve of my sweater as I drove.

"Dev's home," I told Sissy and Viv as I sat on the coffee table and lit a cigarette.

"I know, he was here yesterday," Sissy said. "Did he even go to his new place before he came to see me?" she asked. "It's too bad. I was hoping both those boys would stay quit this time."

"What do you mean?" I looked up from my preoccupation with the bleach spot staining my jeans.

"Mick was here yesterday too. He put his wedding ring in hock for money to get high," Viv explained as Sissy was dialing the phone.

"I thought he was going to be on meth for two years," I said. Disappointment gnawed at me. At least we weren't alone I thought, ashamed of the relief I felt that Mick was using again too.

"Oh he's still drinking his meth every day, 'cept now he chases it with a needle full of dope," Sissy said, her hand over the phone receiver. "He goes to a self-pay clinic instead of the Welfare clinic, so they don't even test for dope use regularly. He ain't gettin' high every day, just a few times a week," she finished, like that made it OK. Was there hope for any of us, I wondered?

"You're in luck, Veena-girl, this guy's goin' to bring your dope here. He has some pills he wants me to get rid of for him." Sissy hung up and I stared blankly at the TV with her and Viv, waiting for the dope-man to come.

***

The October wind brought a cold rain to the city. In a week we would set the clocks back an hour and it would be dark at five, I thought as I made my way down the wet, leaf-plastered sidewalk to Dev's apartment building. Life had returned to normal with frightening speed after Dev came home from rehab. The only difference was that I had stopped caring about any of us getting clean. The last of my hope had died when Dev picked up the syringe the same day he came home and I stopped humoring myself with fantasies of a happy life. Mick met us a few times a week to get high but always left soon after. We were all subdued and quiet during our evenings together, solemnly cooking and shooting our heroin as if we detested the action and just wanted to get it over with.

"I need a tie," I said without looking at Dev as I strode into the small room. He picked up his belt from the floor and tossed it to me then handed me a filled syringe without leaving his chair.

"You're home early today," he said. He closed his eyes in exhaustion and rubbed the back of his neck.

"I left work early. I feel sick." Nothing seemed important to me anymore. I trudged through each hour, feeling oblivious to my surroundings. My job, my friends, family, everything took a back seat to getting my dope. The high I used to enjoy eluded me but I still waited for it, like a lost kid waiting for a parent who never shows up to kiss the bump and comfort the hurt. The most I got now was a deeper feeling of numbness. Which was exactly what I needed to get through each second of every day.

I seemed to be fueled only by the bitterness that burned in my heart. It kept me just barely going, like the last ember in a dying fire. I hated my life, Dev, Mick, my own weakness. I ignored my family's phone calls. I avoided Lynette as much as possible. Rachel had left Amy and was busy courting a new lover so she was easy to put off. Laurence kept his distance, there in the periphery if I needed him but not pushing to contact me. I managed to isolate myself completely.

I sat on the bed, wrapped the belt around my arm and shot relief into the bruised vein in my right wrist.

"I'll get more jobs from the labor place," Dev replied without moving. He was sitting in the chair, his head tilted back to rest on the wall behind him. The dark circles beneath his closed eyes gave his gaunt face a skeletal appearance. We were tired to our bones, both of us, from the stress of keeping our habit fed and the burden of carrying the regret we felt. Dev's hands were raw and cracked from working outside in cold wet weather. He took any job he could get now and had been working over time. Half the guys he worked with were hiding their own heroin addiction he said, so when he disappeared at lunch time to get high no one even noticed.

I pulled the needle from my arm and leaned back against the headboard of the bed. The radio on Dev's small desk was tuned to an all-talk station and I couldn't follow the topic. Voices droned in and out of my hearing then faded to a pleasant buzz in my ears. A sinking feeling over-took me.

I was descending slowly into warm thick fluid. *Just let go ...* It was quiet. The light was fading as I sank like a ship, gradually going deeper beneath the surface until finally I came to rest in the soft sand of the ocean floor. My surroundings were dark and comforting. A stillness settled over my being as if I were in suspended animation, like a TV with a static screen. I receded, becoming a tiny awareness, a spark barely flickering in a swath of cumbersome tissue. *Rest ... just rest ... and ... let go ...* the awareness communicated. I retreated further, going deeper. Blackness surrounding, quietness, nothingness ... ... Then, as if from somewhere far away, the world began shaking. People were calling out, their voices muffled and fuzzy. I tried to fight them but couldn't swim up from the depths that covered me. I wanted to push their hands away. *Stop bothering me, I want to stay here*, I longed to tell them. The shock of freezing cold against my skin brought my disconnected being back together and in response the awareness leaped from a sputtering flame into a fire. I sat up and took a deep ragged breath, like someone breaking the surface of the water after having been under for too long. Dev's terrified face loomed in front of me.

"Jesus Christ," he swore and expelled a gush of air through his pursed lips. He was kneeling beside me holding my hands tightly as I lay sideways over the bed. I watched Mick sink to the floor beside the bed and run a shaky hand through his hair. Dev continued in a strained voice. "Goddammit Novena, I thought we lost you. How the fuck did that happen?" He shook his head violently to the side, his jaw tight.

"What are you talking about," I asked, pulling my hands from his grasp. I pushed myself to sit up and looked at Mick. My breathing was still heavy and I shook as if I were freezing.

"I walked in, Dev was sleep in the chair and you were blue on the damn bed," Mick stated, his eyes still wide. "I don't know how long you were out but I threw ice down your shirt and you finally took a breath."

"Why the Hell didn't you just slap me?" I asked. I put my hands to my face, feeling the need to verify my solidness after what they had just told me. "Or better yet, why didn't you just let me go." Tears came to my eyes in a strange rush of emotion. Mick and Dev looked horrified. Dev swore under his breath and hauled himself to his feet. He dragged me up off the bed by my cold hands and wrapped my coat around me.

"You still look dusky, let's go for a walk," he insisted. We stepped into the freezing dark night. The stars overhead were bright and sparkly through the clearing clouds. I shoved my hands in my pockets and walked beside Dev. "You should quit Novena," he said. His tone was firm and quiet. I looked up at him.

"I can quit anytime. I just don't care to anymore," I lied. He stopped and faced me, grabbed my upper arms tightly, forcing me to look at him. I tried to shrug him off but couldn't get out of his grasp.

"I want to shake you, to make you stop this," he said, and gave me a little shake as if to demonstrate. "I want to toss you out of my life, so you can make a real attempt to get clean," his voice was harsh. Then he paused, looking at the sky. He dropped his hands from me. "But I'm just not strong enough. I can't push you away. As long as you'll come to me I'll take you and that means you'll keep shooting dope. I'm responsible, I know that. You'd have never done it if it wasn't for me and I live with that every day. Just please, I want you to know that if I could, I would make it different." His eyes held mine, and his face was hard under the locks of ragged dark hair that hung in front of his tired features. I looked at the ground, understanding that this was as much as he could give. I tugged the edges of his worn leather jacket closer around him hesitantly, not sure if I wanted even that small intimacy. He pulled me to him and I let him hold me.

"Remember how happy we used to be?" he murmured. "'Member how we used to hang out and talk, just be together? How that was enough?"

"I used to love listening to the sound of your voice, the stories you told," I answered against his chest.

"I used to make you laugh," he said with a smile in his voice, drawing out the last word.

"I miss those days so much," I said, realizing for the first time that it was useless to hold on to the past. I'd been gripping memories in hopeless desperation, thinking that if we stopped using heroin I could open my hand and release them, and just pick up our lives where we'd left off. I pulled away, angry with myself for letting him touch me, for letting myself go soft in his arms. "But it'll never be like that again," my voice was hard and I turned from him. We would never be the same people and our relationship was changed forever. We walked toward his building but instead of going to the door with him, I went to my car. He stood on the curb looking at me. I watched him in the rear-view mirror until I turned the corner.

I was so tired. Too tired to continue this way. Tired of hating myself and hating Dev. I felt like I didn't have even one more day left in me. My accidental overdose hadn't scared me but the fact that it didn't was what *did* scare me. There was no question anymore in my mind about my own dependence and no doubt that I had to stop. Just quitting would not magically transport us back in time to the way we were. This stark fact settled into my heart and I knew I could finally let go. There was no reason to hold on any longer, fearing change. The changes had been occurring every day while I remained purposefully oblivious. I ignored the strangers Dev and I had become and trudged on in hope that the ghosts of who we'd been would miraculously gain substance and live again.

I went home that night and sat in front of the window like I had so many times before when I'd be waiting for Dev to come home. But this time I wasn't waiting for Dev.

"I don't want to get high right now," I told Dev over the phone the next afternoon. The silence on his end lasted only a half-second.

"Do you want to come over here for a while?" he asked. I twined the phone cord through my fingers, silently searching for words.

"I can't stand to even look at you anymore. You just remind me of what my life has become, of what we gave up," I finally replied, my voice like a knife. "I need some time away from you, to deal with my own problem." Surprisingly, he didn't put up a fight. I guess he's tired too, I thought.

"Are you leaving me for good?" Dev asked. Another silence.

"I don't know," my voice was a hard whisper. I sucked furiously on my cigarette, waiting for him to say something.

"Well, call me if you need anything," Dev said hesitantly, and then I heard the click of the receiver.

After hanging up with Dev I pulled my heavy old bike from the basement and peddled five laps around the neighborhood, slowly so I wouldn't fall over from exhaustion like last time.

A decision had finally been made for me, it seemed. The desire to change and survive had at last overpowered the obsession to continue and die. It felt as though I was a bystander, observing from outside myself. I had gone to work and asked for a week off, hardly knowing while I did it what words were coming out of my mouth. My boss reluctantly granted it, she had no choice since I had so much vacation time saved up. I planned on being clean before I returned to my job. Lynette and I had kept our distance since that day in the staff lounge and I didn't even leave a note at the time clock to tell her I'd be gone.

As I peddled my mind became still. For once I felt no fear, just an acute awareness of my present. There was no traffic at that time of the afternoon. I didn't stop riding until my legs felt like rubber and my hands ached from grasping the handlebars.

Later that evening I set up the canvass Laurence had given me and painted white over the original sketch I had done then set it out to dry and turned on the little radio. I fell asleep on the floor listening to the news. Dev strode into my dreams. He looked like he had when we first met except the light in his eyes was gone. I couldn't read the thoughts behind them … they looked for a moment lost and bewildered then went dark. He stood in a doorway. My mind reached out to his for the comfort and laughter I'd found there before. Through the mist of my dream world our gaze met and I felt the familiar joy we had always shared and a piercing sorrow. Then he turned away and I felt the weight of my loss settle on me again like the burden of a heavy hand. I woke up shaking and crying. Hurriedly I wiped my face and got off the floor. My hands shook as I lit a cigarette.

My hand looked thin and pale to me as I lifted the phone receiver. It had been two days since my last heroin use.

"Novena how you doin'?" It was Mick. I shifted on the chair to cross my aching legs.

"Fine Mick." A short silence followed. "How are you?" I asked after he said nothing. I didn't feel like talking to anyone, especially he or Dev.

"You need anything? I'm calling Wilbur and wondered if I could stop by your place. I'll bring you something …" he said.

"No, I'm leaving in about three minutes. I don't want anything right now," I lied. I couldn't explain to myself why I didn't want to tell anyone I was quitting. Not even Mick or Dev. It seemed more likely to happen if I didn't say it out loud.

"OK … well. Dev says he hasn't seen you in a couple days. Everything's OK, isn't it?" he asked. Another silence lapsed between us.

"Yeah, it's good. I've just need some time to myself, you know?" My voice was cool, I knew. I couldn't help it. Hiding my feelings had never been something I was good at.

"Yeah. Well, see ya," he sounded unsatisfied but hung up anyway. I pushed myself from the chair and shivered involuntarily with a slight chill. In the bedroom I pulled on two pairs of sweat-pants, two shirts, my old boots, gloves and a hat, strapped on the banged-up bike helmet and trudged down the stairs to get my laps in before the early darkness settled. Outside the wind blew against me, numbing my face. My lungs felt frozen by the cold but I knew in a few minutes the sensation would become searing pain in my chest and then diminish altogether. My ears ached when the wind raced past and my hands were stiff on the handlebars. I rode steadily and waited for my system to warm up. Soon I was puffing with exertion and welcomed the burn in my thighs as I pushed the pedals. Sweat soaked my inner layer of clothes and they chaffed my skin as I moved. November was a harsh time to be biking but it seemed to be the only thing that cleared my head and I actually looked forward to this daily torture. Besides, I wanted to be as tired as possible before I laid my head down to sleep. So tired that no dreams would come.

By the morning of the next day my joints were aching like someone had beaten me with a baseball bat. My body felt stiff, my limbs creaky and reluctant to move as if I were a machine that was badly in need of oil. I rocked back and forth with the pain of my muscles and I breathed through tight lips, dreading each movement I had to make but unable to sit still. My eyes burned and my head felt feverish. The weight of my clothes against my skin caused me agony. My stomach did flip-flops occasionally but the nausea was mildly uncomfortable in comparison to the joint pain which was excruciating. The shivering was becoming uncontrollable and my hands and feet felt numb with cold, yet I dripped with sweat. To make matters worse the day was cold and misty, deepening the expected depression to the point where I cried for no reason and for every reason. I remembered the days when I would've enjoyed the drama of the scene but things had become so dark in the past few weeks that drama was the last thing I wanted. I had all the lights on in an attempt to brighten my mood.

Dev called again that day asking in a polite voice how I was. He seemed to know what I was doing and didn't pushed me to visit or ask me to get high. I wasn't sure which was worse, quitting heroin or leaving him. I had known what to expect I just hadn't thought it would be so bad. After that call I unplugged the phone.

I sat on the sofa with an electric blanket and a book, a box of tissues, and a cup of chamomile tea. I longed for Dev to put his warm arms around me and ease the suffering of my body. He was always so caring when I was sick and in my depression I mourned for him. Then a rush of anger overtook me as I remembered that he was the reason my TV wasn't here to comfort me in my time of need. The ache of my joints was nothing compared to the pain in my heart, I thought with a spark of my old self.

With a grimace of pain and tears of weakness I pulled myself to my feet and limped on stiff legs across the room. In the cold bright bathroom I struggled to get my clothes off with as little movement as possible. The water flowed into the tub in steaming torrents and sounded deafening in my sensitive ears, like a huge waterfall. I stepped gingerly into the water feeling it burn my skin but comfort the ache. It was my fourth bath of the evening. Hot water seemed to be the only thing that gave me relief. I eased myself into it letting the water swirl around me and cover me up to my chest. I leaned my head back and sighed raggedly as the water soothed my aches.

My mind wandered into a daydream of Dev and I immediately envisioned myself pulling a thick steel wall down around me. I used all my strength to hold the heavy thing in place but soon felt my grasp slipping. I took a deep breath and held it, tightening my muscles in defense against the memories. Pushing Dev's insistent image from my mind I rose from the now tepid water. I stepped over the edge of the tub but the room began to spin wildly and dark walls were closing in from above and from both sides. Grasping at the towel rack I tried to steady myself, but couldn't stop the spinning and soon the darkness surrounded me.

I raised my head, wincing at the throbbing of my temples. I had no idea how long I had been on the floor. I sat up and willed the roaring in my ears to subside. Using the sink, I carefully pulled myself to a standing position.

I was shaking. My skin was cold like the skin of a corpse. Glancing in the mirror, I scared myself; I was ghost-white, my lips were pale and a purple bruise was forming at the outer edge of my left eye where I'd banged my head on the sink as I fell. I grabbed my robe, wrapped myself up and padded to the bedroom on wobbly legs. I fell into the bed and shook with coldness and fear for a few seconds then gradually realized it had just been a black-out. I had spent the past few days exhausting myself physically and not eating much. Bunching the covers around me, I sighed and tried to force sleep to come.

I was leaving Dev. The words wrote themselves into my head. My thoughts the past few days had centered on the coming physical struggle. Any feelings of doubt or sadness had been put to bed and I had been tip-toeing around so as to let them sleep. Now in my weakness the monster they'd become was waking up. It was a hulking toothless beast with clinging fingers and when it opened its mouth it swallowed itself, becoming a vast empty plain. The horizon stretched brown and treeless and barren to each direction under a stark white sky. I stood small and naked in the middle of the featureless land and stepped into the pain I'd been avoiding, letting it engulf me. I felt my face twist into a grimace and I opened my mouth to let silent sobs shake my body as thoughts of Dev poured over the wall I was trying to maintain.

My head was bowed and my shoulders slumped. My chest ached with the intensity of my crying. I wanted to curl into a tiny ball and hold myself tight against the pain. At the same time I could hardly stand to be in my skin and longed to run and jump, shake the pain from me. I sat in bed, gripping my quilt, hiccupping the last of my sobs and gearing up for a second round. I just had to get through the night.

I writhed through the dark hours, alternating between the pain of missing Dev and the pain of heroin withdrawal. I lit cigarette after cigarette, the rolling nausea letting me get only half through most of them. By morning of the fourth day my nausea was passing, the body aches were bearable and I could get out of bed without my head spinning. But a deep depression and desperate longing for relief consumed my mind. Every cell in my body screamed out for a shot of dope. The obsession was inexplicable. I felt like I couldn't survive without it yet I knew it was killing me.

I got through the day by crying and holding on the belief that I would feel better. I glanced at the canvas and gave fleeting thought to the bike in the basement. They had been part of the plan to keep my mind off getting high, but I couldn't muster up the energy or desire to put a hand to either. It was enough to sit in the bed smoking. I was afraid if I moved at all I'd jump into the car and run to Sissy's, begging for a hit.

By four o'clock I decided I couldn't do it. I didn't have it in me to stop. Who cared if I stayed off dope. I plugged in the phone and lifted the receiver intending to call Sissy. My fingers dialed Lynette's number instead.

"Hello," her deep mellow voice rolled into my ear.

"Lynette I need help," my voice broke and I began to sob. I hadn't meant to call her and when the words came out of my mouth I was shocked at what I'd said.

"Don't move Baby, I'll be right there."

Twenty minutes later Lynette's large form was climbing the stairs to my apartment. I met her at the door.

"I don't want to die, I thought I did but I don't and I just can't stop, I don't know what to do," I rattled on in rushed words trying to explain without actually saying what was wrong. Lynette sat heavily on the sofa and pulled me down next to her.

"You got to tell it to me straight girl," she said while trying to catch her breath.

I looked away. It was so hard to say the words.

"I've been getting high, shooting dope. I want to stop, God I'm so sorry I started, I don't know what to …" she cut me off with a wave of her hand.

"Baby you really want to quit? 'Cause I can't help you unless you want it."

I nodded, tears starting again.

"I can't live this way. Dev and I started and I thought it was his problem but then I couldn't quit and it all just got worse and worse." I wiped my face and my shoulders shook.

"You'll be alright honey," she soothed, putting her arm around me. "You just need some support. When did you get high last?"

"Five days ago."

"You doin' good. You just need to hold on and get through the depression. It ain't real baby. That's just the dope callin' you. It'll get less loud after a while. I know some people can help you. You put some clothes together in a bag. You can stay with me for a few days so you're not alone with your own mind."

I nodded, so thankful someone was taking charge that my legs felt weak with relief as I stood. I packed a bag and locked the door on our way out.

I stayed with Lynette for three weeks. The first night she told me that her husband had died of an overdose seven years previously. She herself had become addicted to drugs also but had managed to stay clean for the last ten years. She said she had dealt with the guilt of raising her children while chasing dope and that over the last ten years her life had changed so much she could hardly remember having lived in such a way. Seeing me brought it all back as fresh as if it were yesterday. She said she was grateful for the reminder, because it helped her strengthen her commitment to staying clean.

Lynette took me to rooms full of other people who gathered to admit their addiction and share their stories. At first I resisted, hearing the name Narcotics Anonymous made me think of smarmy self-help groups and goofy positive-affirmations.

These people were different. They had a hard-worn, self-depreciating quality to them but they also beamed with happiness and serenity. They welcomed me with hugs, telling me everything would be alright, telling me to keep coming back. I drank lots of coffee, stuck close by Lynette and marveled at how many people told stories that were just like mine. From their shame they had salvaged strength and their faith in each other made me want what they had. I was shocked to meet doctors, lawyers and even a nuclear engineer in those rooms. Lynette laughed when I commented on this.

"Baby," she said, "addiction don't care who it chases, and it catches you no matter who you are." Slowly I began to trust them and eventually told my story, feeling such relief at pouring it out that I felt almost high afterwards.

In a few weeks the rooms of NA became the place where I belonged. In the early days of our addiction I treasured the intimacy Dev, Mick and I shared as we practiced our secret ritual together. Now I felt an even deeper connection to the other members of NA. They not only knew what I'd suffered during the worst of my addiction, they nodded their heads knowingly as I struggled to stay clean and this familiarity was the mortar that cemented us. I began to look forward to seeing them every evening.

I returned to work after a week, glad to be back in a safe routine. Under Lynette's instruction I prayed at night and in the morning for God to keep me on the right path and gradually the strong cravings for heroin began to pass. Lynette took me to my apartment and together we threw away all the old blackened spoons, syringes and any other reminders of the ritual. She hugged me close and pressed her lips to my forehead before she left. We knew we'd see each other that night at a meeting but her action was a symbol of my starting anew.

***

Laurence blew a smoke ring and focused all his attention on me. He wanted to hear every detail of the weeks since Dev had come home from rehab, especially about my withdrawal. We were sitting at Jon's kitchen table drinking tea. I had been clean four weeks.

"I still have some depression. I'd cry watching a Hallmark commercial if I had a TV but the worst is over," I told Laurence. "Every now and then a craving for dope hits me like a rogue wave but I just chain smoke and hold on till it passes. My friend at work introduced me to some people who've had the same problem and I can call them if I get squirrely. That helps. I feel like I'm getting a second chance and I don't want to mess it up."

"You're one lucky girl," Jon said as he came down the stairs. "Most people don't get that chance. How's Dev doing?" My hand shook a little as I smashed out my cigarette.

"I haven't seen him since the day I decided to quit," I told Jon. My throat tightened with the mention of his name. Jon poured himself a cup of coffee and sat beside Laurence.

"I really hoped Dev would come out of this alive. Thank God you did." He sipped his coffee daintily. "How do you feel?" I had to think about it for a second. How did I feel?

"That's a good question. Let's see, I feel like ... like I just woke up from the dead. I feel like I'm wrapped in a shroud, stumbling around and trying to figure out where I am. Still numb, really," my voice trailed off.

"And you don't feel at all tempted to get high?" Jon asked, leaning towards me.

"It's not so much being tempted, it's an obsession that takes over. When it comes now I remind myself that I can live without heroin and it eventually passes. I've gotten through a few days without it I know it's possible. And I know people who have stayed off for years." I tried to explain. I took a deep breath. "My problem is going to be staying away from Dev. My heart was filled with Dev for so long. When he was happy, I was happy. When he was upset, I was upset. I used to think that without him I would just dry up and float away like a little bit of dust from a crumbled empty shell." I couldn't look at either of them. Laurence put his hand on mine.

"And now what do you think?" he asked. I raised my eyes to his tentatively.

"I guess I'm waiting to see what happens when the wind starts blowing," I laughed a little but it came out sounding hollow.

"Hey Novena," Dev's voice over the phone sounded like he was smiling. I had summoned up the courage to call and tell him I was clean for a whole month. Hearing his voice made my hands shake.

"Hi," I said. "How are you doing?" I shifted in the chair to cross my legs and reach for my ever-present cup of tea. Hot tea was the only way I could stay warm in my cold attic. Money was too tight to turn up the heat so I was relying on tea and my electric blanket. With some cooperation from the weather and a willingness to suffer just a little more I figured I could get through the whole winter without turning the furnace on.

"Novena where have you been? I banged on you door every day for a week. I thought you were dead," Dev's voice was a mixture of confusion, relief and anger. "No one knew where you were, I couldn't get in touch with Rachel, Laurence hadn't seen you, I was going to have the police breakdown your door but since your car wasn't there I thought maybe you had just left."

"I'm sorry I made you worry Dev. I just couldn't do it any more. I couldn't live that life. I quit getting high. It's been a whole month." I stopped myself from explaining too much. I didn't have to make excuses for quitting.

"That's great Novena," I could hear the uncertainty in his voice. "You miss me?" he asked. I stayed quiet for a minute.

"It's kinda like some bad country music song. I'm so miserable without you it's almost like you're here." He chuckled and my breath caught with the pain of knowing I might never see his smile again.

"You want to come over tonight? I really miss you. You don't have to stay, just come and sit with me for a while." His voice was warm and soft like a familiar old blanket. I swallowed my tears and pushed my longing for him to the back of my brain.

"I can't. I can't stand to see you killing yourself. If you want to try and stop I'll support you but I can't take the chance of falling back into it with you," I said, trying to convince us both of my resolve. Lynette had warned me to stay away from him that seeing him would be like having a big syringe full of dope handed to me.

"I wouldn't get high in front of you Novena. I just want to see you," he coaxed. I lit a cigarette and sucked at it hard.

"Look. I'm done with that life and everything in it. As long as you're still using drugs you're part of it." I gripped the receiver tightly and listened to the silence on the other end of the phone.

"I never thought you'd leave me," he tried. I sighed heavily, rolling my eyes.

"Drama is my department," I stated. "I'm done getting high." My voice gained strength as I continued. "And if you're a part of that life then yeah, you get left behind too." Silence again. "Anyway, it's not like we've really had a relationship in the last year. We've just been torturing each other," I said, realizing that I'd left him long ago.

"Novena ..." he began then stopped speaking.

"You felt good when you stayed clean in jail," I said quietly. "Lynette at work is an addict and she's been clean for ten years. She introduced me to some people who've been through it. It helps me to be around them. They could help you too. If you want to go to a meeting tonight I'll go with you. You'd feel better if you just tried," I pleaded.

"I don't need you to preach sobriety to me. Haven't you realized yet that you have nothing to do with my getting clean?" His voice had become hard. I bit my lip and felt the burn of tears in my eyes.

"Then just leave me alone," I said. He was quiet and I could hear his breathing.

"That'll be best for both of us," he said bitterly.

"Take care of yourself," I whispered before I hung up. My emotions were still raw. I had to get used to feeling things without the dulling effects of heroin. Since quitting I seemed to be flying in the light one minute and wallowing in darkness the next. I took a deep breath and released it. Then I bundled up, dragged the old pink monstrosity of a bike from the basement and peddled like hell around the neighborhood. The effort of physical activity in the cold left no room for the pain in my heart.

***

The vibration started in my abdomen just below my belly button, same as the high from heroin. It bloomed and traveled up towards my throat and down to my toes. I was on my back, the floor supporting my spine evenly, my arms out-stretched, hands open, eyes closed. My heart was pounding in my chest and my body seemed to be pulsing with the same rhythm. I was wholly focused on the sensuality of the moment, each nerve highly attuned to the specific sensation it was programmed to transmit, my brain receiving each transmission with complete awareness and appreciation. I shivered uncontrollably in delight.

Then the song ended and the radio-station went into commercial break, reminding me that I had to be at Rachel's in thirty minutes. Music! What a rush, I thought. As my mind thawed out I began to remember the pleasures I had sacrificed when heroin took over my life and even the mundane seemed miraculous. I sucked in the wind as I left the house, smiling as my breath took form and hung in the cold air. This would be my first visit to Rachel's since quitting and I was a little apprehensive as I entered and took off my coat. I accepted the cup of tea she offered and followed her into the next room.

"You haven't seen him in how long?" Rachel asked in disbelief.

"Six weeks," I replied. We sat on the floor of her living room playing with the new kitten she had brought home from the shelter. I smiled as it hopped on unsteady legs after the toy I dragged in front of it.

"Why didn't you tell me on the phone when we talked last week?" She sounded hurt. I lit a cigarette and blew a cloud of smoke, preparing to explain why I hadn't called her with the news.

"I wasn't ready. Things were too unstable," I said.

"What the fuck does that mean, 'unstable'? A life-shattering event occurs and you don't call your best friend?" She continued to sound mortally wounded.

"More happened than you know about," I said in a dark tone. Rachel eyed me without blinking.

"Like what?" Her voice was low and implied that she had a pretty good idea. I hesitated and held her gaze for a moment that seemed to span the life of our friendship. We both jumped when the door opened.

"You can read about it in my memoirs," I said as her new girlfriend passed through the room into the kitchen, greeting us brightly on her way. Someday I'd tell Rachel about my own heroin use but not yet. Everything was still too new and difficult. I needed to deal with one painful problem at a time.

Rachel picked up on my cue and let the moment pass. She leaned against the wall and pulled the kitten off the windowsill above her. She held it close to her chest and looked at me over its squirming body.

"Have you talked to him or anything?"

"I have conversations with him in my head constantly," I told her. "Some days I miss him so much it gives me chest pain, other days I fantasize about running him over with my car. I figure if I just keep yelling at him in my head I'll get over it." I didn't tell her how I rode past his apartment a few times a week hoping to catch just a glimpse of him. My heart would pound as I drove by, not returning to normal until I was blocks away. I hadn't seen him once.

"Is that like the patch method of quitting cigarettes? You get the nicotine diffused through your skin instead of directly into the lungs?" She asked with a sideways look at me. I rolled my eyes and shook my head.

"At least I left him! Don't I get any credit for that at all? Do you realize how hard this is for me? Five years is a long time to be with someone," I said in exaggerated disgust, trying to hide the tears that formed every time I mentioned Dev's name.

"I know, I know. I'm not judging you. You don't know how glad I am to hear you're done putting up with that shit. Do what you have to do to get by and it'll get easier as time goes on." She attempted to sooth me. "Is he still using drugs?" she asked and pushed her brown curls from her forehead. I sighed and let my shoulders slump forward.

"I'm sure he is. He chose heroin over me after all. I just thought if I held on long enough I'd get the old Dev back," I said, trying to explain the years of suffering. She reached out her hand to touch mine but I pulled it back. Tears would start if I let her comfort me and I wasn't ready to be that vulnerable yet.

"At least you're free now," she tried. I shrugged.

"I resent him so much I don't know if free is the right word," I said.

"You still love him." Rachel made it into a statement instead of a question.

"Of course I do, but I hate him too. And I know I can't be with him and I'm miserable. So I give him Hell every couple of minutes in my mind to make myself feel better," I explained.

"And do you?" she looked from the kitten back to me.

"Sometimes."

"So what are you going to do with yourself now?" Rachel asked, her eyebrows raised.

"What do you mean?" I avoided her eyes.

"Well, you'll have a lot of free time on your hands. How're you gonna fill it?"

She changed position on the floor. "You and Dev read the same books, saw the same movies, you were always together. Then you spent a few years taking care of him, now what?"

I changed position too, sighed, and changed position again trying to buy myself time to think before I answered.

"I guess … I guess it'll be like having an adventure. I'll have to go out and try some things. Maybe meet some new people … I don't really know," my voice dropped away. It sounded exhausting but not as scary as I expected.

"You'll figure it out," she replied encouragingly. I nodded in pretend agreement, anxious for the conversation to be over.

Rachel got up from the floor and crossed the room. She came back carrying an exquisite old lamp with a crystal base and silver accents. The shade was faded but she had sewn white silk roses to cover it and crisp white ribbons decorated the edge. It was beautiful in an old-fashioned romantic way.

"Did I show you my newest masterpiece? I found the base in the trash, all covered with black spray-paint. It cleaned up pretty good. I bought the shade at the thrift store. The roses came from the bouquet I carried in my sister's wedding. Surprising how easy it is to make something out of nothing if you use a little imagination isn't it," she asked in an off-handed way, primping the roses and straightening the shade. I nodded again, smiling slightly this time. Gayle, Rachel's new lover came in carrying a plate and the moment was broken.

I took a cookie from the plate Gayle offered me, marveling at the texture and exquisite taste of the food. "Jesus this is incredible, what kind of cookies are these?" I asked, continuing to utter 'mmms and umms' as they both stared at me.

"They're week old generic shortbread, not exactly first class fare," Rachel said, perplexed. I just smiled and reached for another cookie.

***

When the first snowflakes of the year flew past my window in December I reached out of habit for the phone to call Dev and tell him to look outside. My heart tightened with pain as I realized my action. I had been off heroin for two months and I was struggling to return to normal life. During the long nights I lay awake staring at the ceiling and crying over my mistakes. I smoked cigarette after cigarette to keep from calling Sissy and getting something to ease the pain as I realized what had happened during all those months. I felt like an accident victim coming out of a long coma and finding out I'd lost my limbs. Methodically I listed all the things and people I had sacrificed, reminding myself of the fate I had just barely escaped. I began to accept responsibility for my own part, realizing that my problem wasn't Dev's fault. Sometimes I would list all the people I still had in my life and all the new ones who understood my past. My heart warmed with the love I'd been shown, and the empty twisting place in my stomach felt full. I thought about seeing my mother when she came home. Eventually the thought of getting high didn't seem so attractive. My mom was right, life was a blessing.

"Hey Sweetie," Laurence called as I climbed the steps to his apartment. "How are you?" He smiled broadly at me and waved at me with the pink-handled scissors in his hand. I sunk onto the day bed and sighed.

"I'm getting by, that's about it," I told him as I rubbed my forehead in an attempt to relax myself. He eyed me from his chair by the window.

"Are you OK?"

"My cravings are much less often as the weeks pass. When I'm tired or lonely I still want it sometimes," I told him. He was scanning magazines for articles and recipes he was interested in and glanced at me briefly before continuing to cut.

"What do you miss about it?"

"It made me not care," I sighed. It was so hard to explain. Sometimes the gnawing hunger for the drug would hit me from out of nowhere and I would be lost in it for a second. Then I'd grit my teeth and remind myself that I was good at going hungry. "I don't see it so much as a way to get relief, anymore. It's more like a pathway back to pain."

"Have you talked to Dev?" he asked, putting aside the magazines and scissors and lighting a cigarette.

"No. I turned the phone off. That way I'm not tempted to talk to him if he calls. He hasn't showed up at my door either," I said, not sure how I felt about the fact that I'd not heard from him at all. Had he been able to cut me out of his life so easily? I studied the bedspread dejectedly. "I miss him most at night. And when I pass movie theaters. And bookstores ... and coffee shops. I guess I associate him with just about every part of my life," I said in morose realization. Laurence continued to study me, a sympathetic smile on his lips. "I know I sound just like every other person who's ever lost someone they love," I said, when I saw his look.

"So what have you been doing to keep busy?" he asked, crossing his arms over his chest.

"Working, reading. Nothing really," I replied. "I'm not quite ready to jump back into things. I'm not even sure how to talk to people anymore. Who do I tell them I am?"

"Who do you want to be?" He asked in return.

"I want to be who I use to be. I want things to be like they were, that's what I want." I felt my face flush with anger.

"I don't have to tell you that's impossible," he said. "You'll never be that girl again and it's a good thing."

"Now I'm a skinny worn-out former junkie in a dead end job with no boyfriend, no interests and debt up to my faded-hair roots." My face twisted into a sneer.

"You are the sum of incredible experiences. You've lived through things most people will never know. You're a walking miracle. Relax, Sweetie and let go of that junkie-girl, you don't need her anymore. You can be anything you want."

"I want to be happy, and beautiful. Most of all I want to not be afraid."

"You're already all those things," Laurence said in a tone meant to convince me. His voice grew in depth and volume as he continued to speak and he lifted his chest as if he were on stage performing. "You're perfect inside. You have to recognize that in yourself then stand up straight, tear off the mask and let your energy flow!" He spread his arms wide and threw his head back, demonstrating the freedom his words promised. I looked doubtfully at him and he smiled and sat next to me on the bed, putting his arms around my shoulders. I stared at my hands in my lap and nodded a little, for his sake.

"You know what you need?" Laurence asked. "A make-over. That'll make you feel better, I guarantee it," he said as he crossed the room and rooted through a drawer. "I got this sample hair color in the mail and it'll be perfect for you," he said, holding the packet out for my inspection. *'Redwood--auburn red for darker hair colors, semi-permanent'*, I read.

"I don't know Laurence," I began skeptically. "This is like a cliché from some bad made-for-TV women's movie: Depressed female character gets made-over by effeminate gay friend and then presto, she bounds out of the bathroom with a new hairdo and new attitude to match." Laurence wasn't listening. He pulled me up from the bed and led me into the bathroom.

"No excuses. You need this. Let me take care of you," he fussed as he turned the facet on and the rushing water drowned out his voice.

An hour later I was patting my dark-red, almost purple locks in the mirror. He had trimmed inches of broken ends from my hair and it looked fuller. My face was still pale but was beginning to fill out some with three meals a day. I had to admit, I felt better.

"At least I'm beginning to resemble a human," I said. Laurence's face broke into a big, toothy smile.

"It's a piss-poor shame but that's the most positive thing I've heard you say in months. I guess it'll have to do!" He squeezed me against him.

***

I dialed my mom's overseas number and my heart quickened when she answered.

"Hi Mom," I said. The little flutter in my heart blossomed into a warm glow.

"Baby I'm so glad you called! When I talked to you last week you seemed really down."

"Good days and bad days, you know. I miss Dev." I was becoming accustomed to being honest about how I felt and it required so much less energy than lies. The fear of exposing my feelings was disappearing. I continued to attend NA meetings daily where I watched tough smart people share the same weaknesses I felt. They bared their souls and remained strong. I was learning that strength came from humility.

"I can't wait to see you next month! Richard and I will be home for three weeks and I want to spend two of them with you, is that OK?"

"Of course Mom, I can't wait to see you too." The ease with which my affection for her flowed surprised me.

"It's been so long I'm not even sure what you look like. How exciting! You sound more settled in yourself, more sure. What happened?"

I had kept her informed of all my ups and downs after leaving Dev without divulging any information on my drug use. Lynette had said that mothers didn't need to know the details. They just wanted to know they're children were happy.

"I don't know that I'm any different, I'm just surprised that I'm a capable person," I laughed. "I'm growing up, I guess."

"Finally!" She joked. "You've always been capable. You're just beginning to believe it yourself."

After we hung up I pulled the canvass Laurence had given me out of the closet and stared at its perfect blankness. Maybe the person that emerged from all this would be worth the pain I'd been through after all I thought, and began to uncap the colorful tubes of paint.

Chapter Fourteen

Leaving the house one morning for work I almost tripped over a young woman sitting on the steps of my apartment building. She looked about my age, had long red hair and was smoking. She smiled at me, and chomped furiously on her gum.

"Hi, I'm your new neighbor, Sandy. I just moved in downstairs," she said in a friendly voice.

"I'm Novena. I live on the third floor," I told her. There was something vaguely familiar about her. "Where did you move from?" I asked, thinking I knew her from the neighborhood.

"I left L. A. a week ago to move here. Better environment for my little girl." She looked up at me from where she sat. There was something odd about her eyes. They were open and asking, yet fearful at the same time and there was a dark sadness to them despite their light-blue color.

"Wow, LA to Pittsburgh. What a change! I'm on my way to work but let me know if you need anything. And good luck," I told her. She stood up and seemed reluctant to let me go.

"Hey, would you like to have coffee this afternoon? If you're not busy I mean," she added.

"Sure, that'd be nice. I get home from work about four so I'll just come down after I change," I said. I held out my hand to shake hers and when she unfolded her thin arm I saw the marks---bright red circles and pink mounds of scarred flesh decorating the inside of her elbow. My mind registered dull recognition and I knew why she seemed familiar.

All day at work I thought about her. Maybe she donated plasma for extra money. Maybe she'd had lots of medical tests, after all, people came to Pittsburgh often for medical care since the University was a world-class research center. There were lots of possible explanations but the real evidence was in her eyes.

When I knocked on Sandy's door later that day she opened it with an engaging smile.

"I'm so glad you came!" She stepped inside and led me to the kitchen. I slid into a chair as she poured me coffee and refilled her own cup. "I've been afraid I won't make friends here. The other mothers in my little girl's class all look like professionals and I don't really think I'll fit in," she confessed in a rush, looking down at her own worn t-shirt and jeans. She was tall and thin, all bones and sharp angles. Her hands shook as she lit a cigarette and she smiled at me as she exhaled the first puff of smoke.

"This is a pretty friendly town, you won't have any trouble," I reassured her. Her apartment was comfortable, cluttered with toys and books. I looked back at Sandy. She was nervously chewing on her fingernail as she chattered about packing up her stuff and coming here and how many of her things she left behind. She glanced out the kitchen window often and only looked at me from the corner of her eye.

"How old is your daughter?" I asked. Sandy's face lit up.

"She's ten and her name's Delia. She's beautiful. And so smart!" She jumped up and ran to the living room then ran back with a paper in her hand. "Look at this poem she wrote, isn't it brilliant for a ten year old?" I studied the piece and nodded appreciatively though I had no idea what constituted brilliance or even mediocrity for a ten year old.

"Are you married?" She asked, tacking the paper to the wall.

"No, I'm … recently separated," I said evenly. "We weren't married but we were together for five years," I explained. Sandy nodded. She had crossed her legs and was swinging her foot. She switched legs and began swinging her other leg. I tapped my fingers a little. Her restless energy was making me nervous. I thought about how I'd felt trying to hide my heroin use all those years. Like I was walking a narrow ridge of sharp rock, one misplaced step and I'd go careening down the steep slope on either side.

"You might as well be married after being together that long," she exhaled smoke. I tried to make eye contact with her but she had grabbed a magazine and was flipping through its pages. "Look at this kitchen, this is what I want to do in here," she said, showing me a picture of an airy green and yellow room with colorful wall paper, shiny fruit in a large sleek bowl and trendy ceramic dish-ware gracing the stylish new table. "I love to decorate and I want to make this place a real home for my little girl," she finished in a rush of words. Sandy jumped from her seat and ran to the living room, coming back with a thick book of wallpaper samples. "I want to redo this whole apartment!" She drew a deep drag from her cigarette and sent a long stream of white smoke curling from her lips when she exhaled. "I think it's really important to show kids you're making an effort to provide stability for them, so they feel loved, don't you think?" She darted a look at me then clapped the book closed and opened another magazine. "Why'd you leave him, anyway?"

"Excuse me?" I was lost.

"Your boy-friend, why'd you separate?" Sandy continued to page quickly through the book, turning it to me here and there to point out something.

Maybe she didn't have to do this alone, I thought. I knew I couldn't have. I had been strong enough to carry my secret all that time now I needed to be strong enough to share it with someone who might need to hear it. Take the risk, a voice told me.

"He's a heroin addict," I said.

Sandy's head snapped up. Her foot stopped in mid-swing. She lit another cigarette but slowly this time, as if she were processing what I'd said. She leaned toward me.

"How'd you get away without getting into it yourself?" she asked, her eyes focusing on me for the first time.

"I didn't," I said, holding my arms out to her. She eyed my scars and met my gaze then held out her own arms. I nodded my head, keeping my face blank.

"How long did you do it?" She asked.

"I shot dope for a couple years and I've been clean almost four months," I told her. "How about you?"

"I've been using on and off for five years. I can't seem to put much clean time together. This time I've been holding on for, what's it been now, five weeks. I'm supposed to get my little girl back if I can stay clean three months. She's in foster care with my aunt here in Pittsburgh. That's why I came. To be near her so I can at least visit," her voice was low and even as she spoke, the high-pitched frantic tone from before gone.

"I thought there was something familiar about you." I smiled at her. Sandy looked down at the chipped, stained tabletop.

"It's so good to hear that someone else has been through the same thing," she said in a husky voice. "Do you go to meetings or drink meth?" Her voice danced on the edge of desperation. "I really want to stay clean this time. I need to. For my daughter." When she looked up her eyes were bright with unshed tears.

What could I tell this woman, I wondered? I didn't have any enlightening advice or deeply spiritual words to give her. The decision to stop hadn't come from me, if it had I would have done it long before I had lost so much. Some divine intervention had occurred, allowing me to surrender and ask for help. My commitment to do what it took to stay off heroin came from remembering how bad it had been and from knowing what I had sacrificed to my habit. What I'd done to stay on heroin had taught me that I was strong enough to live without it. It wasn't much but Sandy continued to look at me imploringly.

"I asked for help. Once I really wanted to quit I tried but I needed someone to help me. I go to NA meetings and listen to how others did it, I stay busy, I pray sometimes, and I spend time with people who love me. If I just keep doing what everyone suggests things seem to go OK." My voice was halting and uncertain in the beginning, gaining strength as I continued. I was only becoming aware of my thoughts as I said them. Sandy sighed.

"Some days I'd leave my baby alone for hours to go out and find dope. I lost her last year when she called the medics because I OD'd." I sat quietly for a minute. Lynette had told me that it helped her to help others, to get away from her own worries. That's why she continued to work at the nursing home. That's why she had helped me. I knew from experience that it made me feel better when I talked about things. And if that talking helped others too … suddenly Sister Raphael the nun from the courthouse came into my thoughts. Her smiling face glowed in my mind, her words echoing in my heart, *"Sometimes the best way to show someone the path is to find it yourself."*

"I met this nun who volunteers at the woman's shelter. Maybe there's a need for people to just come around once in a while and visit the women staying there and to listen to them without giving counseling or advice.

We could just sit around and talk about things that happened, exchange ideas, maybe help each other. It wouldn't have to be centered on drugs, just people getting together to talk." I liked the idea more and more as I spoke. Sandy's face showed promise.

"That sounds great! I bet lots of those women have kids, too. Let's call her today," Sandy was already reaching for the phone book and I was anxious to hear Sister Raphael's soft voice again.

***

My arms ached as I lugged my canvass and paint box up the stairs to Laurence's apartment. I had told him about my painting and he asked to see it, telling me he always thought I had artistic leanings.

"What's that smell?" I asked, stopping dead as I entered his room. A tingle trailed up my spine as a faint but familiar spicy scent wafted under my nose.

"It must be the chai-tea I made. And I had some incense burning earlier," Laurence added as he glanced away and busily straightened a pillow on the chair. I observed him closely for a minute but he just smiled and lit a cigarette. "Show me," he pointed at the painting in my hands.

"Here she is," I said, propping the canvass against the wall. He stood back and took a long look.

"Not bad, not bad at all," he murmured, still assessing it. "What made you start painting?"

"Boredom. And I liked all the little squishy tubes of paint and the way the turpentine smelled," I told him.

Laurence continued to study my work.

"Now it seems like I have to do it," I continued. "I never know when I sit down what I'm going to paint and I can't stand the suspense. It's like it comes from someone else," I said quietly. This still puzzled me. "Some days I feel compelled to sit at the canvass, like the paints demand it. Like I'm just a tool for the colors. And then at the end of the evening I feel so satisfied, like I could nod my head and say, 'that's it, that's exactly how I've been feeling all day in gold and blue and red or whatever, there on the canvass'. And I put it away and go to bed and sleep like I've never had a care in my life." Laurence was looking at me seriously.

"Sounds like you have a real passion for it Novena," he said.

"I guess I do," I answered, thinking about the times when I became mesmerized by the way the paints created shades and moods and density on the white background and the hours would pass unnoticed.

"You also have real talent. With that combination you could really do nice work." He turned back to look at my painting again. "So many artists have talent but no real desire or they have the passion to create but lack skill." He backed up, standing almost across the room. "You have an interesting perspective."

"What's perspective?" I asked him. He smiled and took out a pencil and note pad.

"It's how you see things. It can be off a little to show your individuality, or a lot if you're Picasso, or it can be true to nature, making your painting as realistic as possible. But it always comes from the artist's view, so even the most photographic-looking painting is still a reflection of how the artist perceives her world." He drew some sketches on the pad to demonstrate. I nodded. "You should take some lessons and hone that talent. You may not ever pay your bills painting but it can be an outlet for your emotions to just take out the colors and put them down on the canvass."

"Would I have to show the whole class my work?" I asked in alarm. He threw back his head with a laugh.

"Well, of course! How else do you think you'll learn, Sweetie?" He rubbed the back of my head and offered me a cup of tea from the hot plate on his dresser. I took the cup and sat on the edge of his daybed, balancing the cup with both hands.

"But I'd feel so ... naked," I said, wrinkling up my face in horror. He chuckled and sipped his tea.

"The more you expose, the less you feel like hiding," he said.

A week later Sandy and I were sitting in a large comfortable room in the shelter's administrative building with a group of women. Sister Raphael had been thrilled with our idea when Sandy and I called her from Sandy's apartment with our idea for a coffee hour. She suggested we open it to all women and call it a 'Coffee Social'. Besides being an emergency refuge for woman leaving abusive relationships the shelter provided housing for up to a year for women who needed somewhere safe to live while they made housing arrangements, took care of costly legal actions or were in the beginning stages of recovering from drug use. Its residents were a diverse bunch and Sister suggested that we all have something to offer each other. Our group consisted of women and staff members from the shelter, women from Sister Raphael's church congregation and others who'd seen the flyers posted in the community.

We sat at a large table drinking coffee and tea. The women from the shelter had baked cookies in the large kitchen they had access to, and the church women brought coffee cake. Conversation had been a little stiff at first, as we eyed each other and tried to find a common thread among us. Sister Raphael tucked a short strand of gray hair back under her habit and passed the cookies around the table.

"These cookies are just like the ones I used to bake when I was a novice," Sister Raphael said, smiling as she took a bite. "I must've made a hundred dozen that first month I lived in the convent!"

"Were you looking for something to do or did you just really like cookies?" A woman named Bridgette asked. She taught exercise classes once a week at the shelter.

"Both!" Sister Raphael laughed. "My divorce had just became final and I was so unsure of my decision to become a nun that I tried to stay busy all the time. Baking just seemed to sooth me and the other Sisters were happy to eat the results."

"I didn't think nuns could be married," one of the other women said.

"I was married at nineteen and divorced by twenty-three. My husband was a wonderful man some days and a demon other days. I often wonder if the thrill of not knowing what would happen is part of why I stayed with him. I still have the scar on the back of my head where he kicked me with his steel-toed boots," she smiled at the woman, her blue eyes clear and calm. "I went into the convent when I was twenty six. That was fourteen years ago and I haven't regretted a day since."

"Did you ever miss you husband even though he hurt you?" A young woman with a pink scar on her chin asked quietly.

"Oh yes." Sister nodded "Every time he beat me I thought it would be the last time and every time he'd apologize and cry after hurting me I thought we'd finally live happily ever after. And I felt guilty for staying with him because those days were the height of the feminist movement and I was supposed to feel like an empowered woman. So I just kept quiet and didn't tell anyone. Then I realized that if I didn't take care of myself no one else would and I left him. God called and here I am," she said.

"I remember those days," a middle-aged woman named Betty said. "In twenty years of marriage, over a span of six dress sizes, four children and a wide range of tax-brackets I always, no matter what, kept a black dress in the closet for my husband's impending funeral. He's still alive, kicking and been sober seven years. It's hard to know how long to hang on; you gamble either way." I nodded. I had kept a black dress too.

As the evening progressed conversation became lively and relaxed and everyone seemed to be at ease except Sandy and I. At some point the organized group dissolved and we milled around as if we were at a cocktail party, talking and laughing. Sandy was glued to my side and when we ducked into the bathroom for a break she whispered that she was feeling overwhelmed among all these women.

"I just feel intimidated," she complained to me. "I wish I could tell who is from the shelter so I can stick with them. I don't want to be talking to someone about all my fucked up problems and then find out she's a staff member or a church woman." I nodded in understanding. I was feeling a little of the same thing.

"It's hard to remember how to be social when you're used to avoiding people," I replied. "But this is a good place to practice. No one knows us. Let's just try to relax," I said. "Maybe we need to set a goal like talking to at least three new people tonight," I suggested. Sandy swallowed and gave a slight shake of her head and we entered the room again. We eased up to a small group and hung around the edge until we were drawn into the conversation. Someone introduced herself to us and I wracked my brain trying to think of something to talk about. I took a deep breath and began telling her about my recent car problems and how every time I took it to the mechanic it ran perfectly. She laughed and told a similar story and I began to relax. I asked her about her job, where she lived, how she heard about the group, why she came and the more I asked the more she talked. I just smiled and nodded. Finally I asked if she felt like she was standing next to Barbara Walters and she tossed back her head and laughed from deep in her chest. Conversation was easier than I expected, I thought.

"When I sent my daughter to school this morning I told her not to buy more than one cookie for lunch and now I've had four," a tall, distinguished looking woman said to Sandy, who was standing silently at my side. I turned to observe Sandy's turn at conversation.

"Yeah, it's so hard to make my kid eat right when I want to eat junk myself," Sandy said, looking terrified.

"When I was pregnant a couple of years ago all I wanted to eat was candy bars. I ate so many I thought my little girl was going to come out in a candy wrapper," she joked. "And I'm a nutritionist!"

"Are you a staff member here?" Sandy asked her. The woman beamed at Sandy and extended her hand.

"No. I've been living at the shelter for two weeks now. My name's Marion." Sandy's face relaxed into a broad smile and she took the woman's hand firmly in hers.

***

"What I really enjoy about your work is the vibrant colors you mix," my teacher said as she stood in front of the canvas propped on the table. The painting classes I took were held once a week in the teacher's basement. She was in her seventies, small but wiry and wore black every week. Her long grey hair was twisted up in a neat bun on her head and she wore extravagant earrings that swung wildly as she moved her head. Myself and six other aspiring artists met, talked, painted and then critiqued each other's work under her direction.

"Yeah, your subject is simple but the colors give the painting a deeper look, like there is more going on here than we realize. I'm drawn in," someone else said. I raised my eyebrows, wondering how these people found such insightful things to say each week. All I had been able to offer in the beginning was a mumbled, 'I like it', or 'nice work', blushing each time I spoke. As the weeks passed I forced myself to look up when speaking, eventually even making eye contact with the person I was addressing.

"Thank you," I said. I took a deep breath and reminded myself to relax as I spoke. "I don't know about a deeper meaning. I just pick colors I like and they seem to do their own thing. I really don't have much to do with it at all." I shrugged my shoulders.

"Take credit where it's due," the teacher told me. "You put yourself in every brush-stroke, whether you know it or not." I shook my hair out of my eyes and smiled. It had been a revelation to me that people would smile back.

"See you next week," I called to the others as class ended. I had been working on the same painting since starting the class two months prior and was close to finishing. The simple landscape was of a tall slim waterfall cascading into a calm pool of clear water lined with smooth round stones against a deep green background of trees. I found myself getting lost in the tranquility of the scene as I painted. It had been slowly revealing itself on the canvas until I felt like I could reach out and wet my hands in the water, feel the smoothness of the leaves. Some days I admired my own work in wonder that I could create something so beautiful, other days I referred to it as 'my piece of crap' and thought about painting over the whole thing. As the class progressed I felt less and less a need to whitewash over the colors and begin again.

A gust of wind hit me as I lifted my paint-case out of the car. It was warm for March and I could smell rain in the air. Inside the apartment I immediately turned on my little radio. Bit by bit I was paying off the overwhelming debt I had accumulated over the past two years and though I was careful to eat three decent meals a day, I budgeted my paychecks and ate thriftily. A financial specialist was going to be a guest speaker at our next Coffee Social and I hoped, with her advice, to pay off my bills and start saving money. The phone rang and I balanced the receiver against my shoulder as I flipped through the mail.

"Hey, monkess, want to come over for a hedonistic night of mindless TV and fatty foods?" Rachel's voice invited.

"Sure but I have to ride first," I replied, and shut off my pan of water. She sighed in mock exasperation.

"Jesus you make my lazy ass feel guilty. All that healthy food and exercise can't be good for you. You need to relax once in a while," she scolded.

"I relax all the time!" I laughed. "Just let me do my ten miles and I promise I'll eat at least three pieces of pizza."

"With pepperoni?"

"With pepperoni. I'll even have ice-cream," I told her.

"Yippee! Honey she's really going to splurge tonight, get out the big bowls!" I heard Rachel call out to Gayle as we hung up. I changed into ragged long-underwear pants, pulling an old pair of shorts over them, slipped a light jacket over my t-shirt and strapped on my helmet. Earlier in the year I had traded in the old heavy bicycle for a used ten-speed. After putting on a new chain and some oil it was in good working order and I had worked up to ten miles a day, riding even in the coldest of weather. Today's relative warmth was going to be a treat.

My ten miles gave me opportunity to think or just to sink into the cadence of my breathing and the feel of my body. Every day I was stronger and planned on increasing my distance until I could ride twenty miles. Maybe further I thought to myself as I stood on the pedals to power up the last hill.

"How are you really?" Rachel asked later that evening as we sat on the porch enjoying the first warm air of the year. I lit a cigarette, and she chuckled, holding out her hand to ask for a drag. "Does all that exercise balance out smoking a pack a day?" she asked.

"Can't I have one bad habit? Besides, I'll quit when I'm ready," I told her, remembering that the last time I used those words I had been referring to heroin. She handed the cigarette to me.

"Back to my first question," she said. I lounged in the lawn chair and exhaled slowly.

"I still think about Dev every day, a hundred times a day. I don't even know if he's alive or dead," I said. "He never tried to call me or come over; I don't know whether to be relieved or upset. I miss him more now than I did in the beginning."

"You're not as angry now. You've had time to cool down and remember the good times. Just keep reminding yourself how bad things got," she looked at me from the corner of her eye.

"I'm reminded every time the bills come in the mail and every time I look around my empty apartment." And every time I catch sight of the fading scars on my arms, I thought. "Besides, I've begun to like my new simple life. I don't think it's wrong to wish Dev the best and hope he is OK, that's all," I said. "I'll never forget where I've been, it may have been awful but I sure learned a lot." Rachel nodded and glanced away briefly, observed a moment of silence.

"So what are you going to do when you see him again? And I do mean *when*, 'cause we aren't living in some booming metropolis where you can loose yourself. What if you run into him at the A&P getting milk or something? What are you going to do?" She demanded.

"I'll deal with it when it happens," I said, waving my hand to dismissing the subject.

"That's a great plan. You'll see him while you're reaching for a bag of spaghetti and piss yourself right there in the pasta isle. I can hear it now," she cupped her hand over her mouth to simulate an overhead speaker, "clean up in isle six, and, uh, bring the mop."

I took a long drink of water. I had thought about the possibility of running into Dev then pushed it to the back of my mind. How would I react? Did I still love him? I was just beginning to find my way alone and was even enjoying it, but …

"Do you think you're still the same person you were when you met him?" Rachel asked.

"I'm not even the same person I was when I left him," I answered.

"Maybe the woman you are now can do better," she said.

"Dev is a good person with a bad habit," I said sharply.

"It's not like he grinds his teeth in his sleep. He's a junkie," she responded.

"He didn't mean for things to get so bad. I have to take responsibility for letting it go so long and get that far too," I reminded Rachel and myself. I put my sunglasses on and crossed my arms over my chest, hunching into my sweater. She was needling me because she cared but it didn't make it any more pleasant. Rachel leaned back in her chair and I gathered my thoughts.

"I don't know if it's important to plan what I'll do if I see Dev," I began. "I think … what's more important is to keep asking questions so I know myself better." My voice gained conviction as the wispy train of thought solidified and I was able to grasp it. "Then it won't matter what comes along. I lived through more than you know in the past few years and I've seen what I can be. And I mean that in the best and worst sense. I just need to keep building on my strong points and recognizing my weaknesses and I'll be OK," I finished, pleased with my sudden enlightenment. I looked confidently at her and I felt gratified when Rachel squirmed a little in her seat.

"Well girl-friend, I'll be askin' you some questions myself. Checking in so to speak. We all need a little prod every once in a while so we stay on the right path," she said. "But I think you should lift a box of those adult diapers from work, just in case."

"You're a real pain in my ass," I told her in mock irritation. She let out a big sigh, looking pleased with herself.

She said, as if I had thanked her, "don't mention it Novena. That's what friends are for," and smiled at me.

Chapter Fifteen

I bounced up the porch steps coming home from work, planning my bike ride and an evening of choosing classes for the fall semester. Going to college would be difficult, but if I had survived the past few years I could do anything, I told myself.

The changes were becoming more apparent. I was rarely tired now. When I looked in the mirror I saw that my cheeks had color and my body was muscled and strong from biking. Even more important than the physical improvements were the changes in my thinking. Each small victory, from increasing my strength on the bike to feeling more secure in painting class, to talking with the women at our Social each week and sharing with other addicts in NA was an awesome revelation. Surprisingly, I was looking forward to starting school and challenging myself even further.

That evening my stomach grumbled loudly even after I ate. I felt restless and moody, and had trouble concentrating on writing out my bills as I'd planned to do. The empty feeling I thought I'd conquered was gnawing away and I remembered how easy it used to be to call Sissy. Now the thought of heroin held no allure for me, didn't provide the promise of relief I used to seek from it. The feeling would just have to be tolerated until it passed. Heaving a great sigh I got up disgustedly from my seat and began wandering around the living room listlessly as if looking for something I could not find. A book Dev had given me caught my eye from where it sat on the shelf. I picked it up and an old grocery list that had served as a bookmark fell out. My eyes clouded and my face felt heavy when I recognized Dev's bold script. Sinking to the floor I held it to me and wept a little, the tears dropping onto the ink and making it run and blur.

"How's school?" Rachel asked a few weeks later. I'd gone to my first class that day.

"I think it's going to be really great," I could hardly contain my excitement. "The subject is world politics and the teacher seems intense. It'll be so interesting to learn new things," I finished.

"Wait till you have to write a paper then we'll see how much fun you think it is." She had dropped out of college during her second semester years ago and was still resentful.

"Why don't you enroll next semester with me? You could finish what you started."

"Oh no, I'm happy doing my own thing. I have enough to keep my busy at the cat shelter, the food bank and whatever job I'm doing at the present. I know what I love. You better just concentrate on getting through world politics on your own."

"If I can't pass this class, I'll try something else," I told her. She nodded slowly, continuing to look at me. Her living room windows were open to the evening breeze and the cats lounged peacefully on the floor, their noses raised to the smells from the city outside.

"You're serious about this school thing huh? Just like the painting and biking. I never thought you'd keep those up but you have. It's like you just pulled that stuff out of thin air and made a new life. I gotta give you credit, a lot of people would still be floundering around in self-pity," she said.

"Well don't be nominating me for any awards. I still wake up crying in the middle of the night and I'm still scared a lot," I confessed.

"Everybody is scared and if they claim not to be they're lying. You're doing things you've never done, it's an adventure. Those guys on National Geographic Explorer always look a little spooked to me," Rachel said.

"Yeah but I'm not chasing down wild Rhinos or hanging off cliffs," I laughed. "I'd just like to get through my painting class without stuttering when it's my turn to speak."

"It's still taking a risk. Besides, isn't it getting easier for you now?" She asked.

"It has to at some point. I want to get on with my life. I've got no time to waste being afraid. I guess I just don't have much patience," I sighed. Rachel rolled her eyes again, then opened them wide and leaned forward towards me.

"No, not you!" She said in an exaggerated tone. I dipped my fingers in my water glass and flicked them at her. "So, do any of the men in your class look interesting?" She peeked at me from under her lashes as if she were afraid to ask the question.

"They're all either young boys or old men!" I replied. The TV Guide had suddenly become of incredible interest to me even though I had no television.

"So what? You don't know who you'll be attracted to unless you talk to them," she said.

"I don't need some man complicating my life right now. Let me get through the semester first then maybe I'll think about … that stuff." I was reluctant to even say it out loud. The memory of Dev's hands on my body was so fresh in my mind that when I let myself go, I could still feel his warmth. "I still miss Dev. After some time has gone by it'll be better," I said quietly, looking down at my hands and effecting what I hoped was a tragic demeanor. Rachel rolled her eyes.

"Look, Tellulah, he didn't die in some heroic battle or even waste away in an agony of sickness. He almost destroyed you with his drug use. You need to get over him before you dry up and become an old woman." She sat back in her chair and clicked the remote for the TV. "If we're going to share a room at the nursing home you better have some good sex stories to entertain me with or I'm gonna be one cranky senior citizen." It was my turn to roll my eyes.

"I have lots of time and I'm not avoiding anything. Let me go at my own pace." She opened her mouth to speak again but I silenced her with my hand. "Conversation closed."

"Tick, tick, tick," she quietly mimicked a clock and continued to innocently watch TV.

The burn in my legs intensified as I pushed the pedals harder. My lungs filled and emptied in a rhythmic, powerful cycle. I lowered my head and focused on the ground passing beneath the bike. If I pushed just a little harder I could beat last week's time, I thought as I prepared to stand on the pedals.

"On your left," a voice called from behind me and I heard the whirring noise of another bicycle approaching. I swerved to the right to give the faster rider room to pass me. Instead of passing the cyclist paced beside me. "How far are you riding?" He spoke easily, his breath not affected by the effort of pedaling.

"I have another six miles," I replied, trying not to gasp while I spoke.

"Mind if I join you?" His voice was friendly and I nodded wordlessly. I looked at him from the corner of my vision. He looked about my age with dark hair, his arms and legs sculptured curves of tan muscle. No helmet and no glasses. Expensive pro-team biking shirt and shorts, funny little bike shoes snapped onto his pedals and his bike was a slim light racing model with an Italian-sounding name decaled on the frame.

"Do you ride every day?" he asked. I nodded again. I didn't want him to see how I had to struggle to keep up with him.

"I'm not used to talking while I ride," I said and smiled. Then I huffed and puffed trying to regain the oxygen I'd lost in those few words.

"That's OK. You set the pace, I'll ride at your speed," he told me. "How long have you been cycling?"

"A few months," I said. My pedaling slowed as I talked. "I just traded my old heavy bike in for this ten-speed and it's much better. It's used but some oil and a new chain and it's good as new," I told him, trying to get a good look at him through the straps of my helmet.

"If you ride a lot you should invest in a good bike, something like this one. It'll improve your training remarkably," he said, eyeing my bike with obvious distaste. My cheeks heated with embarrassment and anger. His bike was probably worth more than my car. I picked up my speed some, pushing hard on the pedals.

"There's nothing wrong with this one," was all I could manage. I tried hard not to gulp air. I could feel him watching me and smiling as he effortlessly rode while I suffered.

"You have good form and your legs look like you ride a lot," he said in admiration. "Have you ever thought of racing?" I shook my head no.

"I ride 'cause I like it," I said. My breath was coming easier now. He had slowed his pace, so I did too.

"You must like it an awful lot to get out and push that heavy machine," he laughed. "My name's Mark. I ride around here six days a week," he told me. I gave him my name and nodded. "The Cycling Federation holds races in the Zoo parking lot every week. You should come watch sometime."

He looked at me but there was an intersection coming up and I focused on the traffic pattern.

"That'd be interesting," I said as we slowed for the red light. "I turn here, it's been nice riding with you," I said as I prepared for the light to turn green.

"You want to meet and ride together tomorrow?" He asked hopefully. I had only seconds to think about before the light was going to turn. 'Tick, tick, tick,' Rachel's voice sounded in my head.

"Sure, I'd like that," I said. He smiled.

"Great! I'll wait for you at the same spot we met today. Six o'clock," he said, and rode off.

I made my turn and pedaled home, my stomach already flip-flopping at the prospect of an almost-date. I hadn't ever had to do this. Dev had been the only man I'd ever been interested in. My mind raced as I carried the bike up my stairs.

"Laurence," I spoke excitedly through the phone. "I have a date tomorrow, I'm panicking!"

"What are you panicking about? Just be yourself!" I could hear the laughter in his voice.

"Who is that again? Remind me," I demanded. He laughed out loud this time.

"Just relax and have fun. You'll be fine," he said as we hung up.

The next afternoon I strapped on my helmet and made sure I was ten minutes early on the corner. I had called Rachel and Gayle and gave them the details then told them I'd call when I got home and if they didn't hear from me by ten to call the cops. They laughed at my precautions.

I saw Mark pedaling toward me and my stomach turned over a little.

"Hey how are you?" He smiled warmly as he stopped next to me. I smiled back and nodded to him.

"Fine, how are you?" Did my voice sound as stiff as I felt I wondered?

"I'm doing well. It's a beautiful day, my legs feel good and I have a riding partner. What more could a guy want?" His eyes flashed hazel at me. "I thought we could ride and then maybe have coffee," he suggested. I nodded again. "Good. I have a ten mile route through the city that's nice. We'll go at your pace." I was relieved to start pedaling so I didn't have to look at him while trying to make conversation. He rode beside me and talked easily about his job as a systems analyst. I didn't have any idea what that was but I continued nodding. I told him I was a nurse's aide and had recently gone back to school. He seemed impressed and my confidence grew a little. By the time ten miles had passed I was laughing and comfortable. We parked our bikes at the coffee shop and I watched as he unfolded his tall thin frame from the bike, admiring the muscles in his thighs. He held the chair for me as I sat and I shivered a little as he let his fingers barely touch my shoulder when he passed behind me. This is going so well, I thought excitedly. I can't wait to tell Rachel and Laurence.

"So have you ever been married, Novena?" Mark asked as our coffee came. I shook my head.

"No, have you?"

"I was engaged to the woman I dated for four years then at the last minute we broke it off. After all that time, living together for a month before the wedding sealed our fate," he said with a smile. Our hands brushed as I reached for the sugar and a pleasant jolt passed through my skin.

"I was with the same man for five years but we broke up about six months ago," I told him as I poured a generous helping of cream into my coffee.

"Why'd you break up?" I wanted to be honest with Mark. He was attractive, well spoken, and I was flattered by his attention. Best to be honest from the beginning, get it all out on the table even if it was hard to say the words.

"He was a heroin addict and he just couldn't stay clean." I concentrated on stirring my coffee, assessing the color to see if I needed to make a cream-adjustment. When I looked up Mark was staring at me.

"The guy was a drug addict?" His voice was flat and incredulous. "I never knew anyone who did drugs." His statement was hard, as if he was telling me he was above such things. "Are you like a motorcycle chick or something?" The laughter in his eyes was gone even though he continued to smile and I detected a slight sneer to his voice.

"No," I said quietly. "I'm just a regular person. It can happen to anyone." I held his gaze steadily and kept my voice even.

"Regular people don't hang out with junkies. Let me guess your daddy was an alcoholic and you were looking for someone to take his place," he smirked. "You almost had me fooled. I'd never guess you were a little wild woman. So what else are you into? I bet you like it rough, huh?" His voice was low and heavy with implications. A panicky sense of confusion began to cloud my mind when his hand gripped my thigh, his fingers biting into my flesh. My shoulders slumped as I tried to make myself smaller, shrinking into helplessness. I wished I hadn't told him, wished I was someone with a clear unblemished past with no mistakes or scars to hide. Then Laurence's words filled my ears: 'You're perfect just as you are Sweetie, stand up straight and let your energy flow!' I lifted my sternum and squared my shoulders to bring my head up to Mark's eye level. As I filled my lungs with a deep breath anger flooded the space I'd made in my chest, displacing my fear. I slapped his hand away and stood up.

"You have no right to make assumptions about me. You have no idea who I am," I said more firmly than I felt. I turned and walked through the café without hurrying, not looking back. Jumping on my bike I pedaled away into traffic. By the time I got home I was crying with hurt at the injustice of the situation. I rode past my apartment house and went to Jon's. As expected, Laurence was in the kitchen.

"Sweetie, what happened?" His look changed from welcoming to concern as I entered and he saw my face.

"Oh Laurence it was awful," I said. I sat down and covered my face with my hands.

"Did he hurt you? Are you OK?"

"I'm alright. He was just so mean when I told him about Dev and then he treated me like trash and I just felt so bad about it." My words came out in a rush as I shook my head side to side in anxiety. When I looked at Laurence I was shocked to see him smiling.

"How dare he not like you!" he said in mock-drama, trying not to laugh. "Sweetie people aren't always nice," he said. "You're going to run into all kinds out there. You've been spoiled, that's all." His face was relieved and he patting my hand, still smiling.

"You don't have to keep smiling like it's all some hilarious joke," I said darkly. "And what do you mean I'm spoiled? Me spoiled, of all people," I huffed.

"You are!" he laughed out loud. "You've been surrounded by supportive loving people. There are so many nasty mean ones out there, you just need to keep living and you'll run into them. Not everyone is going to pat you on the back for having been a drug addict. You have to be ready for that." He got up to get the boiling teapot from the stove.

"So I'm going to have to lie if I want to make new friends who are normal people." I stated, then sighed dejectedly. "It's always us and them in some way. I'm always on the wrong side no matter where I go or what I do," I complained. "I'll always be different." I stared at my hands and pouted. Laurence sat down, handed me a cup of tea and rolled his eyes.

"Sweetie you're missing the point. It's not 'us and them', it's just 'we'. Everyone is different and that's what makes us the same. We're all fucked up in our own special way. Some show it, others hide it but that makes no difference." He stopped and sipped his tea daintily and giggled. "I can just see you. You probably stood up and did that princess thing where you throw your head back and shake it. I've seen you do that a million times when you're pissed off!" He laughed, imitating me. "Did you fling your drink in his face? That would have been perfect!" I tried to stop the smile that insisted on curving the corners of my mouth and dropped my chin to my chest in an attempt to hide it from Laurence.

"No, I wasn't thinking fast enough or I would have," I confessed. "That would have been a great ending to the story, huh?"

"Just like in the movies! All you needed was the handsome hero to run to, you know, the one who sweeps you into his arms and comforts you?" He continued to laugh.

"That's what I have you for Laurence," I was laughing too and let my eyes go soft when I looked at him. He blushed and crossed his arms over his chest, one hand placed delicately over his heart and blew me a kiss.

***

Strong calloused hands caressed my skin. I drew a deep breath and moaned a little as I felt Dev's warm lips on my neck. A hot sensation spread through my lower abdomen and into my limbs. My breathing came in soft gasps as I begged in a whisper for him to come into me. His body was close and I arched my back, feeling his hardness against me, trying to get to what I wanted. Suddenly the same hands were holding my arm straight and I cried out with longing as a fat syringe filled with heroin came close, teasing me with the open point of the needle. I writhed on the bed, trying to get closer yet holding myself away, knowing how good it would feel but fearing the consequences. Just before his body came into mine, just before the syringe pierced my skin, I woke up panting and sweating, my heart pounding against my chest wall. Sitting upright in bed I clutched the covers and steadied myself. I brought my breathing to normal and wiped the dampness from my neck with shaky hands. The dreams had been getting fewer and farther apart in the last ten months but every once in a while I was still caught off guard by a vivid reminder of my dependencies.

I got out of bed and placed the new canvass I'd bought on the easel by the window. I uncapped the tubes of color. My hand flowed over the white canvass and the colors chose themselves. My body relaxed and I sighed with some relief. I painted through the rest of the night knowing better than to try to sleep. By dawn the colors had begun to take definite shape. Part of the form was boxy and linear, shown in strong blue and red. Another part was swirling and dancing in shades of fertile green and gold with flecks of flamboyant purple. Waves of pink and peach gave the painting some softness. But part was blank. I could find no color to fill it, as if the space was a question waiting for an answer that had yet to be provided. I stood back, tired but satisfied and found that I was looking at my own image on the canvass.

I pedaled slowly down Dev's old street watching the door to his apartment building and searching the curb for his car. I hadn't seen any evidence of him since I'd started looking two weeks prior. His phone number had been disconnected and now I could see the 'for rent' sign in the window of his old apartment. I turned my bike for home, feeling dissatisfied and hungry.

"Simon its Novena. I wondered if you've heard from Dev," I chewed my thumbnail as I spoke into the phone.

"No darlin' I'm, sorry. He hasn't been in touch since last December. And then it was to beg me for money. I told him no of course and haven't heard from him since." Simon's voice was heavy with regret and sadness and I felt a pang of guilt for bringing Dev's name up to him.

"Sorry Simon. Some days I still think about him a lot and I hadn't asked you in a while." We exchanged kind words and a promise to meet soon before hanging up. The blank space in the painting I'd started two weeks prior taunted me from across the room. My hand lingered on the receiver for a second. Then I picked it up and dialed again, the number coming to my fingers from memory. I lit a cigarette as the phone rang on the other side.

"Sissy," she answered in a clipped tone.

"Hey Sis, this is Novena." I exhaled smoke as I spoke.

"Veena, Honey! How are you? You still clean I hope?"

"Yeah it's been ten months now," I told her.

"That's great! Hey Viv, it's Vee. No she's still OK," I could hear her talking over the phone. "What's up honey?"

"Um, have you seen Dev around?" I wrapped the phone cord around my hand, watching the coils get caught and intertwine. "I just, you know, was wondering if he's OK or dead or what. It would just ease my mind to know."

"You don't know where he is?" Sissy's voice was incredulous.

"No. I haven't seen him since I got clean," I answered, feeling my stomach twist at her tone of voice.

"Vena I haven't seen him in that long either. We just figured you both got clean together." Her voice rose at the end in an expression of wonder. "I don't know where he is." I was quiet for a minute as disappointment crept over me like a chill.

"Well if you see him, could you call me?" I asked.

"Sure honey. I'll put the word out and see if anyone knows anything. You take care of yourself." She hung up and I sighed. Maybe it was for the best that I not know, I thought, as I pedaled to Rachel's. This thought didn't stop me from fantasized about finding Dev as I rode. After all, maybe things could be OK between us now and anyway, it didn't hurt to think about it. As the pavement passed under me the scene grew clearer.

In an apartment a young woman is reading. She looks up as a knock sounds at the door, rises and opens it. A tall handsome man stands smiling in the doorway and the woman covers her mouth with her hands. She shakes and steadies herself on the doorframe then throws herself at him. The man drops the bouquet of pink roses he is carrying and catches her in his arms. He lifts her off the ground and hugs her to him tightly, whispering her name. Then he sweeps her into his arms and carries her to the bedroom. The door closes and the words 'The End' appear on the screen.

I sighed heavily and smiled to myself. But wait. Cut to the bedroom. Is the man clean or does he pull out a few bags of dope? If he is clean, does the woman like the man he's become? Do they still love each other or is it just one set of hormones calling out to the other for memory's sake? Is the man working? Will he fall back into the same bad habits? Will she? Will the woman have to change her life to accommodate him? What does she really want?

My brow wrinkled as the questions popped one after the other into my head, spoiling my happily-ever-after scenario. So many uncertainties. The movies never deal with this part, I thought resentfully.

Rachel and Gayle were on the front steps blowing bubbles in the late afternoon sun.

"Look honey, it's that freak who has a car but rides a bike instead," Rachel said to Gayle as I stopped in front of them. I kicked dust from the sidewalk at her and she stuck her tongue out at me. "What's go'in on?"

"Nothing," I replied. I dropped the bike to the sidewalk and eased onto the cement step beside them. "I just wondered if anyone was up for ice cream." I lit a cigarette and stared at the bubbles bursting wetly on the pavement.

"That's like asking if I want to win the lottery," she said. "So have you found anything out about Dev?" I shook my head. Rachel gave the bubble soap to Gayle who went into the house, then held her hand out for a drag of my smoke.

"I talked to Simon and he hasn't seen him. And I called Sissy." I had begun to tell her bits and pieces of the past two years, mostly stories that I could make sound funny. And there was definitely a lot of raw material where Sissy was concerned so Rachel was well acquainted with her character. "Sissy hasn't seen him either."

"At least that tells you maybe he isn't getting high," Rachel said.

"If he's not getting high he's probably dead." My voice was even. I was surprised that I didn't feel the old catch in my throat I used to when I said his name. "I'm not sure why I even want to know," I confessed.

"Because you loved him for five years that's why. I think it's perfectly normal. But once you find out, then what? I mean, are you doing this because you want to get back with him if he's clean?" I sighed and shrugged.

"I don't want that, I don't think."

"Are you pissed that he never called you or tried to see you? Maybe you just want to needle him a little, hurt him like he hurt you," she said.

"No, that's not it. He didn't mean to hurt me and I certainly was no saint myself. I think maybe I just need to see what my reaction is. It would be the like the real test for me. I thought I couldn't live without him and now I've been getting along really well without him because I have to. But what if I don't have to, then what? Will I still be as strong? Or will I go back to being that clingy little girl with no identity that hid behind her boyfriend's personality?" My voice gained animation as the questions formed themselves in my mind. "Have I really changed and grown or I am just fooling myself? Will I just fall into the same pattern with the next guy I like? Inquiring minds want to know." Rachel turned to me.

"Girlfriend, I know you're really into this whole challenging yourself and facing your weaknesses thing," she said, and put her hands out, palms up like she was placating me. "And I think that's great. But maybe this is one of those things you can get through life without needing to find out. Put it in the same category as say, the question of weather a thirty-foot python can swallow a hundred pound woman whole. Sure you'd *like* to know, but do ya *need* to?" She cocked her head sideways, raised her eyebrows and set her mouth in a firm line.

"You think the risks outweigh the benefits."

"That would be it," she answered in a clipped voice. "It's like playing with fire."

"Maybe I'll be enlightened," I said and lit another cigarette, the match glowing briefly in the darkening evening.

"Yeah, and maybe you'll be incinerated," Rachel replied.

Rachel drove me home that night, my bike crammed in the hatchback of her small banged up Ford. As I waved goodbye to her from the porch, a familiar scent caught my attention and I lifted my head like a dog to sniff the wind. It was spicy and slightly exotic and brought a rush of memories to my mind. I peered into the darkness at the edge of the porch, my heartbeat picking up. My knees felt week and I swallowed reflexively as I heard a shuffling noise.

Mick stepped out of the shadows wearing Dev's old leather jacket. My hand dropped from the doorknob and I stared blankly at him.

"Hi Novena," he said, and shoved his hands in the pockets of the jacket. He was thinner than I remembered and his face was pale.

"Mick, how are you?" I stammered a little. His appearance was not what I'd expected.

"I'm pretty good Novena. You look great. How long's it been now?"

"Ten months," I replied. I stood at the door, not sure what to do. "How's Francesca?" I asked, to fill the silence.

"She's fine, working me hard. The business is going really well. We're doing all Victorian renovations now, restoring houses back to their original look." He pulled his hands out of the pockets and rubbed his face then dropped his arms to his sides. "I came to ask you if you'd seen Dev lately," he said, looking into my face.

"No I haven't. I've been wondering about him too." I tugged on the sleeve of the jacket, inhaling Dev's scent from it. "How'd you get this?" I asked, smiling at how the sleeves hung down, covering his hands and making him look like a child wearing grown-up's clothes.

"Dev gave it to me the last time I saw him, a few months ago. He said he didn't need it anymore." Mick's voice wavered a little. "He told me he loved me and that he was thinking of moving on and probably wouldn't hang around here much longer. That's the last time I saw him. By the next week all his stuff was out of the rooming house and no one knew where he'd gone." Mick's eyes were sad and his face fell as he told the story. I held my arms out to him and he clutched me tight. We parted and sat on the steps. Mick slid the jacket off and placed the worn out old thing carefully beside him as if it were a sacred object. "Do you still miss him?" He asked me.

"Of course I do. But I miss the man he was before he started shooting heroin. I probably wouldn't even know him now. And he wouldn't know me." A light breeze fluttered the sleeve of my t-shirt and I shivered.

"You do seem different," Mick said, turning to look at me. I smiled a little at the discomfort his tone conveyed.

"I feel OK. Not always great but not bad either. Are you still getting high?" I asked after a bit of time. He looked away.

"Here and there," he evaded. "Things are ... stable at our house. Except for Dev leaving not much has changed since the last time I saw you."

"That's good Mick. Stability is good," I said, wondering to myself if that statement was true.

"Yeah it is, I guess," he said. I tried to think of something else to say, something that would connect us like in the old days but my mind remained blank. Mick fidgeted, wiggling his foot, shifting position, then he stood up. "It's been good seeing you Novena. I'm glad everything worked out for you." He held my eyes for a minute then let his gaze fall to his feet. He shuffled his work boots and looked out into the dark street. "If you ever run into Dev tell him I asked about him, OK?"

"OK Mick," I said. He lingered a moment longer then disappeared into the dark at the end of the steps. I let him go without saying another word.

As I pulled to the curb outside Jon's house to visit Laurence, my heart jumped when I saw a car like Dev's driving away. I watched it turn the corner realizing that this car was shinier and in better condition than Dev's had been. I sat on the steps of Jon's house waiting for Laurence to join me. I gazed at the summer sky as the bright orange-red sunset melted into soft pink and purple. I could smell the honeysuckle that grew next to the curb and the lazy buzz of an airplane high above provided the perfect soundtrack to the slow change of color in the sky. The screen door banged closed as Laurence came out at sat next to me.

"What are you thinking about?" He asked. He was looking at the sunset too.

"I was thinking that I've done the things I'd dreamed of doing as a young girl. I've visited exotic places without even leaving my own city. I've had adventures and taken risks. I always wanted to be worldly and wise. That's what I was looking for." Laurence smiled at me.

"As usual you have an interesting perspective," he said.

"I just wish I knew if Dev was alive or dead," I said, remembering how he used to point out the beauty of the sky to me. "I always thought we were connected by some cosmic bond and that I'd know if he died. I figured I'd get some awful pain and clutch my chest like in the movies." I chuckled. I glanced at Laurence and took the honeysuckle flower he handed me.

"You did have a cosmic bond Sweetie. You loved each other," Laurence told me.

"But it wasn't enough." I held the flower to my nose and then tossed it into the yard where the light of the rising full moon made it glow against the dark of the grass.

"Yes it was. You loved him enough to stay with him through a lot of trouble and he loved you enough to let you go." Laurence turned to look at me.

"Dev wasn't my savior after all. If I'd realized that from the beginning maybe neither one of us would have gone so far. Maybe I made Dev into a hero he couldn't live up to being and he had to do something to break away," I said, thinking out loud. Laurence nodded.

"Or maybe things just happened," he said. I smiled and leaned against his shoulder.

"My buddy the Buddha. What would I do without you?" I asked him. He put his arm around my shoulder.

"You'd find your way. Of course the journey would be much less exciting without a friend like me," he said.

"So true," I nodded and smiled in agreement.

"What if you never find out what happened to Dev?" Laurence asked. I leaned away from him to stretch. I smiled and arched my back, lifting my arms and taking a deep breath.

"Then I never find out. My life isn't dependent on whether he's alive or not. My life's not dependant on anything except waking up in the morning," I told him.

"And you never know when you wake up in the morning what the day is going to bring," he said then lit a cigarette and passed it to me.

The next morning at work I felt antsy and restless, like I was waiting for something. The crimson dawn gave way to a flat gray day but by mid-afternoon the wind began picking up and dark clouds gathered to the west. A late summer storm blew through, rumbling the windows of the nursing home. Hail pounded loudly on the roof and the novelty of such a violent storm made the residents clap and whoop with excitement, bringing them to life with an exhilaration they rarely demonstrated. Even the staff was enthralled by it and I ran out to scoop up some hard little balls of ice with a kidney basin so the patients could touch it.

The sun was breaking through the clouds as I drove home from work and it glinted off the raindrops clinging to the open windows of my living room when I walked in. The wind had scattered my morning newspaper around, tangling the pages in the legs of a chair. One of my plants had been blown over and when I righted it I was glad to see that no leaves had been damaged. Surprisingly it remained firmly rooted in its pot despite the disruption. As I slipped off my shoes I noticed the blinking light on the answering machine and pushed the button to receive the message.

"Novena!" Dev's cheerful voice sung to me from the little plastic box. I sat hard on the floor in front of the phone table. "Novena it's me, Dev. You probably knew that huh? Well I've been clean since December and I thought I'd finally give you a call. I'm living across the state, I made some new friends and I have a steady job," his voice was boisterous and happy-sounding. He continued in a quieter more serious tone. "I know we really had a bad time. We each had to come to an end alone with this thing. I just hope you don't hate me. I'm not going to call you again but I want you to know that I'm OK." His voice paused for a second. "I still love you, no matter what." He left his new phone number then the machine beeped off. I held my breath preparing for after-shocks, holding on for the chaos to come. I replayed the message expecting to feel my muscles tighten in fear and worry. I waited to suffer through the clenching of my stomach and the sick queasiness that always followed. Surely my heart would flutter and skip. The old comforting habit of transferring real life into a movie kicked in:

The woman picks up the phone …

Wait I thought. *Cut.* I don't need to be in a movie anymore. I'm in the director's chair now. Dev was alive. He was off heroin and sounded happy. I was growing and becoming confident. This is what I'd wanted all those long painful nights I'd spent trying to fix myself with the needle. He was OK and I was … I was the same person I had been before his call. No reaction had shaken my foundations, made me crave dope or even made me ache for Dev. My chest rose and fell in a simple sigh and in my mind the blank space in the painting across the room infused with a serene solid aqua, completing the picture. I was free. My legs felt strong and steady as I rose from the floor.

I changed my clothes and headed out for my bike ride. The late afternoon sun streamed through the dissolving storm clouds in a blaze of orange and pink and the rain washed air smelled like fresh morning dew as I pedaled solidly into the promise of all my tomorrows.

The End

About the Author

Gineen Dutkovic works as a home health nurse and writes as a hobby. She currently resides in Pittsburgh, Pennsylvania, with her husband, Greg, and their pets. All My Tomorrows is her debut novel.

Printed in the United States
By Bookmasters